Christopher Fowler is the director of The Creative Partnership, a film promotion company based in Soho, and is the author of the novels *Roofworld*, *Rune*, *Red Bride*, *Darkest Day*, *Spanky*, *Psychoville*, *Disturbia* and *Soho Black* and of the short story collections *City Jitters*, *The Bureau of Lost Souls*, *Sharper Knives*, *Flesh Wounds* and *Personal Demons*.

D I S T U R B I A

DISTURBIA

Christopher Fowler

A *Warner* Book

First published in Great Britain by Warner Books 1997
This edition published by Warner Books 1998

Copyright © Christopher Fowler 1997

The moral right of the author has been asserted.

A CIP catalogue record for this book
is available from the British Library.

ISBN 0 7515 1909 X

Typeset by Solidus (Bristol) Limited
Printed and bound in Great Britain by
Clays Ltd, St Ives plc

Warner Books
A Division of
Little, Brown and Company (UK) Limited
Brettenham House
Lancaster Place
London WC2E 7EN

WARNER BOOKS

Dedication

For Bal Croce, whose energetic pursuit of London's hidden histories inspired this tale.

Acknowledgements

The solidarity and support of Richard Woolf made this book possible, and for this I am eternally grateful. Jim Sturgeon is the sensible half of my brain. Our creative partnership spans almost a quarter century, and that's where the ideas come from. Thank you, James. Maximum love, as always, goes out to parents Kath and Bill, superbro Steven, Sue and family.

FAQ: How do I find the time to write when I have a day job? With the help of great friends like Mike and Sarah, Jo, Twins Of Evil Martin and Graham, David and Helen, Damien, Sebastian, Alan, Jeff, Richard P, Sally and Gary, Pam, Maggie, Poppy, Amber, Stephanie, Di, Kevin, Lara, Michele. My agent Serafina Clarke may not be entirely *au fait* with the Internet but makes a superb champagne cocktail, a far more desirable skill. Editor Andrew Wille and Nann du Sautoy are as essential as Wordperfect, and I suspect represent the 'X-Files' end of Little, Brown; my kind of folks, as are Jenny Luithlen and Pippa Dyson, international rights and UK film rights respectively, and Joel Gotler at Renaissance. Thanks also to fellow authors Graham Joyce, Nick Royle, Kim Newman and Joanne Harris.

Part One

'Si monumentum requiris, circumspice'

– Wren's inscription for St Paul's
('If you seek a monument, look around')

Prologue

'All That Mighty Heart Is Lying Still.'

Taken from the Foreword of City of Night and Day *by Vincent Reynolds.*

NO LIVING person has seen London. Its meadows and pastures are buried beneath layers of concrete, brick and bone, its topography and history crushed by the sheer weight of events. Within an ever-changing circumference is concentrated such a tumultuous deluge of life that the palaces of the Bosphorus seem dull in comparison.

London is a city of myth. Its buildings hold and hide legends. Its rivers are lost underground. Its backstreets vanish into fable. Its characters are blurred between fact and fiction. Truths have been twisted by fantasy. Tourists are rendered blind, stepping around beggars to photograph the past, and sit in parks reading of a city that only springs to life in the mind, for in reality only the faintest outline traces now remain.

London is a cruel city. Beneath the rosy veils of lore and imagery its architecture is at best grand and callous, at worst patched, shabby and vulgar. It gives no guidance to the lost, no comfort to the lonely, no help to the abandoned. It has no truck with sentiment, and no interest in its own mythology. Its buildings, like its people, are often defined by the negative shapes they leave on the retina. They lack both the florid invention of the French and the bland utility of the American. London is muddling through and unavoidable, like a garrulous drunk making uncalled-for conversation. Whereas its form once sprang from a collective energy of purpose, it is now defined by the manufacture of money. If its parks were not protected, they too would now be built upon, and out to the very edge of the street, in order to maximise office space.

Its residents are divided; secretive and arrogant, briskly condescending, or confused and gentle, slightly disappointed. For some it is still a sanctuary of civilisation, to others a living Satanophony. There are no glitzy showtunes written about this city, only a handful of rumpty-tumpty music hall dirges.

Once, though, it was a living, breathing thing, its buildings homogenously palladian and baroque, its roads spacious, its parks tranquil. This is the London of collective memory; warm solid buildings of dirty white stone, dingy soot-streaked stations with a curiously sharp metallic smell, children trudging through wet green parklands, low sunlight in narrow streets, and people, people everywhere. A city traversed by railway cuttings and canals, and at its heart the curious silence of a broad grey river, glistening like dulled steel.

The war, the developer, the councilman, the car, each has taken a turn in London's destruction. It is a city scoured by perpetual motion. All that is left now are pieces of brilliant brittle shell, the remnants of a centuries-long celebration of life, fractured glimpses and glances of what was, and what might once have been.

And yet . . .

There are places that still catch the city's fleeting spirit. Little to the West, and not much in the centre, where only visitors stroll on a Sunday in the Aldwych. But there's Greenwich Park at early evening, the river mist settling below the statue of General Wolfe. The silver glow of St James's Park after dark, gothic turrets beyond the silhouettes of planes and chestnuts, above lakeside beds of tulips and wallflowers. Charing Cross Road beneath early morning drizzle. Bloomsbury in snow. The dolphin-entwined lamps of the Embankment, when a hesperidian sun ignites the Thames and the lights flick on like strings of iridescent pearls. St Paul's at daybreak, stark and unforgiving, less barren than Trafalgar Square but just as immutable. Sicilian Avenue, ornately silent on a hot, dead afternoon. The arches of Regent Street like stone sunrises, sweeping across sideroads. These and a thousand other points of brightness remain, skin-prickling intersections on a vast spiritual grid.

And there are its people; resilient, private, wilful, defiantly odd. There's little can be changed in them. Their ability to trust is the city's greatest strength – and its most devastating curse.

London is a city only halfway in light. Not all of its walls are bounded in brick and stone. Its mysteries are diminished but not gone. Its keys are well hidden because the key-holders are invisible to the public. A few last selfish truths still remain here, cushioned and sheltered by power and class and money. They are protected by nothing more or less than the will of the landowners to survive for one more century. Nothing you can do will ever bring them out into the light, for the enemy is too elusive. He shape-shifts among the buildings, daring you to find him, knowing your task is quite impossible.

'Dear God! The very houses seem asleep, And all that mighty heart is lying still!' wrote William Wordsworth at Westminster Bridge early one morning.

Perhaps one day, some brave Prometheus will carry the light into the city, and bring the sleeping giant fully back to life. Then, reader, beware.

CHAPTER ONE

The Brigands

APART FROM one niggling annoyance, Sebastian Wells felt at peace with the world. He had just ignited a particularly fine cigar of Cuban extraction, and had drunk the decent portion of a magnum of Bollinger, albeit from a plastic cup. He was leaving one pleasurable venue, a box at the Royal Festival Hall where he had been attending a charity recital of Offenbach arias, and was heading for another, the Palm Court at the Waldorf Hotel. The violet dusk had settled into a late-summer night that was warm and starless. Ahead of him, confident couples fanned across the walkways of the South Bank and awkwardly climbed the stairs to Waterloo Bridge to collect their cars. Others strolled in evening dress beside the river, transforming the barren concrete embankment into a set for a champagne commercial. There was an air of gentle joviality. Sebastian felt unusually stately and benevolent, willing to be swayed in his argument, although perhaps not ready to concede it.

'The point, my dear Caton-James, is that the man was successful before he was twenty years of age.' He flicked the ash from his cigar and blew on the end until it was glowing.

'Not wealthy, though,' said Caton-James, searching the crowd.

'What do you expect? He had five children, and he lived extravagantly. His music was throwaway, full of topical parody, and yet here we are one hundred and twenty years later still listening to it.' Sebastian located the source of his annoyance and pointed his cigar to the figure emerging from one of the Hall's entrance doors. 'I think the gentleman we're looking for is there, at the back. He's alone.'

'Opera was invented for a closed society,' said St John Warner. He had the misfortune of speaking in a high, strangled voice that irritated everyone in earshot. 'It was never meant to be understood by the proles, but Offenbach made it accessible to all. I thought you'd be against that sort of thing, Sebastian.'

'Not at all,' Sebastian replied magnanimously. 'It doesn't hurt to give your workers some little tunes to hum. Besides, I defy anyone to resist *La Périchole's* "Letter Song".' He pointed in the direction of the entrance doors again. 'Look, will somebody stop this chap before he simply wanders off?'

Caton-James eased his way through the last of the departing audience and slipped a friendly arm behind the startled man's back.

'I wonder if we might have a word with you.' He attempted a pleasant smile, revealing a rictus of grey pegs that could make a baby cry.

His hostage, a smart, dark-complexioned man of twenty-two or so, checked the firm fist at his waist with an outraged 'I'm sorry?' and shorthanded such a look of violated privacy that he failed to see the others closing about him.

'Not that the working classes could comprehend such music now,' said Sebastian testily as he joined them. 'They make a sort of mooing noise in their public houses when Oasis comes on, wave their cans of Hooch and busk along with a few of the words to "Wonderwall", but ask them to remember the chorus of "Soyez Pitoyables" from *Les Brigands* and see where it gets you.'

Moments later their victim found himself separated from the concert stragglers and forced into a litter-strewn alley at the side of the Hall. The area seemed to have been designed for the facility of brigands. In front of him were five imposing young men in Edwardian evening wear. Alarmed and confused as the shadows closed over him, he was still considering the correct response when Caton-James punched him hard in the stomach. To everyone's surprise, the boy instantly threw up.

'Oh God!' squealed St John Warner, jumping back, 'all over my shoes!'

'Hold him still, will you?' asked Sebastian. 'Where's Barwick?'

'Over here.'

'Keep an eye out. There's a chap.'

Caton-James waited for the thin string of vomit to stop spilling from the young man's mouth onto the concrete, then punched him again, watching dispassionately as he folded over, moaning. Sebastian drew back his shoe and swung it hard at the frightened face beneath him. The shoes were new, Church's of course, and the heels still had sharp edges, so that his first kick removed most of the skin on the boy's nose. He was haematose now, his eyes dulling as he kicked and kicked, his mind in another place. The body beneath him fell back without resistance. Even from his position at the alley entrance, Barwick could hear the sharp cracking of bones, like explosive caps being stamped on. Sebastian lowered his leg and bent forward to study the cowering, carmine-faced figure. Blood was leaking from his ears.

'Looks like you've fractured his skull,' said Caton-James. 'We'd better go.'

'You're right. We'll lose our table if we don't get a move on.' The light returned to Sebastian's eyes as a chorus from *La Chanson de Fortunio* forced its way into his head. Nodding along with the melody, he reached forward and pulled the young man's cracked head up by his hair, then gently blew on the tip of his cigar. Forcing his victim's mouth open, he pushed the glowing stogie as far into his retching throat as it would go.

'Christ, Sebastian.' St John Warner grimaced, turning away.

With the annoyance taken care of, Sebastian rubbed the toecaps of his shoes against his calves until they shone, and straightened the line of his brocaded waistcoat. The Offenbach chorus rang on in his head, unstoppable now.

'I'm famished,' he said, glancing back at the convulsing body with distaste. 'Let's eat.' He led his men from the alley-way towards the bridge as Barwick attempted to lighten the mood, regaling the group with a scurrilous story about Sir Thomas Beecham. As they left the dying man behind, their dark laughter was absorbed in the gaiety of the dissipating crowds.

CHAPTER TWO

The Assignment

'BECAUSE I saw you trying to nick it, smartarse,' shouted the stallholder. The name of his stall was Mondo Video, and supposedly sold cult trash/rock/horror items on VHS, but these days his stock had been decimated by the need to conform with tougher censorship restrictions. It didn't help being sandwiched between a woman selling secondhand children's jumpers and a falafel takeaway, either.

'I wouldn't be caught dead nicking anything from this stall,' Vince countered, waving one of the video boxes in his hand. 'Check out the picture-quality of this stuff, it's burglary.'

'Burglary?'

'Yeah, like watching the screen with a pair of tights pulled over your face. You got a nerve trying to offload it onto the public.'

'Well, don't bother trying to half-inch any of it, then.' The stallholder rested his hands on his hips, amused by the boy's cheek. Maybe he'd seen him before; it was hard to tell. The worn-over sneakers, the clipper haircut, the ever-shifting eyes and the sallow complexion of a fast-food diet were common juvenile stigmata around here. But this one had a freshness, a touch of charm.

'Wouldn't give you the benefit of my custom, not for this load of pants. Of course, you probably dosh up from your export stock.' 'Export' was the universal code for videotapes that had not been classified by the British authorities. It was illegal to sell such merchandise to the public unless it was for export. It would have been especially foolhardy trying to offload such material in Shepherd's Bush market, which was constantly patrolled by police. The stallholder feigned shocked indignation, a skill he had practised and perfected long ago.

'I hope you're not suggesting I break the law.'

'Well, you ain't gonna make your money back flogging fifth generation copies of *Black Emmanuelle Goes East* with the good bits cut out, are you?' said Vince. 'This technology's dead, anyway. If you're gonna market cult videos, you need old BBFC–certificated stock, something the DPP can't touch, and I have the very thing.' He looked about for signs of the law, then dug into his leather duffel bag and produced a boxed tape. 'Check that out, mate.'

Vince had travelled the country buying up stock from dealers who had withdrawn tapes following advice from the Director of Public Prosecutions. 'First generation rental, and – technically – totally legal,' he explained, pointing to an original copy of *The Exorcist*. He opened the lid and displayed a dealer stamp from an Aberystwyth public library as proof. 'There you go. That's so clean it belongs in a photo-opportunity with a politician.'

Vince knew he had made a sale the moment the tape passed into the stallholder's hands. It was easy to spot the fanatical zeal in the eyes of a true collector. In the next few minutes he sold the remainder of his stock for six times what he'd paid, and left behind a grateful buyer. As he strutted between the crowded railway arches, back towards the entrance of the market, a little mental arithmetic confirmed that he was within sight of his financial target. He could now afford to reduce his hours at the store and concentrate on his assignment for Esther Goldstone.

He took a last look back at the boisterous crowds. Not so long ago the transactions taking place beneath the railways of London involved Jacobean candlesticks, Georgian silver and Victorian paintings of dubious provenance. Now they teemed with housewives who had been forced into scouring stalls for cheap children's clothes. Only the contumacious energy of the multitude remained.

An hour later, he kept his appointment at Goldstone's cluttered Covent Garden office, situated above a mediocre Italian restaurant in Floral Street. Esther was an agent, and the mother of a boy he had befriended on his journalism course. An editor of her acquaintance named Carol Mendacre was preparing a volume of new London journalism for her publishing house. Esther had read several of Vince's unpublished articles, and had been sufficiently intrigued to pass them onto the editor, who in turn had expressed an interest in commissioning a more substantial piece. If the finished product worked and the book did well, it would lead to further assignments. Esther was happy to offer guidance to her protégé. She felt that his writing had conviction, although his style was a little wild and ragged.

Now she listened patiently as he explained what he wanted to write about. She was a good listener, smiling and nodding as she absently touched her auburn hair. Glitzily maternal, she wore rings set with bulbous semi-precious stones on almost every finger, and sported an array of gilt ropes at her bosom. This may have given her the appearance of being Ali Baba's business manager but she was, in fact, a highly respected agent with a fondness for nurturing new writers.

'I don't see why nine per cent of the population should own ninety per cent of the land,' Vince told her heatedly, 'or why the country needs hereditary peers. It astonishes me that a city of nine million people selects its living options from a shortlist of outmoded ideas; that politicians are working for the common good and that the state has the welfare of all at its heart. The state is supposed to be there to uphold a sacred trust; to protect what rightfully belongs to its people. That concept disappeared when everything was sold off. How did we let it slip away? Isn't it time politicians learned that you can't excuse an incompetent career by having your picture taken with your arms around your children?'

'You're ranting, dear; I don't like that,' Esther gently chided him. 'Opinionated rhetoric is the province of the elderly, not twenty-five-year-olds. I read the piece based on the interviews you conducted. It was interesting enough, in a hectoring way. What Carol needs for this anthology is balanced reportage, not mere vocalised anger. No kneejerk stuff. Nothing in life is as clear-cut as you think. Don't turn this into a bleat about the class system; it's all been said before, and by writers far more articulate and experienced than yourself. Let's discuss practicalities. What I'll need from you fairly quickly is an outline of your intended piece.'

In the street outside, the Garden's performers were calling to the crowd, encouraging them to chant a set of comic refrains. Beyond this chorus, Vince could hear a coluratura soprano singing scales in the rehearsal room of the Opera House. A peppery cooking smell was wafting through the open window. There was an undertow of garlic in the air; restaurants were preparing for their evening sittings. On the roof above, someone was having a barbecue. So much life crowded on top of itself.

'You want me to pick something else to write about,' he said moodily.

'Not at all! The subject of class fits perfectly with what the editor has in mind, so long as you find an involving approach to your material. Don't just create a patchwork of facts and opinions. Find a vessel in which to present your argument. Don't forget – if she likes what you write, a quarter of the book will be yours. The other authors in the anthology all have extensive previous experience. You'll be her wild card, her new face. I'm counting on you to do this, Vincent.'

He sat back in his chair, chastened and feeling foolish. He wanted to leave her with a good impression. Esther reached over and placed a plump hand on his, her bracelets chinking. 'Stop looking so worried. You'll do fine, I'm sure. Just go back and concentrate on the project. Ask yourself if you've chosen your topic for the right reasons. It's obvious to me that you care, but that's nowhere near enough. Everyone feels passion about something. Everyone has ideas about their world. You need to refine yours through individual insight and experience.'

Her business manner returned as she withdrew her hand. 'It's not official yet, but this book is going to be part of a more ambitious project. Carol is hoping to sign a deal for a whole series of volumes, probably twelve in all. Each will feature the work of between four and six authors. They'll be setting out to chronicle the state of the world at the end of the twentieth century. She's come to me to help her find fresh young talent, and I don't want to disappoint her. You know I like your style, Vincent. I loved your London pieces and I'd love for you to become one of the series' regular authors. But you're not a recognised journalist. You're young, and the ideas of the young are not always thought through. You've only been published in fringe magazines. It all depends on you getting this first project right. I don't want to interfere editorially, but if you have problems with your material, bring them to me and I'll be happy to help you sort them out.'

'You have more faith in me than I have,' he said quietly.

'My interest isn't wholly philanthropic, I assure you.' She twisted a thick gold band on her finger, a gift from her divorced husband. 'As you know, I left the agency to set up on my own. This office is expensive, and Morris's settlement only goes so far. I promised Carol I'd find her fresh talent. I have to make this work. I search the literary backstreets for new blood, and what I find rarely holds promise. When I get someone like you, I hang on in hope. That you'll come through, that you'll be different from the rest. So write about London, if that's what interests you.'

'It's just . . . finding where to start.'

'Listen to that.' Esther sat back in her chair and nodded in the direction of the open window. 'What do you hear? Street vendors, tradesmen, punters, hawkers – and ranging above them, the opera singers. The centuries haven't overturned their roles. You talk about class. If the class system is so terrible, how come it's still here? What keeps it in place? Money? Breeding? Sheer selfishness? Perhaps you can find out.'

She rose suddenly, closing the session. 'Make it human, Vincent. There's much you won't understand unless you can find someone who'll explain from the inside how the system works. Try getting to know such a person. Assemble facts and figures, by all means –' she leaned forward, smiling now, and prodded him with a varnished nail, ' – but filter them through that pump in your chest. Give your writing some heart.'

The Elite

AS HE emerged from Esther Goldstone's office and crossed the road, clearing clouds released the afternoon sun, gilding the terraced buildings of Floral Street in brassy light. Vince knew he could not spend the rest of his life studying. He had taken night courses in photography, advanced English, history and journalism, with varying degrees of success. He had written and published sixteen poorly-paid articles on London, its history and people in a variety of fringe newspapers and desktop-produced magazines. Now at the age of twenty-five, he felt himself in danger of becoming a permanent student. He did not have enough cash saved to go travelling, and he was too tired to consider the prospect of backpacking across the campsites of Europe in search of sensation.

His mother wanted him to find a regular job, start a family and settle down, or at least stay in one place long enough to save some money. He wanted to work at a single project instead of half a dozen, to pick a direction and stick with it, but so far writing had earned him nothing, and the spectre of hitting forty in a ratty cardigan and a damp flat surrounded by thousands of press clippings filled him with depression. He did not want to fight his way into the media world determined to produce award-winning documentaries, only to wind up writing video links for cable kids' shows. He was more ambitious than that.

His brother Paul had screwed up royally, telling everyone he was holding down a highly-paid job at London Weekend Television as a technician. Far from being gainfully employed, he was caught breaking into a stereo component factory in Southend, and served four years of a six-year sentence for inflicting damage to one of the security guards. He was now working on an army base in Southampton. Vince was determined to do better than that, just to convince his mother that she hadn't raised her children in vain.

He rubbed a hand through his cropped black hair and looked back at the tourist-trammelled Piazza, at the gritty haze above it caused by street-cooking and car exhausts, then at the quiet curving street ahead. It was his afternoon off from the store, and he planned to visit Camden Library to raid their reference section. Now that he had set aside his misgivings and accepted the commission, he needed to develop a working method that would allow him to deliver the assignment on time. More than that, he needed a human subject to interview, but had no clue about how to find one.

As he passed a newsagent's shop in Charing Cross Road, he glanced in the window and idly studied the incongruous array of magazines. Between copies of *Cable TV Guide* and *Loaded* were a number of sun-faded society magazines, including a copy of *The Tatler*. On its cover was a laughing couple in evening dress, attending some kind of hunting event.

It made sense to purchase the field-guide to his chosen subject. As he thumbed through the pages, checking the captioned photographs, he felt as though he was facing an enemy for the first time. His knowledge of the class system's upper reaches was minimal and, he knew, reactionary, but studying a display of guffawing nitwits tipping champagne over each other in a marquee – 'The Honourable Rodney Waite-Gibbs and his girlfriend Letitia Colfe-Burgess, raising money for Needy Children' – filled him with an irrational fury that deepened with each page he turned. There were photographs of silky, bored debutantes seated beside improbable floral arrangements in Kensington apartments, drunk young gentlemen collapsed over wine-stained table-cloths, elderly landowners awkwardly posed at their country seats, their slight smiles hinting at perception of their immortality.

They struck Vince not as sons and daughters and brothers and sisters, but as dwindling continuations of lines buried deep in the past, barely connected to his world. Their forefathers' determination to civilise others had certainly earned them a place in history. Thumbing through *The Tatler* though, he could only assume that their children had collectively decided to abandon themselves to less altruistic pursuits.

One series of photographs particularly intrigued. They showed a handsome, haunted man with a contrite look on his face shying from cameras as he entered a grime-covered granite building. The caption read: 'The Honourable Sebastian Wells puts his troubled past to rest over a conciliatory dinner with his estranged father, Sir Nicholas Wells, at the Garrick Club.' In the entire magazine, this was the only hint that something was wrong in the upper echelons. He found himself wondering what sort of trouble the honourable Sebastian Wells had got himself into. He planned to write about London from the view of his own working-class background, but it needed someone like this to provide his ideas with contrast. What were the chances of getting a member of the aristocracy to talk to him? How did he even set about obtaining a telephone number? Wells's father belonged to the House of Lords, which at least made him easier to track down.

Vince closed the magazine and headed off towards the library at a renewed pace. He had found his human subject. And his method of choosing Sebastian Wells could not have been more constitutional if he had simply stuck a pin in an open telephone directory.

The Meeting

'**AND YOU** must be Vincent Reynolds.'

Vince squinted up into the sun, raised a hand to his brow and saw a slim-shouldered man with floppy chestnut hair and green eyes smiling down at him. He knew at once that this was the person he had arranged to meet, and smiled back. He thought later that it had been the preposition in that intro-ductory sentence which had given the stranger away, turning Vince's name into the postscript of some deeper thought.

'Sorry, I was nearly asleep,' he explained, nervously closing his book.

Sebastian Wells held out a manicured hand. The skin was pale and traversed with bulging veins. 'Nice to meet you at last. All those messages going back and forth, all that modern technology and we still couldn't connect.' He looked around at the gardens, the sloping lawn. 'I've not been over here before.'

'I'm sorry, I picked it because I understood you lived nearby.'

'My father has several houses in the area, that's correct, but I spend very little time here.' He didn't pronounce the *r* in *very*.

The late summer afternoon had begun warm, but its lengthening shadows were chill. For the last half-hour Vince had been sitting on a wooden bench just below the cream wedding-cake façade of Kenwood House, in front of a gnarled and ancient magnolia tree. He had vaguely registered the man walking up from the dank green lake at the bottom of the slope. Sebastian Wells was styled in that self-consciously English manner Americans sometimes affect when they move to London. The navy-blue cable-knit sweater over his bespoke blue and white striped shirt was almost parody-Brit, and had the effect of setting Vince at a disadvantage in his Mambo sweatshirt, jeans and filthy sneakers.

'You're reading about the Jews?' Sebastian tapped Vince's book cover. 'Fascinating stuff. The great majority of English Jews are Ashkenazim.' He joined Vince on the bench. His clipped enunciation suggested the speech of an elderly member of the aristocracy, and seemed false in one so young. 'From Germany, Holland and Poland. Edward the First banished them from England in 1290. Oliver Cromwell let them back in three and a half centuries later. What exactly are you researching?'

'How do you know I'm not just reading this for pleasure?'

Sebastian tilted the cover of the book and narrowed his eyes. 'Societal Group Structures In Nineteenth-Century European Culture. What, you thought you'd get through it before the movie version came out?'

'It's for research, you're right,' he admitted. 'I'm studying for a course.' He was determined to speak nicely and not drop his aitches, something he always tried when meeting new people but only managed to keep up for twenty minutes or so. The difference in their speech alone suggested an unbridgeable gulf between them. Sebastian's consonants were cut crystal.

'Oh? And which course are you taking?'

'History of London. It's just three nights a week. An aid to my writing.'

'Oh, a *night* course. The Open University. How exciting. And that subject interests you, does it?'

'All journalism interests me.'

'So why aren't you taking a course in journalism?'

'I've already taken one. Now I'm on the creation and maintenance of British social divisions.'

'Goodness, that sounds like heavy going. Your manner of speech is very clear. I like that.'

Vince thought this an odd sort of compliment. 'My parents taught me to enunciate clearly,' he explained. 'They felt it was important to be understood. My dad needed to be for his job. He was a bus conductor. He used to shout out the destinations. I was a bingo caller for a while last summer. You have to speak clearly for that. A lot of the customers are deaf.'

'How interesting.' Sebastian placed his hands behind his back and nodded, adopting the kind of pose Prince Charles holds when a foreman describes the cubic capacity of a drainage outlet to him. 'Of course, one mustn't confuse diction with clarity of intention. Did you know that there are as many accents in an English street as there are in the whole of America?'

'No, I didn't,' said Vince. 'Anyway, what you say is more important than how you sound.'

'True, but it's advisable to speak properly if you wish to be taken seriously. Listen to that.'

He looked down towards the lake. One small child was hitting another with a large section of torn-off branch. Even from there Vince could hear them screaming 'fuck off' at each other.

'Of course, one's language has a tendency to reveal one's class, doesn't it? Which position in society's beehive do you occupy?'

Vince closed his book and rose from the seat with more aggression than he had intended. 'I'll give you a clue. My dad rode Routemaster buses down the Old Kent Road. He died of a heart attack at forty-eight. My mum still works in a shoe shop. I grew up in Peckham.'

Sebastian dismissed the reply with a wave of his hand. 'Oh well, it's a classless country now, if the television is to be believed.'

'What class am I to assume you are, then? Upper middle?'

'Me? Heaven forfend. There's nothing remotely *middle* about it. Nobody in our family has ever held down a proper job. We just own land. Lots and lots of it.'

Vince studied his companion carefully. He looked to be about twenty-seven.

'Yeah, but you must do something.'

'Why must I? We socialise, support charities, run societies, that sort of thing. My father works for the WBI, an organisation that is attempting, wrongly in my opinion, to remove all trade barriers between European member countries. As a lord he cannot represent in parliament, of course, and as the House of Lords exists primarily to delay legislation, he has to find other ways of filling his time. At least that way we don't have to rush about raising money for the upkeep of the family pile.'

'And you?'

'Oh, I chair debates. Hold parties. Play all sorts of games. I like games.'

'Games get boring after a while. You must wish for a more substantial occupation sometimes.'

'Yes, perhaps even in the same way that you do. I suppose in that respect our lives run on parallel lines.'

'Which implies that they never cross over.'

'Except at moments like this.'

'But I work to eat,' said Vince. 'It's not a diversion from being bored. It may be stating the obvious, but I do it because I don't have any bloody money.'

They studied each other, equally intrigued.

'I take it you are in employment, then.' Sebastian made the idea sound disreputable.

'I work in a home entertainment store. Just to pay the rent.'

'Home entertainment.' He savoured the concept for a moment. 'What is that, exactly?'

'CDs, videos, laserdiscs, interactive CD-Roms, play-stations, you know.'

But one look at Sebastian's face told Vince that he didn't know. He masked his ignorance with a brave smile. 'Well, Mr Reynolds, I passed a coffee shop on the way in here. Would you think me exploiting the social orders if I offered to buy you a cup? As I'm to be the subject beneath your microscope, perhaps we should get to know each other a little better.'

Somewhere on the green slopes below, a bird was startled into singing. And somehow, through some mysterious osmotic process, Vincent Reynolds allowed himself to be gently drawn into a different world.

Friends

THE OFFICES of Stickley & Kent were located in a parade of shops heralded by a long purple-painted brick wall with the words 'Shambala Skins' decoratively sprayed on it. On his afternoon off, Vince headed to the Kentish Town estate agency to share lunch with his two oldest friends.

'Men are like taxis,' Pam was telling Louie as he arrived. 'You think the one you get inside is all yours until you realise that the seat is still warm from the last passenger.' She held a steaming plastic beaker at eye level and examined it, turning over the contents with a plastic fork. It was the first time she'd paused for breath in twenty minutes. 'You know, a simple anagram for Pot Noodle is Not Poodle. I shudder to think about what people stick into their bodies. Come to that, I shudder to think about what I stick in my body. Or rather, who.'

'Your choices take some explaining, I'll give you that,' said Louie.

'The trouble is,' Pam continued, 'everyone's become so *knowing*. Men are adept at making each girl they date feel special for a set period of time before moving on, like waiters. Hi, Vince.' Pam immediately broke off the conversation when Vince entered the office. She would never speak of other men in his presence because she loved him with every fibre of her being and longed to monopolise his every waking hour. The object of her adoration could not reciprocate, however.

'That's 'cause we've read all those magazine articles about what women really want,' said Louie. 'We know all the right moves.' Louie was a velvet-voiced Antiguan who had been raised in the neighbourhood and was now studying at the University of North London. The real problem was that the three of them knew each other too well. Vince, Louie and Pam had grown up a few streets apart. Vince was amazed that they were still friends, given the different directions their lives were taking. He was aware of Pam's infatuation with him – how could he not be when her eyes followed him around the room like peepholes in a gothic painting – but he also knew that they were not suited for each other. She entirely lacked imagination, a minor fault to many but a fatal flaw in Vince's eyes.

Louie had piercings and a white strip of hair running down the centre of his stubbled black head, a look he had designed to accentuate his independence and nonconformity. Everyone he hung out with sported this look except Pam, who as an estate agent was excluded from the world of exotic personal statements. Louie was six feet, two inches tall and wore tight black leather, a common look in North London but this leather was expensive, not the usual rocker-tat they sold on the high street stalls. Instead of skull rings he sported enough gold jewellery to suggest that he was the advance scout for a Barry White revival. The other estate agents in the office barely noticed Louie's attire; in this cosmopolitan section of London it labelled you a Neo-Punk, and was virtually treated as a job description.

Of course, neither Pam nor Louie expected Vince to be

fashionable. Vince was Good Old Vince, dependable, down-to-earth and durable, like a pair of workboots. He cut his own hair, shopped in street markets and never bought a shirt without telling you how much he'd saved on it. He wore his background like a badge, so much so that he sometimes seemed almost a parody; a forgotten cockney caper, a throw-back to a more innocent time.

'Well, I've had enough,' said Pam. 'I'm really tired of this city.'

'You've been saying that since you were fifteen.'

Pam provided a total contrast to Louie. Her hair was cut in a tight blonde bob, its hue discreetly elevated. Her suits were pastel, and her earrings (always ovals or drops) comple-mented her pearlised nail varnish. She idolised the corporate women she saw on American soaps, copied their clothes and read their magazines, but was unable to duplicate their aggressive behaviour. Vince reached over and dug a spoon into her lemon cheesecake.

'Good to see you two haven't run out of things to talk about.'

'I just need to get out for a while, go somewhere where there's some light and air,' said Pam, finishing her cake and carefully brushing the crumbs from the desk. 'The three of us could go away together.'

'Oh, I don't think so.' Vince waved the idea away. They had this conversation twice a month.

'Where would you go if you left London?' asked Louie, filling three cups of coffee on Pam's desk.

'I don't know. There are other cities. I've got to leave the flat. The council's busy stocking my building with rehab-ilitated sex offenders and refugees who've not quite broken the habit of street-cooking. I'll go somewhere where the men haven't wised up yet. Eastern Europe. Prague, maybe.'

'Prague's full of American students doing Europe.'

'Germany, then. I can't stay here. London is finished. It's dying under the weight of its own past. Look at the place, filthy, run-down, the roads permanently dug up, ugly new buildings cropping up like weeds, the public transport system collapsing, the politicians useless. And everyone's so – *angry*.'

'It was always like this,' said Vince, accepting one of the coffees. 'Take a look at the old photographs. Barely controlled chaos. That's what I like about it.'

'We know you do,' said Louie. 'Pam was telling me about this Sebastian Wells character. What's the deal?'

'He's a genuine toff, photo in *The Tatler*, pile in the country, father in the House of Lords. My passport to fame and fortune,' replied Vince. 'When I finally managed to track him down I left about a million messages on his machine, but he didn't answer any of them. Then I wrote to him and explained that I was working on a book – well, he doesn't know it's only a quarter of a book – about the British class system, and he agreed to be my live study subject.'

'What does he do?'

'He plays games.'

'Games? What kind of games?'

'Chess, mah-jong, ancient blocking games, puzzles, word games. I guess he has too much time on his hands.'

'Upper class and idle. And a rich bastard too, I suppose.'

'I don't know, I only just met him. He looks rich. Manicured. His clothes have –' he hunted for a suitable word.

'Linings,' suggested Pam.

'His father's some big shot in the European community. He bombards you with information all the time, like he's teaching you stuff. He likes facts. Exactly what I need.'

'I'm surprised he agreed to let you question him,' said Louie, 'considering your chosen subject.'

'He doesn't know anything about the angle I'm taking,' Vince explained. 'He's gonna let me conduct a series of interviews, but he's asked to vet the manuscript once I've finished.'

'What if he doesn't like what you've written? He could screw the whole thing up. You're better off being honest right from the outset.'

Vince dropped his chin into his hands and looked out through the plastic sale-cards that dangled in the windows. 'I don't know. This is the first break I've had. People aren't prepared to talk about the class system when it works in their favour. They're wary of making enemies. As it is, I feel like I'm writing this under false pretences.'

'You won't be if you have to show him everything you intend to publish. So long as he has final approval, you might as well be employed by him.' Louie checked his Swatch, then hefted a sports bag onto his shoulder and rose, turning to Vince. 'There's a simple way around that, of course. Take what you can from this geezer, lie yourself blue in the face to get his confidence, drain him of information, don't show him what you've written, then do a real slag-off job in print. That's how the tabloids do it. What do you care? He can't sue if it's all true.'

'Nice attitude, Louie,' said Pam. 'Can't you see that Vince feels uncomfortable about using someone?' She did not understand his choice of career, but was always ready to defend him. To her, writing seemed a peculiar way to try to earn a living, as did any job without set lunch-hours.

'He's unlike anyone I've ever met,' Vince tried to explain. 'His accent is so refined I can barely understand him. He can trace his ancestors back hundreds of years, to the House of York, John of Gaunt, all the Edwards and Richards. I can't trace mine back two generations. If I was him, I wouldn't even consider passing the time of day with me.'

'You're in awe of him, you wanker,' shouted Louie glee-fully. 'You've gone all proley and apologetic. He's already got to you. That's how it works, don't you see? They come on all superior and charming, and moments later you're wringing your cloth cap between your hands and making excuses for getting in the way of their horses.'

'You do always put yourself down, Vince,' said Pam, clearing away the cartons, cups and paper bags that had held their lunch. 'It's such a shame. You've no self-esteem. Of course, neither have I, which is probably why I haven't had a date this year unless you count Darren Wadsworth, and I don't. Wait until I've finished my business management course, though. I'll be a new me.'

Vince doubted it. Over the years his oldest female friend had not changed one atom. She was still hopelessly shy and inward-looking, and clung to the idea that the courses she took would eventually provide her with a dynamic person-ality, a change of character that would finally enable her to marry him and settle down.

'It's great that you're getting a break on your project. I'm very pleased for you. You just don't look too happy about it, that's all.'

'It's because we got on so well. I didn't think we would.'

'Where's the problem in that?'

It was so hard to put into words that he felt uncomfortable even discussing it with Pam. 'I don't get it,' he said finally. 'I'm the only one who benefits. Why would he bother to help me? What's in it for him?'

'You wanna watch it,' Louie said and laughed. 'It'll be up to his club for tea and crumpets, a fine claret and a spot of buggery, and before you know it you'll be back on the street with a sore arse and a gold sovereign for your troubles.'

Vince laughed too, but the questions in his head remained unanswered.

CHAPTER SIX

Q & A

THEY HAD arranged to meet for the first of their formal interviews in three days' time. But here he was, standing before Vince in the reference room of Camden Library, the honourable Sebastian Wells himself. He had been seated across the room, making notes from a stack of what appeared to be gaming manuals. He was paler and thinner than Vince remembered, dressed in a superbly cut black suit and club tie, far too immaculate for grungy old North London.

'Well, we meet again!'

'Jesus! Sorry,' said Vince, jumping. 'You always seem to catch me unawares. What are you doing here?'

'I must admit it's not my territory, but I needed to look up the rules of a rather obscure Polynesian blocking game, and Highgate Library recommended a book held here. Saves spending hours at the British Library. What about you?'

'The usual, research.'

Sebastian pulled out a chair and sat opposite. 'I've been doing some thinking.'

He's changed his mind, thought Vince, he doesn't want to be interviewed.

'The day before yesterday I agreed to answer your

questions, didn't I, but you know, perhaps you can help me just as much.'

'I can? How?'

'In our brief chat you made me realise just how little I know about working-class London. Forgive me, but you did admit to being working class.' He smiled pleasantly, anxious not to cause offence.

'Absolutely.'

'So you can teach me something as well.'

'What would you want to know?'

'Facts, Mr Reynolds, facts. The more one is in possession of them, the better one's overall frame of reference. How long are you going to be here today?'

'Another hour, I imagine.'

'I'll tell you what. I've got all I need for now. I'll come back for you in an hour, unless you have another appointment? We could go for a drink.'

'I think I'll be free then,' said Vince. *Like I have another appointment to go to,* he thought as he watched the elegant subject of his interview stroll from the room, leaving the gaming manuals scattered across the table for someone else to put away. There was a charming air of vagueness about Sebastian, as if each thought he had was freshly plucked from the ether. He trusted everything to fall into place in its natural order. People like that never had to worry about landlords or night buses. The mundane clutter that separated most people from their dreams did not exist for him.

An hour and a quarter later they were sitting outside the Dingwall public house in Camden, watching bargees operating the canal lock below them and discussing Vince's determination to be a successful writer. Sebastian had once attempted to write a technique manual on contract bridge, but had lacked the necessary drive to finish it.

Vince was unnerved by his new friend. Considering his argument for the equality of the classes, it was absurd to be in awe of someone like Sebastian, but he could not help himself. Perhaps this built-in respect for social order was a genetic thing. Looking at their surroundings, he felt embarrassed at the dirt and shabbiness, at the tattooed tribes folded up against walls, nursing their cans of lager.

'I wonder if you have any idea how unique this is,' said Sebastian, sipping his pint with a delicacy that suggested the experience was new to him. 'Nobody I know would ever do anything like it.'

'Then why are you?'

'You asked the same question when last we met, remember? Surely you've acted out of sheer curiosity before.'

'I do it all the time.'

'There you are, then. The "class divide information exchange" starts here. I'll ask you something, then you can ask me something, how about that.'

Vince dug around in his bag for a notebook and pencil. 'All right,' he agreed. 'You start.'

'Vincent. May I call you that? Were you named after Van Gogh?'

'Nah. My dad liked Don McLean.'

Sebastian searched the air. 'I'm not familiar . . .'

'The title of a song. My turn. Why are you willing to do this? Why talk to me? Be honest.'

'You're not going to let it go, are you?' Sebastian sighed. 'For the same reason as you, to learn. Besides, you asked me if I would do it. Nobody's ever done that before. You're clearly a man of some insight and intelligence. I would have refused if I'd found you not to be so. My view of the world is every bit as limited as yours, I can assure you. We all need to expand our horizons, don't you think?'

'Fair enough.' Vince made a note on his pad. 'First of all, let's find out what you don't know.'

'Fine. Ask me anything.'

'Here's an easy questionto start with. Pulp, Oasis and Blur are all – what?'

This was not what Sebastian had been expecting. He pursed his lips and thought for a moment. 'Nouns?' he asked desperately.

'Wow.' Vince was amazed. 'They're bands.'

'Ah. Popular, I suppose?'

'Very popular.'

'I rarely listen to the wireless.'

'Remind me to send you a tape. Now it's your turn.'

'Okay. Our family motto is *Ad Astra Per Aspera*. Do you have one, and if so, what is it?'

It was Vince's turn to think. '*Don't Get Caught*,' he said finally. '*And If You Do, Don't Lag On Your Mates*. When Manchester United plays Liverpool, who usually wins?'

'I don't know anything about football.'

'I suppose you play rugby.'

'No, polo.'

'All right. If Robocop fought the Terminator, who would win?'

'Ah, now I know this,' said Sebastian confidently. 'The Terminator. He's a boxer, isn't he?'

'He's more of a liquid metal cyber-android,' Vince replied. 'Remind me to send you another tape.'

'Which after-school societies did you belong to?'

Vince laughed. 'You don't mean gangs, do you?'

'No, I don't.'

'We didn't have any. It was as much as the teachers could do to keep from getting stabbed during the day, without extending the risk into the twilight hours. What did you belong to?'

'Oh, the usual,' Sebastian said airily. 'Operatic, Scientific, Debating, Badminton, Christian Union, Stampfiends, *Quo Vadis* –'

'What was the last one?'

'Oh, you know, "Whither Goest Thou", meetings about one's future. Gilbert and Sullivan –'

'They had their own society?'

'Of course. Tennis, Numismatics, Bridge, Chess – and I was a moderately empassioned Lysander in *A Midsummer Night's Dream.*'

'I'm surprised you had any time left over for smoking and shagging behind the bike sheds.' Vince drained his glass. 'Although I suppose you went to a boys-only school.'

'It made no difference on that front, I can assure you. The pupils of public schools are every bit as rebellious as their counterparts. Whose turn is it?'

'Yours.'

'Okay. Why do so many working-class people look for handouts all the time? Why can't you organise yourselves properly?'

'Because if we did, you'd all be murdered in the streets. The French got rid of their toffs, and look at them now; a national railway that works, great grub, unspoilt country-side, gorgeous women.' Vince nodded at his empty glass. 'Your round.'

Over the next hour they argued the merits of popular food-stuffs, authors, football versus polo, films, architecture, art and music, although in the last category Sebastian proved to

Disturbia

be woefully unaware of any post-Offenbach developments. Vince carefully steered the conversation clear of politics and religion; he was wary of damaging their relationship at such an early stage.

Sebastian seemed to especially enjoy telling Vince about his games, and launched into a series of complex abstractions about rule-making that were almost impossible to follow. Vince usually found it difficult making conversation with strangers. He lacked confidence, and yet a stubborn streak made him stick to his guns in arguments, even when he knew he was utterly, incontrovertibly wrong. This annoying character trait was an inheritance from his father, but with Sebastian it found no need to surface, because he made Vince feel that he was contributing something valuable to the conversation. Sebastian listened. Not even all of his own friends did that.

Even so, he made a conscious effort not to be charmed. It was important not to lose sight of his intentions. He was using his subject to garner material that might damn him. He could not afford to lose his objectivity.

When Vince finally announced that he had to go home, Sebastian offered to drive him in his Mercedes. The offer accepted, Vince made his chauffeur slow down as they arrived so that the bloke in the shop downstairs would see and be impressed.

The Barrier

SEBASTIAN WAS three years older than Vince, an isolated, unfathomable man of twenty-eight who had strong opinions on all kinds of esoteric subjects, and no knowledge at all of more populist topics. He never watched television, and had missed out on all of the social phenomena associated with the medium. He had never been to a rock concert or a football match. Vince spent an amusing hour explaining the appeal of TV shows like *The X Files* and sorting out the scatalogical implications of various football fans' songs.

In return, Sebastian explained the structure of the House of Lords, the benefits and limitations of hereditary peerage and why Conservative MPs had to know about pigs and mooring rights in order to keep their constituents happy. His arguments convinced with a beguiling mixture of wisdom and naivety.

Three days after they had last met, Vince invited Sebastian over for something to eat while he conducted a more formal interview at the dingy first-floor flat he rented in one of the great damp Victorian houses behind Tufnell Park tube station.

He kept everything neat and freshly painted because he

had briefly shared a flat with Louie, and their apartment had ended up looking like it was in the process of being searched by the SAS, as well as being decorated in a manner that showed influences of rave culture, *A Rebours* and colour blindness. While his host clattered in the kitchen, Sebastian wandered from room to room, appalled that people could actually live like this. Still, it was clean if nothing else, and the neat stack of books and videos on Vince's bedside table revealed a bewildering array of interests: Patrick Hamilton, Virginia Woolf, *The Usual Suspects*, Evelyn Waugh, Irvine Welsh, *Pulp Fiction*, Dickens, a Manga video, Mervyn Peake, Fortean Times and VIZ. A quick flick through a pile of battered street-style magazines revealed a world as mysterious and lost to him as the ancient wisdom of the Pharaohs.

One thing they shared in common was a fascination with their surroundings. Vince was captivated by the city, had been ever since his father had walked him along Shaftesbury Avenue at the age of four. He had passed his childhood lost in the delights of the printed page, his fingers remaining firmly in his ears to block the sound of his parents fighting. By doing so, he had amassed an alarming amount of detail about his habitat. Reading Pepys and Boswell had provided him with reasons for wanting to become a journalist.

'So you know all about London, then?' asked Sebastian, turning over a volume of photographs entitled *The Changing Metropolis*.

'That's impossible,' Vince called back. 'I defy anybody to do more than scratch the surface. The city is older than Christ. Dig, and all you ever find is the layer below. It's like peeling an onion. But I had a summer job as a tour guide for London Transport once, and picked up a lot of stuff. For example, do you know what's so special about the lamps at the corners of Trafalgar Square?'

'I've absolutely no idea,' Sebastian laughed.

'They're the original oil lamps from Nelson's flagship, the *Victory*,' Vince said, walking into the room. 'Do you know why Dick Whittington had a cat?'

'I have a feeling you're about to tell me.'

'It was a metaphorical feline. A "cat" was a medieval nick-name for a coal-barge, and Whittington made his fortune in coal. Shit –' There was an explosion of steam in the kitchen. 'I think we're gonna be eating out.'

Sebastian was also something of an expert on the subject, and during the interview unveiled his discoveries before Vince like a series of moves in an obscure memory game. He talked about the past, but never the future. He seemed closed off in so many ways that Vince could never tell what he was thinking – but he was always thinking.

'I've got one for you,' he said suddenly. 'Officially there's no such place as Westminster Abbey, did you know that? It's actually the Collegiate Church in Westminster.'

'All right,' Vince countered, 'why isn't there a single statue of Dickens in London?'

'Easy. He was a modest man, and forbade it. For many years there was a statue of a fat boy near Smithfields, marking the spot where the Great Fire finished. What did it represent?'

'I know this, I know this. It's supposed to be the sin of Gluttony, because the fire started in Pudding Lane and ended at Pie Corner. One more, come on, hit me with your best shot.'

Sebastian thought for a moment. 'All right. Why was St George's Church in Southwark built with three white clock faces and one black?'

Vince knew he was beaten. 'I don't know,' he conceded.

'The people of Bermondsey refused to contribute towards the church. The black clock face pointed in their direction. Impossible to read in the dark.'

'Is that true?'

'Absolutely,' Sebastian said and grinned.

They met again on September the 16th, two weeks after their initial meeting.

'Have you ever encountered real royalty?' asked Vince as they sat in the lounge bar of the Queen's Head & Artichoke with the microphone of his cassette recorder propped between them.

'Oh yes, on several different occasions.'

'Go on, then, who've you met?'

'Well, Her Majesty.'

'What, Liz?'

Sebastian winced. 'Please, Vincent, have some respect. I was presented to Queen Elizabeth the Second when I was thirteen.'

'Wow, what was she like?'

'Regal.'

Vince closed his notebook. 'Did you ever notice that whenever the Queen is asked something she doesn't have a favourable opinion of, she replies in a single word answer? You know, "How does ma'am find this painting?" "Disagreeable." "And the sunset?" "Lurid." "And the prime minister?" "Bovine." That sort of thing. You're like that a lot of the time. It must be a class signifier. Us proles have a hard time shutting up.'

'Really.'

'You see what I mean? But I figure if I keep asking you little things about yourself I can slowly build up a composite picture, like an Identikit. Tell me what you dream about.'

Sebastian smiled mischievously. 'Fire.'

'What do you like to do most?'

'Challenge.'

'What are your plans for the future?'

'Promethean.'

'How much is your family worth?'

'Oodles.'

'What quality do you value above all else?'

'Leadership.'

'How do you get on with your father?'

'Pass.'

It was obvious that Sebastian would rather have his teeth pulled than discuss anything about his private life. It was a barrier Vince knew he would have to break down if they were to make any real connection with each other. He enjoyed his subject's company immensely. The man never stopped explaining the rules; how to behave in a fancy restaurant, why good clothes cost so much, how to order wine, when and how much to tip, what to look for in a good cigar, how the old London streets were laid out, how to play Pelmanism, how to win at poker, chess and a host of strange games whose complex subtleties escaped him. But he adroitly sidestepped intimacies, and the one subject he never offered advice on was women. He seemed only tangentially interested in them. Perhaps he had been badly hurt in the past. Didn't wealthy families sometimes arrange that side of things for their offspring?

Sebastian's town apartment overlooked the Snowdon Aviary in Regent's Park and was stuffed with elegant impersonal furniture, more of a showflat than a home. The only room with any character was the games room, a large spare bedroom filled with board games and puzzles of every description. His 'country pile', he assured Vince, was an altogether more prepossessing sight, a vast Georgian estate in Hertfordshire. He occasionally rang someone called St John Warner, and someone else called Caton-James, and apparently spent evenings playing board games with his friends, but never invited Vince to meet any of them. There was little evidence of the network of powerful connections one imagined every honourable young gentleman to maintain and exploit.

Minor caveats aside, their meetings continued to yield fascinating rewards. One cliché appeared to be true; the isolation of Sebastian's upbringing as he passed from nanny to boarding school contrasted sharply with the warmth and chaos of Vince's childhood home. He was particularly determined not to discuss his relationship with his father, or to set out his hopes and fears for times to come.

Vince taped the interviews, carefully labelling each cassette and indexing it for later reference. Sebastian paid for lunches and dinners, lent cash and cabfares he clearly did not expect to be repaid, and generally behaved like a decent friend. It was a lifestyle to which Vince felt he could easily become accustomed.

Still, an unspoken barrier remained firmly in place between them, preventing any true closeness from developing.

Research

`CONSTITUTIONALLY, England no longer exists. It is not mentioned in the title of its sovereign. The English people have no special rights, not even a separate set of official statistics. England retains its separate identity in just two areas: religion – the Church Of England – and sport – cricket, rugby and soccer. England occupies more than half of the United Kingdom's land mass and contains over four fifths of the population. It is one of the most densely populated countries in the world. And yet Scotland and Wales have both been more successful in securing their own institutions. For example, the BBC has special Scottish and Welsh broadcasting councils, but England has none. So how do we define Englishness? By history, by art, by character? What is the spirit of England, and how can we embody it, empower it?'

Vince didn't like the sound of the last part. He had been digging out old speeches in an effort to uncover something more substantial on Sebastian. He knew virtually nothing about his subject's immediate past and had hoped to unearth details about the Wells family background, but this was not entirely what he had expected to find. Turning to the front of the article, he checked the author's name again. Sebastian Wells, right there in black and white. There was even a moody little photograph that looked as if it had been taken at university.

'England is a compact country. All its destinations are within a day's land travel. Consequently it maintains a national character despite the extraordinary diversity of its people. It is dominated by the vast central city of London, a city older than Christianity itself, but almost completely reinvented in the New Elizabethan age. For the Blitz caused far more destruction than mere damage to bricks and mortar. In 1939, London was still the greatest city in the world. This rich royal capital, so absolutely sure of itself, was changed forever by the incessant rain of bombs. Its traditions were lost, its centuries-old sense of national mission replaced with confusion, loss of civic responsibility, bureaucratic muddle and argument, a state of chaos from which it has never fully recovered. It is no coincidence that the post-war years saw a rise in factors contributing to that chaos: immigration, divorce, motiveless crime.'

Vince knew a little about the so-called New Elizabethans, the first generation of post-war university graduates. The name had never really caught on. Closing the book, he recalled seeing Sebastian's name somewhere else, on another item culled earlier from the Political Science section. The curse of a photographic memory. A glance at the clock confirmed that the library would be closing in fifteen minutes. Just enough time.

He found what he was looking for in the sidebar of an article about political extremism that he had photocopied for his original course essay on London and the class system. Sebastian Wells had been thrown out of Oxford for something referred to as 'Incitement to Hatred', which presumably meant encouraging racism. If that was the case, what on earth was he doing answering Vince's questions?

It was hard to believe that the two people were actually one and the same. In person Sebastian was perfectly reasonable and rational. On paper he was a torch-wielding fanatic. According to the press he was billed as one of the emerging new leaders of the intellectual far right, but his birthright seemed to deny him as much as it offered. As an MP he would have had the power to promote his ideas. As an Honourable destined to adopt his father's title, his only power lay in preventing the ideas of others.

An alarming new picture of Sebastian Wells drew into focus. He had certainly covered the far-right corners of the political waterfront in his brief life. He considered both the Monday Club and the Disraelian Society too liberal and 'wishy-washy'. He advocated forced repatriation, an end to the Health Service, the return of capital punishment, further tax incentives for big business. More sinister motives were hinted at.

Sebastian had not advanced a single extreme opinion in any of their interviews. On the contrary, he had evinced such naive courtesy that it was tempting to avoid the dark areas of his psyche, to enjoy his easy charm, his louche manner, his casually reckless expenditure. Vince was ashamed to admit that it was fun hanging out with someone who wasn't penniless for a change, someone with a car and money to spend. This was what half of him had always wanted: stability, order, respect, social standing. So what if it required making a few moral sacrifices?

He had not even begun his professional career as a writer, and already the question of compromise was slapping him in the face. He decided that Sebastian would have to be told about his misgivings. He would give him a chance to explain, warn him, possibly even stop the interviews. In a way, finding out something like this was exactly what he had hoped for. But he *liked* the man, for God's sake.

And there was something else. He made photocopies of the articles he had just read and headed towards his apartment, making a mental note to ask Sebastian about a phrase that had cropped up a number of times, his connection to a society known as the League of Prometheus. Instead of confronting him immediately, Vince decided to do some more reading up on the subject of the beliefs and proclamations of the Hon. Sebastian Wells.

'It seems like you're here every day, man,' said the Rastafarian desk clerk as he arrived at Camden Library the following morning.

'Yes, you're right, I have no life,' Vince admitted, shaking out his umbrella and stowing it in a corner. He had stepped on a paving stone that had tilted, soaking his jeans, a typical street-hazard in Tufnell Park. As usual he was the first customer, and would probably be alone until the down-and-outs arrived when they were cleared out from the local hostel. At the battered Apple Mac in the corner of the reference section, he logged onto the Internet and began a subject search for items located under the references *Wells, Sebastian* and *League, Prometheus*. The latter organisation had been mentioned most recently in a *Guardian* article. God knows how much this could cost me, he thought, praying for speed as he checked the loading times and pulled down a couple of text-only articles.

There were a number of old newspaper and magazine pieces to choose from, mainly concerning Sebastian's early fundraising days for the Tories, when he had organised special events at his school. One concerned his putative friendship with a notorious Nazi sympathiser, a professor whose new book set out the theory that the Holocaust had not happened. The other featured the text of a speech he had given at the opening of a right-wing bookshop in South London. Mildly nasty stuff, yet no one had anything critical to say in print. On the contrary, the tabloids seemed to champion him as the voice of common sense, and he was generally considered to have the ear of a number of influential figures. This was a different image to the vague game-playing charmer presented to Vince.

There were no societies listed under the reference *Prometheus*, so he printed hard copies of the articles and logged out before the bill had a chance to climb too high. As he checked through the classical section, distant thunder rumbled above the rain-washed skylight in the centre of the room and it grew so dark that the librarians had to switch the lights on, something they were always reluctant to do, as if they considered eye-strain to be a beneficial part of the learning process.

Prometheus. Greek demi-god. Son of Iapetos, brother of Atlas. The name meant 'forethought'. The wisest of his race, he was credited with bringing knowledge to mankind. He had been given the task of distributing powers and abilities on earth. He stole fire from the gods and gave it to mortals, only to be punished by Zeus, who had Prometheus chained naked to a pillar in the Caucasian mountains. Each day an eagle tore out his liver, and each night it grew back . . .

This was no help. It shed no light on the League of Prometheus, if such a thing even existed. Well, he thought, there's more than one way to skin a cat. He would simply call up Sebastian and ask him a few casually-phrased questions. But even as he considered the idea, he knew he would not do it because – the realisation came as a shock – he sensed that Sebastian would make a dangerous adversary.

He would ask Esther to help him find some back-up contacts, and if Sebastian's society proved to be some kind of neo-Nazi organisation he would base the proposition of the book around it, maybe even sell serial rights to a newspaper as an exposé. Even though he found it hard to believe that Sebastian was such a Jekyll and Hyde character, he knew that the time had come to cool their friendship. It was the only way to avoid further duplicity, and it would free him to write whatever he pleased.

Having made the decision, though, he had an uncomfortable feeling about the possible outcome. As a small child he had read a book called *Where The Rainbow Ends*, an Edwardian adventure in which some children witnessed St George's battle with the dragon. Years later, he had been shocked to discover that the book was a thinly disguised fascist tract. Even now he found it hard to recall those eerie evanescent illustrations without feeling a sense of betrayal. It was a sensation he was starting to associate with Sebastian.

Playing Games

THE RAIN was drifting across the trees of Regent's Park in silent undulating veils. Sebastian sat before the great mahogany board set up beside the window and considered his position. Exposed, he decided, but not precarious. He shifted one of the ceramic and ivory counters towards him, protecting his most vulnerable piece. He had been playing for five hours without pause.

Strict but fair. That was how he would describe himself if someone asked. Disciplined. Moral. And bold, as bold as Prometheus thrusting his unlit torch into the sun.

But of course, many people feared crossing paths with the truly unafraid. There were those who saw him as a threat. Many lies had been told, but in his mind the truth and the lies were quite separate.

It was true, for instance, that he had been invited to leave university. It was true that he would have graduated with honours had he stayed. It was true that there had been some unfortunate business with a hysterical young woman, and that this perceived – and publicised – blot on his escutcheon would prevent him from ever attaining a position of power. It was true that the death of an interfering journalist had become linked with his name, providing a source of future embarrassment and another skeleton for the family cupboard. The fact that he would eventually inherit his father's title meant further disruption to his political prospects. He had been forced to consider a less high-profile entrance into the state arena.

It was not true that his family cut him off without a penny. It was not true that he kept the company of common criminals. It was not entirely true that he had squandered his family's allowance on parties and drugs. It was not true that he had been forced to resolve a stimulant dependency (he had chosen to admit himself to the clinic in order to tackle a genuine psychiatric problem). It was not true that he had become the '*fin de siècle* wastrel' recently described in an unflattering feature entitled 'The New Bad Boys' in the *Guardian*. It was not strictly true that he had had a nervous breakdown when the aforementioned hysterical girlfriend had died in so-called mysterious circumstances on his grandfather's Devonshire estate.

These days, at the grand old age of twenty-eight, his greatest pleasure in life – apart from his league meetings – was the creation of, and participation in, games. All kinds of games. Strategic puzzles. Peg and board amusements. Elaborate ritualised entertainments. Linguistic riddles. Intellectual anomalies. And sometimes, more overtly sexual charades involving the hiring of prostitutes and the testing of their personal tolerances. As a child he could complete *The Times* crossword in under seven minutes. He quickly worked his way through Scrabble, go, pta-wai, mah-jong, sabentah, poker and bridge. Then he began to invent his own games. As an adult it amused him to add new layers of role-playing and gamesmanship to an otherwise dreary life. And the best part of playing these games, of course, was setting the rules yourself.

He had already attempted to involve Vince in his game playing, although the boy had no natural skill, no guile. Those honest blue eyes were picture-windows to his soul, incapable of hiding secrets. As opponents they were poorly suited. Some kind of handicap would have to be applied. He had studied his quarry at lunch the other day. They were dining at L'Odeon in Regent Street, a restaurant far too modern for his tastes but selected to impress the boy, and he had asked Vince what he was really writing about, and the boy had fiddled with his microphone-gadget nervously, unable to hold his eye, fobbing him off with some nonsense about the state of the capital. He should have recognised the signs then and interrogated Vince more thoroughly.

Unfolding his long legs, he leaned across the mahogany board and shifted another white piece so that it imprisoned his opponent, then removed the appropriated counter to the brass railing at the edge of the board. He sat back and surveyed the battlefield. The war was all but won. The best way to capture an enemy was to let him think you had no interest in capture at all.

It amazed him to think that the boy had no inkling of how he was being used. Proles were like that: broadly honest, reasonably decent, breathtakingly naive. Indignant, of course, upon the discovery of any detrimental deception. But ready to empty their purses before you, should you call upon their assistance.

He felt sorry for Vincent. The boy would never get to the heart of the matter. It simply wasn't something you could catalogue on paper. It was far too perverse for his algebraic thinking to comprehend, a perversion of character, family and finance that ran deep inside and underground, to the very core of the nation. It only surfaced when those close to power found a way to control and make use of it; why else, he wondered, shoving aside the board, would organisations like the League of Prometheus be allowed to exist?

Too bad the boy wasn't a bit brighter. He rather relished the possibility of being found out. But that, of course, would defeat the entire purpose of the game. He did not want to have Vincent killed. Indeed, with no other candidates in sight he could not afford to. His fellow Prometheans would not allow him another chance to make good his promise.

The rain was clearly in for the day. The finale of *Der Rosenkavalier* came to its melancholy end. With a sigh, Sebastian heaved himself from his armchair and switched off the tape. He wasn't sleeping well. Lately his mind was filled with visions. Everything was coming to a head. Anger burned dully within him, and nothing, it seemed, not even the game, could assuage it.

Background Information

IT TOOK a lot of phone calls to track down Caroline Buck-Smalley. She had dated Sebastian Wells during his Oxford days, and had been photographed (and labelled with a helpful caption) arriving at a charity auction with him, draped in a Union Jack. Caroline now handled PR for her mother's Knightsbridge dress business, and was reluctant to discuss anything else. Figuring that dishonesty was the best policy, Vince explained that he was writing an article about Sebastian for *The Tatler*, only to have her demand that a formal request for an interview be submitted in writing.

Vince argued that he would miss his deadline for the next issue, and just needed a couple of quick answers.

'Look, Mr Reynolds, I simply don't have the time to waste on this sort of thing,' she heatedly insisted, 'besides which I can tell you very little about Mr Wells, beyond the fact that he enjoys playing extremely childish, spiteful tricks on people and would rather spend his weekends with his pals figuring out stupid character-testing rituals than doing anything useful or constructive.' The line went dead.

Texts of the following speeches and monographs by the Hon.

Sebastian Wells are available upon request:

A Question of Race: Nationality and Identity
Why There Must Always Be An England
Breaking the Jewish Power Ring
The Murder of Innocence: Tackling the Abortionists
Prometheus and Power: Responsibility to the People

He accessed the last article; he had read the others.

The name Prometheus is a Greek corruption of the Sanskrit word Pramantha, meaning a fire-drill. The symbol for this invention is the Swastika.

On the unseasonably fine evening of September the 23rd, Vince and Louie had an argument that started because Vince showed his friend photocopies of the speeches Sebastian had authored, and Louie got on his high horse and virtually accused him of collaborating with Nazis.

'You have to confront him now that you know all this,' said Louie. 'He advocates forced repatriation, for Christ's sake!'

'I thought you were in favour of quote lying till you're blue in the face unquote,' Vince explained.

'Yeah, but I changed my mind. He's a racist, and he has the money to back up his views with action.'

The more Louie shouted, the more Vince opposed him. Sebastian had plenty of good points. He behaved with more maturity than this nitwit spouting agitprop at him in his own flat, a decently-kept place, unlike Louie's bug-infested rubbish dump in Chalk Farm.

So they argued and got drunk and argued some more, and

Vince explained that he would end the interviews with Sebastian when he was damned well good and ready and not a moment before, and Louie could tell him that he chain-sawed the heads off babies and ate them for all he cared, it wouldn't make a blind bit of difference.

'Fine,' shouted Louie, 'but while your fascist pal acts as an errand boy for the far right, filling his speeches with Victorian rhetoric, stuff about shining shields of truth and honour and duty, he operates in the kind of corrupt port-and-stilton circles designed to keep wealth and privilege where it belongs – in the hands of the rich.'

'You're sounding like a really naff angry student, Louie,' he pointed out. 'Why don't you go and bury your rage in an unusual haircut? Go and have your nose pierced again.'

'I have no argument with you, man –'

'Or me with him. I could easily find something else to write about.'

'You're not very convincing,' Louie replied. 'I think he interests you because part of you secretly wants to be like him. Only you don't even realise it. Now, you have to decide whether you're gonna do the right thing.'

He knew Louie was right. The deadline for delivery of his manuscript was December the 10th, and he had most of the information he was likely to get from Sebastian.

'Esther's given me the telephone number of this guy she knows, a Doctor Harold Masters,' he explained. 'He lectures at the college. A couple of years ago he had a run-in with Mr Wells and his pals. Esther had a word with him and he said he'd be happy to talk to me. Besides, there's some other stuff I need to dig out.'

Guardian July 1996

. . . As the son of a lord who has long refused to declare his reputedly conflicting business interests, Sebastian Wells found himself ideally suited for withstanding interrogation by the police recently, when he was held in custody over his suspected involvement in a brutal murder upon a young black concertgoer. Upon being cleared of suspicion, Wells promptly sued the police for wrongful arrest and now looks set to win his case. – Jeremy Tyler

New Statesman February 1994

'. . . Traditional clubs don't follow through on the liberal trends set by university societies,' explained Dr Harold Masters, in his annual Edinburgh address. 'While it is not surprising to find a lack of ethnic diversity in such very British institutions, it is more disturbing to note the return of wealth and class restrictions.'

Societies like the hyper-secretive League of Prometheus remain so well protected by the silence of their members that it is impossible to gauge the club's influence on the city's financial institutions. Indeed, Prometheans make Freemasons look like chatterboxes. Yet for years this supposedly philanthropic institution has been dogged by rumours of its members' violent behaviour, its links to the world of organised crime and illegal government-sanctioned sales of arms. All press enquiries are met with curt dismissal. Arrogance and secrecy, it seems, are but two weapons in the league's power arsenal. – Jeremy Tyler

Guardian August 7th 1996

. . . Privately, though, questions are still being asked about how investigative journalist Jeremy Tyler came to be found dead at the foot of the Westminster Bridge steps after apparently slipping on them during a drunken altercation. The outspoken Tyler had recently conducted a series of acrimonious interviews with members of a society known as the League of Prometheus, and was seen in the presence of several league members on the night of his death.

The league's chairperson, the Hon. Sebastian Wells, insisted that none of his members were still in contact with Tyler, and the police chose to accept his statement at face value. No investigation ensued in the wake of Tyler's death, and no evidence of the journalist's recorded conversations with league members was found in his personal belongings.

With apparent ease Tyler's life's work has been erased – but perhaps this is merely the symptom of a larger public malaise.

With apathy so endemic in our nation, it is hard not to speculate that the dying century's conservatism has created a fertile new home for the spectre of Nazism to once more take root. The message is clear; messing with the Far Right's brash new boys can be hazardous to your health.

Vince noted that there was no author to the final piece. Given the fate of Jeremy Tyler, perhaps it was just as well.

CHAPTER ELEVEN

Breaking The Bond

'ARE YOU Vincent Reynolds?' the boy at the cafeteria counter called across to him. 'There's a phone call for you.'

'I thought I'd find you in there,' said Sebastian. 'I tried you at the entertainment place and they said you'd gone for the day. Listen, I can't make our appointment on Friday, but I can do lunch tomorrow. Would that be convenient?'

Say no, the voice inside his head hissed, if you see him in person you're bound to say something dumb and give the game away. You know too much about him now, and you're a crap liar. *Say no*. But it would be the last time they would hang out together, and his growling stomach got the best of him. It wasn't as if Sebastian was a convicted murderer or anything. Vince was really going to miss the lavish meals of the past month.

'That would be good,' he heard himself saying.

They dined in a busy Cal-Ital restaurant in a Kensington backstreet. Meeting in a crowded area seemed the safest thing to do. Recently Sebastian had taken him to a very old dining club just off Threadneedle Street where he was treated like a visiting member of the royal family, and Vince – after he had been fitted with a stained club tie – was pointedly ignored.

The experience had left him feeling very strange, like a paid escort getting caught out in a smart hotel.

This place was full of young media-types with switched-off mobile phones beside their wineglasses. Everyone looked the same: smart and confident, Gap-advertisement bland. As the waiter showed him to the table he had a fleeting fantasy, that all these diners were friends of Sebastian's, all members of his secret club, and that they were simply awaiting a prearranged signal to fall upon his gratingly common companion like a pack of starving vampires.

Sebastian arrived wearing his usual immaculate black suit, white shirt and crimson tie. He looked like a wealthy man dabbling in the stock market because it amused him. Vince watched warily as they ate. It seemed bizarre that Sebastian had not stopped talking since they'd met, and yet he had revealed less about himself than could be gleaned from a single newspaper article. It was impossible to find anything in his appearance or his gestures that indicated the kind of man he really was.

Vince, on the other hand, had proven to be an open book, describing his disastrous engagement at the age of nineteen, his brushes with the law over a missing van and some stolen computer software, his parents' endless arguments and his father's unexpected death. He now felt uncomfortable about having been so forthcoming.

For a while the talk was even smaller than usual. Sebastian remained circumspect about his own political beliefs. Indeed, Vince could hardly recall a single serious discussion on the subject. He had always taken care to avoid such topics himself; at home, religion, sex and politics were the three things the family never discussed, for fear of initiating one of his father's apoplectic rants about Catholics and Communists.

He knew Sebastian could sense the change in atmosphere

between them. When their conversation finally grew too laboured he returned to safer discussion ground.

'Strategy games are best, but it's hard to find worthy opponents. Obviously, the sides must be well-balanced. Great historical battles are always interesting to recreate, just to see if you can change the outcome. Waterloo, for example, becomes much more interesting if one removes Napoleon's fatal half-hour of indecision. Gallipoli's a good one for the novice, an outcome changed if you allow our artillery bombardment to continue for another ten minutes.' He grew more animated when embarking on a favourite subject. 'I've always wondered what would have happened to the course of the Second World War if Hitler and Churchill had actually met one another. They very nearly did, you know. As early as 1932, in the Regina Hotel in Munich. Churchill had been befriended by a man named Hanfstaengel, who told him the Fuehrer was coming to the hotel at five that day, and would be pleased to meet him. Churchill ruined his chances by asking Hanfstaengel why his chief was so prejudiced against the Jews, and Hanfstaengel immediately cancelled the meeting. So if it hadn't been for Churchill's insensitivity, the Second World War might even have been averted.'

This was an ominous turn in the conversation. 'Churchill was right to speak out,' Vince said. 'A man can't help how he's born.'

Giving Sebastian grounds for an argument, he realised, was not the smartest of moves under the circumstances. Vince could sense the side that was closed off from public view. He wanted to leave, to push aside his meal and get out into the night air, just as much as he needed to hear the truth.

'I want to ask you some things, but I don't know the right way to go about it,' he said finally.

'Just go ahead and ask. I won't bite.'

He took a deep breath. 'It's about the *New Statesman* article, the one where they called you a Nazi.'

'Why didn't I sue them, you mean?'

'Well, there's that, yes.'

'I knew they would find enough fuel to justify the claim. No smoke without fire and all that. They only had to look at the company I was keeping in those days.'

'So you don't see the same people now?'

'Good God, no. One grows up, moves on. Anyway, you mustn't believe everything you read. Journalists have hidden agendas, too.'

He wasn't apologising for his past, Vince noted.

'What happened to your girlfriend? I read there was some trouble –'

'I don't consider that a matter for public discussion,' he replied, steel entering his voice. 'Is there anything else you feel the need to ask?'

'Your involvement in the League of Prometheus, I don't understand what that's all about.'

'Oh, *that*. I wonder you haven't brought it up before. We meet informally,' Sebastian explained, 'just a group of like-minded individuals, as they say. The one thing we have in common is a passion for debate and a desire to see reform. I thought I'd mentioned it to you.'

'No, never. I read about it.'

'I wasn't aware we were written about.'

'On the Internet. Perhaps I could attend one of your meetings.'

Sebastian refused to catch his eye. The shutters had come down once more. 'I'm afraid there are no outside members allowed – it's an old rule, there's nothing I can do about it.'

'An old rule. Then this society of yours isn't new? I mean, you didn't start it?'

'God, no, it's been around for generations. I'm merely the present chairman. The custodian of the League's charter.' He thought for a moment. 'What else have you been able to discover about our little club?'

'Nothing much, really. But I have my suspicions.'

'Oh, really? You'd better make sure you have proof to back them up before you publish. I'd hate to see you get into trouble. Legally, I mean. You've barely touched your meal.'

'I'm not very hungry.'

'Then leave that and we'll have some decent brandy.'

'No, Sebastian. I have to go soon.'

'Tell you what, I'll get the bill and we can have a snifter at my club.'

'I really can't. Too much to write up.'

He cooled instantly, sensing the change. 'All right. If that's what you want. I'll get you a taxi.'

'I just want to walk for a while and clear my head,' he replied a little too fiercely, rising from the table.

'Well, you must do as you feel fit.'

Vince stood awkwardly at the corner as Sebastian hailed a cab. After entering it and shutting the door, he pushed down the window.

'I think I've disappointed you, Vincent. Not something I intended to do.'

'We'll stay in touch,' he said, shamed by the lie.

'It's probably best that I should wait to hear from you,' said Sebastian civilly. 'Take care, old chap. Don't leave it too long, eh?'

The cab pulled away and disappeared into the afternoon traffic. Vince knew that this was an official end to their meetings, just as Sebastian knew that there would be an unofficial continuation. He should have been relieved, but one thought kept running through his mind. *What if I've made a mistake? Suppose he's reformed since those articles were written, does it really matter what his politics are? What right do I have to judge him on the events of the past?*

On the Tube back to Tufnell Park he found it hard to shake the terrible sense of foreboding that had descended upon him. Suppose there was some kind of comeback from all of this?

Some things in life were dangerous; that was knowledge quickly learned. A burning cigarette-end flicked from a car. A bad neighbourhood late at night. The sound of breaking glass. Voices raised in drunken anger. These were reasons to be fearful. When Vince was a child, his father used to show him how his open razor would slice through a sheet of paper just by resting the blade on the top of the page. Its casual power appalled the sensitive young boy; it was intended to.

He had been an easily frightened child. His world was darkened with dangers. His father's timidity was as inoperable as cancer, and it had turned him into a bully. His endless warnings destroyed the little confidence his son possessed. Harm was found hiding in the most mundane events; the turn of the tide could transform a beach stroll into a race against the incoming sea. A picnic in the woods could conjure images of the family lost and starving among lightning-blasted trees. In his father's world, the simple act of replacing a three-pin plug became a feat so fraught with electrical hazard that only a fool would attempt it. The destruction of his confidence, Vince came to realise, was the most damaging childhood loss of all.

When his father died, Vince cried because they had not been able to resolve their differences. He had wanted to show his father that all those years of cautionary advice had been wasted, that far from being scared to live he was now ready for anything the world could throw at him. One week after the funeral, Vince left his mother's house to seek adventure in the city. Now that he had finally found it, he began to realise that there were bigger things to fear.

The Academic

'YOU WON'T find much written down about them. They're not the sort of organisation that likes to leave hard evidence lying around.'

Vince finally managed to collar Dr Harold Masters on the steps of the British Museum, where he had just delivered a lecture on the celebrations of the Inca calendar and early Mayan beliefs, and was now hurrying through the early evening drizzle, anxious to get home. Vince was late and lucky to have recognised him at all, considering he only had Esther's description ('absurdly tall, unsuitable tortoiseshell glasses') to go on.

'You'll have to walk with me, I'm afraid,' said Masters, striding ahead. 'My wife will kill me if I'm not on time. We've some Egyptian ceramics people for dinner and they're unfamiliar with the concept of fashionable lateness. Come under shelter. Pity about this weather. It was so nice yesterday.' He was carrying a gigantic green and white striped golfing umbrella.

'In the twenties they were known as the Young Prometheans. Information on them is all rather hazy. No idea why they linked themselves to Prometheus, except of course

Mary Shelley's *Frankenstein* is subtitled *The Modern Prometheus*, isn't it? Enlightened man, and all that. The heyday of such societies was in the Victorian era, of course. They always picked classic-sounding names with quasi-mystical connections. The League is almost certainly Edwardian in origin, although it seems to have a group of founders rather than one single leader. It began as little more than a splinter group of an Oxford debating society, that much is sure, but its character changed during the Second World War.'

'Why was that?' he asked, hopping ahead to keep abreast of the doctor.

'Oh, for the simple reason that they supported Mosley during the conflict. Around this time they gained the support of the British Union of Fascists, oddly enough through their mutual admiration for Edward the Eighth – the BUF were royalists to a man – and of course the Mitfords began throwing money at them. But the alliance with the Blackshirts marked a move to the far right from which they never recovered. Of course, all sorts of odd things happened in the war. That forecourt, for example,' he indicated the museum at his back, 'was full of onions, runner beans and cabbages, a victory garden dug up by the wife of the Keeper of Coins and Medals.'

'There's something I don't understand, doctor.' Vince paused with him as they reached the kerb. 'What exactly does the League do?'

'That's an interesting question.' Masters rolled his eyes knowingly. He looked slightly mad. 'Their actions certainly seem to be more negative than positive, rather like a radical mini-version of the House of Lords. Basically, they prevent things happening that they don't agree with. From the wealthy backgrounds of their associates I imagine they operate some kind of privilege system that allows their members to get on at the expense of others. You know, do subtle, appalling misdeeds to the underclass and always manage to hush them up, place favoured sons into the jobs their fathers had before them, that sort of thing.

'A few years ago I ran afoul of them when I wrote a monograph on the later history of the city guilds. In the course of my research I upset a few younger members of the Oxbridge set by suggesting that the City of London corruption cases of the eighties could be traced to the exclusion practices of the old boy network, and I went as far as to name a few of the culprits. I had no idea they were Masons. Next thing I know, this chap Wells calls me up – on my unlisted number, no less – and actually has the audacity to threaten me, in the most affable manner conceivable, but still a threat. Tells me my research is based on false assumptions, perhaps I'd care to rethink my proposals, or he'll be happy to have some of his colleagues come around and help me with the revisions.'

'What did you do?'

'What could I do? I'm an academic, not a gladiator. I amended the document to exclude them. Funny thing, though, I was introduced to Wells at a party a few months later and he was charm incarnate. I didn't much care for him, swanning about as if he owned the place. The city, I mean. Struck me as your classic bright boy gone to the bad. A head full of silly ideas and no practical abilities. Wealthy people always assume they have the right to be eccentric.' He halted at the corner of New Oxford Street and peered beyond the edge of the umbrella. 'If you're thinking of getting mixed up with these people, I'd bear in mind that they have some pretty powerful friends. And I should think they can be dangerous. I don't know that they've actually ever *killed* anyone, although there was some speculation about a journalist who died slipping on some steps, but over the years they've exerted a lot of pressure on specific targets. Still, you can't be too careful. There's nothing more harmful than an opinionated intellectual with too much money.'

'Thanks for the advice. I'll bear it in mind. Just a couple more questions.'

The doctor was busy searching the rainswept street for a cab. 'Fire away,' he said, distracted by his need to find transport quickly.

'How many members of this society are we talking about?'

'There you have me, I'm afraid. Could be five or fifty, although if it's the latter, I imagine there's an inner circle that makes all of the more contentious decisions. An organisation like this tends to have a highly developed internal pecking order providing different levels of information on a need to-know basis. If you look at the early structure of the Nazi party you'll find pretty much the same thing.' He spotted a cab with its light on and threw out his arm. 'What was the other question?'

'Where do they operate from?'

'I'm sure they recruit at the main universities, and I imagine their membership is swollen by sheer osmosis.'

'What do you mean?'

'Oh, that like-minded individuals naturally drift towards them.'

Funny, Vince thought, that was the same phrase Sebastian used.

'It's pretty much public knowledge that they have a central London meeting-lodge not far from the Holborn Masonic Temple,' the doctor went on. 'I don't have an address for them, though. Didn't get that far, but I daresay I could find it for you easily enough.'

'If you do come across it, could you phone it through to me?'

'Yes, I suppose so. On the condition you don't go doing anything stupid. God, I'd love to see it all brought out into the light. Mind if I ask you a question now? Why would you want to get involved with these people in the first place?'

'I'm a personal friend of the ringleader,' he explained apologetically.

CHAPTER THIRTEEN

Weighing In

ON A CERTAIN kind of rainy October night some London streets fall back into the past, and it becomes impossible to pinpoint their exact year, like stumbling across an old photograph without a date. On such nights, the dingy dwellings of Spittalfields and Whitechapel still seem to belong to the Huguenot silk-weavers, the prim backstreets of Kensington appear eternally Edwardian, and the houses of the Chelsea embankment, primped with gothic trimmings and standing in Sunday finery like a charabanc of ruddy-faced matrons, remain the province of the Pre-Raphaelites. It is among these latter buildings that the members of the League of Prometheus had set their headquarters.

Although the house itself only dated from 1865, the grounds in which it stood held ancient secrets. Buildings change; sites do not. In later decades London's luminaries attended fashionable parties on its candelabra-filled first floor. Conan Doyle, Whistler, Elgar and Wilde had all taken tea in the Oak Room, a large dark lounge made more depressing by a series of staggeringly ugly morality paintings rendered on fourteen separate oak panels.

Above this room, in the rather inaccurately named

Temperance Gallery, Sebastian Wells sat, as was his habit, and watched the setting sun. The air over the river had turned to the clear violet hue that had once been so common above the city before the Industrial Revolution. In those days the seasons were plainly designated, temperatures rising and plunging with clockwork precision. In the winter, the Thames froze over. In summertime, tinder-dry fields caught fire in East London, the billowing pale smoke drifting down to choke the maze of bookshop-filled streets behind St Paul's. But here in this reach of the Thames, at this time of the year, it was impossible to look out and not be reminded of Turner's hazy, iridescent river.

Sebastian stared through the hand-rolled diamond panes, sipping the porter Barwick had fetched him from the kitchens, and thought about Vincent Reynolds.

There could be only one explanation for the young man's sudden change of heart – he had discovered something damaging about the activities of the league. Unease showed in his face, his composure. At their final meeting Vince had avoided pushing for more detailed answers to his questions, as though he was afraid of what he might hear. He had cast his eyes aside, fidgeting like a cat unable to settle, awaiting the payment of the bill.

What had he discovered, though? The league's business activities existed in an area between the land's laws, a mysterious region of favour and reciprocation, of imperceptible nods and understanding smiles, of quietly stopped documents and discreetly passed bills. Isolating a single piece of firm evidence was like sifting through sand. God knows, some very clever journalists had tried and failed.

No, it had to be something personal. Sebastian was aware of several exposed chinks in his armour. The business with the girl was years ago and long forgotten. The pissed old hack who had fallen down the steps then? Or the idiot they had taught a lesson after the concert? The worst part was not knowing.

Sebastian had been careful to show no anger or suspicion that day at the restaurant, but carried out some careful surveillance later. He persuaded St John Warner to check inside the apartment in Tufnell Park. The photocopied notes which lay in his lap made depressing reading.

Perhaps it had been a mistake, trying quite so hard with Vincent. His conversation skills were minimal, his ambitions were low and his background was so common as to be untraceable. Encouragingly, he had a decent reputation among his night-school lecturers for – here he checked St John Warner's notes – 'determination and tenacity'. Not especially popular (any imbecile could be popular, as five minutes spent staring at a television testified) and of course his interests were awash in a groundswell of studenty left-wing ideals, the kind that eventually got crushed out by life's practicalities, but Vince's deep-rooted interest in the history of London manifested itself in the passionate articles he had written. He had earned money in his spare time hosting guided tours through places of historical interest, and had worked for the pleasure of it.

What drew him to study such an unfashionable subject? Why wasn't he out there consuming vast quantities of drugs at raves like every other moron in his social class? Did he manifest some glimmer of originality that rendered him a worthy opponent? The hardest part of any game, of course, was finding an appropriate challenger.

There was an additional personal element to this: Sebastian, the injured party, had been misled, which left him free to nurture a desire for revenge. Any game between them would therefore become a grudge match, for the city they loved and the deceit that had passed between them. Oh, it had the makings of a French prose poem.

Still, there was something tenacious about Vincent that might transform him into a formidable opponent. He was hungry; that was good. The boy had envy in his eyes, and despite his high ideals would probably switch places with him if he could. His biggest flaw would doubtless prove to be his hesitancy; in the moments he wasted deciding what to do, he would forfeit the game. If Sebastian chose to issue the challenge, he would inform his opponent that he intended to play fairly, in strict accordance with the rules. The gentleman would battle the barbarian in the arena of the city they both shared; if nothing else, it would provide an interesting contrast in their playing styles.

He drained the porter-pot and set it down on the sill. The challenge grows, he thought. It is, as yet, unformed. But it is there. It is simply a matter of planning every last detail and waiting for a window of opportunity.

Meanwhile, it had become important to find out what exactly Vincent had uncovered, and if necessary, to stop him from exposing the information.

CHAPTER FOURTEEN

Background Information

THE FOLLOWING afternoon, Vince visited Louie's disgusting flat in Chalk Farm, and they posted a series of enquiries on the Internet. While they were awaiting replies Louie made coffee the colour of pre-war nicotine, which he poured into mugs bearing the lip-imprints of generations of users.

'There are some serious considerations to take into account,' said Vince. 'If I do uncover conclusive evidence about the League and denounce Sebastian in print, I could wind up having an accident down a flight of steps. Besides, someone's bound to point out that we were friends, and that's going to make me look pretty stupid.'

'Why?'

'I took money from him, you bozo. He didn't seem so bad when we first met. He wasn't one of those toffs you instantly loathe, like Jeffrey Archer. He had a lot of charm.'

'You have to expose this guy,' Louie insisted. 'People like him always get away with it. Doesn't that make you angry?'

'Not particularly,' he replied. 'It's the way things are, the way they've always been and there's not much we can do about it. Or at least,' he added, 'if I have to stir up trouble, I could try exposing someone who can't afford to have me killed. '

'If it worries you that much, maybe you should go back to writing nice little history pieces about London,' said Louie sarcastically. 'Go for a milder kind of exposé. Start with Kentish Town. Try and figure out why they put the local florists next door to a wet fish shop. You have to stick with the class piece, man. You've got the perfect way of bringing your ideas to life.'

'Might I remind you that just a few days ago you were warning me to stay away from the man?'

'You were his friend then. Now the gloves are off, you can make a monumentally disgusting spectacle out of him.'

The screen between them beeped and started downloading typewritten material.

'Whoa. Look at this shit.'

*87 Articles Located/Prometheus League/see
searchrefs@Mosley/Fascism/January Club/Disraelian
Society/Freemasonry/Hermetic Orders/Modern
Paganism/Crowley/Book Of Enoch/Wheatley/Borley
Rectory/'Blue Flame'/Corpse-Blindfolding/'Girl In The
Lake' mystery/ Monk's Parlour/NAACP Bombings/
Anti-Semitism Accusations/CIA links/Blunt/Burgess/
Jack The Ripper/Star Trek:TNG*

'I can see some of the links there,' said Vince, 'but I can't imagine what the Bible's lost chapter on fallen angels has to do with Sebastian.'

'That's the trouble with newsgroups,' said Louie. 'They spend too much time discussing crappy old sci-fi TV shows. They probably accuse the League of alien abductions somewhere. There's no point in going through all of that conspiracy stuff. It's knocked together by lonely fat guys who can't get dates.'

'It could happen to you.' Vince eyed the tantalising list. 'I think I might check out some of it, though, just for fun. You never know.'

'Be my guest.' Louie pushed his chair back from the monitor. 'It'll make you crazy after a while.'

'I'm going to have to buy myself a modem. Meanwhile, I need you to keep looking out for related material. Anything that helps explain what the League actually does.'

'Hey, what are friends for?' asked Louie.

On the morning of October the 22nd they met up at a deserted Tex-Mex cafe in Camden Town, and after ordering beers and nachos, Louie leaned forward, checking about himself with an air of exaggerated caution. 'So tell me, Secret Squirrel, how are your burrowings? Get any good stuff yet?'

'I'm three quarters of the way through the first draft now, about 16,000 words in.' Vince accepted a beer, waving away a glass. 'To think that just a short while ago I was eating off bone china. Now I'm back to drinking out of a bottle. Anything good come through on the Internet?'

'I downloaded a ton of stuff, but haven't had the chance to read much of it. It's mostly rubbish. Users who've come across the odd snippet about the League and want to convince you that they've uncovered another Roswell conspiracy, but nobody has any hard information. It's just the usual mystic mumbo-jumbo theoretical bullshit.'

'Well, I may have something.' Vince hunched down over his beer and gave a secretive smile. 'My contact, the good doctor, rang me last night. He made a couple of calls and found out that the Prometheans are holding their next meeting in chambers behind St Peter's Church, Holborn in nine days time.'

Louie made a quick finger-count. 'That's October 31st, man. You're not gonna tell me they're really into witchcraft ceremonies and stuff like that.'

'I don't know, but I need to be in the room where they're holding the meeting.'

'Do you think they'll let you attend? Hallowe'en and all. Could get strange.'

'I'm not going to wait for an engraved invitation. With any luck they won't even realise I'm there.'

'Couldn't you just put a bug in the room?'

Vince threw up his hands. 'How, Louie? How the fuck do you bug a room?'

'I thought you might know.'

'Well, I don't.'

'Okay, if you have to hide inside, try not to get caught, 'cause you'll be the one who's trespassing. They could take you to court.'

Somehow Sebastian thought that would be the least of his worries.

Ceremony

'YOU'RE NOT allowed to go in there,' the porter had told him, holding up his palm. 'Nobody's allowed in. Nobody.'

Vince responded well to a challenge. He had found a way in. He had entered the unassuming Holborn building to find a series of banqueting suites and meeting rooms that were leased out to special interest groups of every kind. He was surprised to find a black felt bulletin board helpfully pointing him up a broad marble staircase to the appropriate suite, but he was early and the great double doors to the meeting room were still locked.

On the opposite side of the corridor someone else's meeting was preparing to get underway. Vince had made himself known to the secretary of the Enrico Caruso Appreciation Society, and had borrowed the cleaner's keys he found hanging from their door long enough to unlock the room. After that, it was simply a matter of finding a hiding place in the chamber and closing the door behind him. He was nervous now, of course, but more in pain than dread. After he had been hiding under the table for almost an hour, his left thigh developed an agonising cramp. He tried massaging the muscle but it stayed locked, tightening further. Just at this moment, as bad luck would have it, they started filing into the chamber.

Ignoring knife-point prickles of pain, he forced the searing leg beneath him and peered out from beneath the crimson altar-cloth. There were twelve of them in all, males of course, no women allowed, and they were clad in rather boring grey suits and sashes. He had been hoping for more exotic attire, something between the Freemasons and the Sons of the Desert, a scarlet fez and a robe for each member at least. The sashes, in opal satin with a silver trim, were particularly camp and inappropriate. Instead of lending them an aura of mystery it made them look like a group of rejected beauty queens. If his leg had not been stinging so badly, he might have started laughing out loud.

What was it with 'clubbable' men? Why did they need to join societies and create funny little rules that only they could obey and understand? Was it a territorial king-of-the-castle thing, or were they so scared of women that they needed to build safe enclaves from them? Why did they need to keep secrets anyway? Who were they hiding them from? The Inland Revenue? At first Vince had assumed it was a class thing, but he remembered his father once taking him to a working-man's club where the wives were not allowed to buy their own drinks.

They were making speeches now, each taking a turn to read phrases from a little leather book that they passed between them. Ritual greetings, a lot of Hail Brother In The Name Of Astaroth gobbledygook. They would be reading the 'Lord's Prayer' backwards next. He had meant to take notes, but the chamber was dark, the space beneath the altar was too damned small, and besides, his dictaphone had packed up for some reason and he had forgotten to bring a notepad; not a good start to his professional literary career.

Six emerald green uplighters illuminated the wood-panelled room so that everything below waist-level was in virtual darkness. The decor in the chamber was telling; Edwardian master-of-the-house (hardwoods, armchairs of green studded leather, tables and chairs with inlaid brass trims), a few Tudor touches (the stone floor, the big gas-powered fireplace with the painted shield), some kind of sporting trophy – fixed on the mantelpiece, a bit of fifties homeliness (cut-glass scotch decanters, tasselled lamp-shades), a bit of eighties yuppie (the uplighters, the huge desk, Charles Saatchi crossed with Albert Speer), a bit of spooky mystical bullshit (the ornately carved altar, the brass astrological symbols adorning the walls) – and the moth-eaten embroidered banners. The *banners*.

Be Sure Your Sins Will Find You Out.
Honour Shows The Man.
Of Cowards No History Is Written.
Danger Is Next-Door Neighbour To Security.
Severity Is Better Than Gentleness.
He That Cannot Obey Cannot Command.

The chamber was rampant with hormonal arrogance. Vince knew for a fact that no woman had ever set foot in here. It was the sort of place where members of a rugby club might come and throw buns at each other before going home to duff up their wives. There was also only one door to the chamber. He wondered if he would be able to get out as easily as he had entered.

There were twelve of them. Was that significant? Zodiac signs, months of the year? Although he could not see clearly from his hiding place, he could tell exactly where Sebastian was standing; their leader was taller than any of the others, and wore a black and silver armband that presumably indicated his higher rank. He looked different from the rest of the gathering; attractive enough to represent their public face, with a fluorescent smile too sincere to be trusted, tall and fashionably pale and very sure of himself. From his vantage point, Vince watched Sebastian standing with his legs planted firmly apart and his muscular arms folded, quietly discussing business with his colleagues. He didn't so much ooze confidence as laser-beam it from every pore. It was the stance of a man who was determined to be taken seriously.

'All right, gentlemen, let's get down to the evening's main business. Who wishes to start the activity reports?' His clear bass tone cut through the general susurration, silencing the room. Vince tilted his head and tried to hear, but the heavy embroidered altar-cloth muffled the replies of the group. Something about 'European treason'. Something about 'initiative'. Snatches of sentences. 'Without borders.' 'Imposing the penalty.' 'Inappropriate behaviour.' 'Breaching acceptable codes of honour.' 'Considerable personal risk.' And then the tone lowered to discuss something that sounded far more serious . . . but he could hear no more.

Great, wasn't it, he thought, that two thousand years of civilisation could bring about this scene; a penniless young man crouched beneath a table, hiding from a gathering of privilege and prejudice. He gripped the hem of the altar-cloth and gently pulled it to one side so that he could see between the legs of the nearest participant. It was hardly the lair of Beelzebub he had been expecting. Where was the dungeon filled with burning torches? Where was the screaming bare-breasted virgin, bound for sacrifice? He had been hoping for the set of a Hammer horror film, but this was more like a mystic sports club, and considering everyone in the room was in their twenties, alarmingly middle-aged in attitude.

Sebastian was standing at the front of the damp-smelling chamber on a raised platform, gravely intoning a list of misdemeanours from the typed page in his hand. Vince leaned forward to try to see more. Unfortunately, by doing so he had one of his Norman Wisdom moments, pulling forward a large Victorian copper bowl that had been set on the edge of the altar. It inched forward and finally fell onto the stone floor with a spectacular ringing clatter. In the shocked silence that followed he froze, desperately trying to think of a response. Moments later hands reached in and grabbed him beneath the arms, dragging him from his hiding place.

Vince realised that his relationship with Sebastian was about to take an interesting and alarming new turn. Some things were dangerous; this much he knew. Being here tonight with these people was one of them.

CHAPTER SIXTEEN

Civilised Men

'AND SO here you are,' said Sebastian, looking him up and down. 'It might have helped if you'd asked to attend one of our meetings rather than just barging in.'

'I tried that and you wouldn't let me, remember?' He attempted to disentangle himself from the grip of the two men who held him down. 'Frankly, it's a bit of a letdown. This is sort of like an adult version of a tree house. I could run it a whole lot better. Get nicer uniforms, modernise the place.'

'How *did* you get in here?' Sebastian stalked down the platform steps towards him. 'You disappoint me, Vincent, you really do. You have no secrets from us. We know everything about you.'

'You like to think you do.'

Sebastian exchanged a smile with a smarmy-looking man on his left. 'No, I think it's safe to say that we do. Where has he stored his work-notes, Barwick?'

Barwick, a man who could have modelled for A. E. Shepherd's *Wind In The Willows* drawings of Mole, studied Vince through thick spectacles that shielded watery eyes the size of drawing pins. A second chin waxed above his shirt collar as he frowned. 'You mean the ring binder labelled "City Of Night And Day"?'

'That's the one.'

'On the table beside his bed.'

'Oh, very secure. Left or right hand side?'

'Left.'

'You bastard,' Vince shouted, 'that's bloody illegal, breaking and entering, I'll take you to –'

'You didn't even notice anyone had been into your flat, so how do you expect the police to find anything? What are they going to do, dust for fingerprints? For God's sake sit him down, someone. Give him a glass of port.'

'Sebastian,' cautioned Barwick, 'you know it's against the rules.'

'Sod the rules for once. He managed to get in here, didn't he?'

The two men holding him pulled a tall oak chair forward and made him sit. He thought of kicking them both in the balls, shouting his head off and making a run for it, but knew that the only way of gathering hard information now was by complying with their wishes. Besides, he was interested in what Sebastian had to say.

'We made a copy of your work to date. I don't think your ideas are going to stun anyone with their originality. All that stuff about conspiracies. Civilisation is, by its very nature, a conspiracy. "Modern life is the silent compact of comfortable folk to keep up pretences. The pity is that the reformers do not know, and those who know are too idle to reform. Some day there will come a marriage of knowledge and will, and then the world will march." Buchan wrote that as long ago as 1915. Still, I shall keep your notes. Better to be prepared when an enemy is planning to attack. You are the enemy, aren't you?'

'That depends on your point of view,' he suggested.

Sebastian scratched his chin thoughtfully. 'Well, which of us do you place on the side of the angels, Vince? Which is the anarchist, which the representative of the status quo? It's confusing, the class thing, isn't it? Never clear-cut. Alan Clark described the *nouveau riche* as "people who bought their own furniture".'

'Yes,' said Vince, 'but Alan Clark is exactly the sort who confuses snobbery with wit.'

'Hmm. Yes, you have a point there.'

This was odd. Here he was, once more face to face with someone whom he had lately come to think of as the devil incarnate, only to find his feelings unchanged. There was still something disturbingly charismatic about Sebastian. Some animals had it; the ability to charm and repel simultaneously. Vince settled in his seat. 'I guess I consider myself to be representative of most people my age.'

'Unlikely, given your background and your fondness for supporting strikes. And what a little marcher you are! You've been on them all! The miners' protests, the Anti-Nazi League, the Greenpeace initiatives, the Gay Pride rallies, the Anti-Racism demos, the Pro-Choice bike-a-thons. They only have to set foot on the streets and you've fallen into step beside them chanting, haven't you? Well, you've fallen in behind the wrong group this time.'

One of the others poured a tall measure of port into a crystal Lady Hamilton goblet and set it on the table before him.

'Do you understand the consequence of your actions, I wonder?' asked Sebastian, sipping at his own glass. The others were at ease now, pouring drinks, lounging in the armchairs. Vince glanced at the door and was dismayed to see two of the largest men in the room standing either side of it.

'You see, my friend, it's always people like you who cause problems. You profess to care about the fate of your country but you don't really care about your own people. You don't care enough to do something. This group, on the other hand, cares very deeply. Ask the average man on the street about the history of his own city and his ignorance will appal you. Few of the rising generation are even capable of articulate speech, or speech of any kind. They only know what they hear and see 'on the telly'. Ask them for a reasoned opinion, ask them for a solution to our troubles, ask them anything and all you will get back is a knee-jerk reaction, a mooing noise, the lowing of an ignorant animal. A belch of chips, a scratching of the head. And although I am loath to do so, I have to include you, Vincent. You're one of the street people. That's where you come to life. You own the street, but we own all the houses.' Somebody sniggered. Vince shifted forward in his chair, growing increasingly annoyed. 'This is all very interesting,' he said, 'but you can't just suppress the things you don't agree with.'

'Of course not, I'd be the first to admit that. People are never prepared to see the error of their ways, their godlessness. All we can do is make sure that those of us with the right intentions have a clear path to power.'

'Besides, you're outnumbered,' Vince persisted. 'There are a lot more of us than there are of you.'

'Really? Then why are you the one standing there alone? Your back-up crew are being a bit apathetic. Something good on the telly tonight, was there? Vince, you just have to accept that we know best.'

'That sounds like the classic attitude of old money. I can't say I blame you, wanting to hang onto it. I'd probably do the same in your position. When I first met you, I thought your lack of self-awareness was engaging. Now I just think of you as deluded.'

Sebastian looked back at the men flanking him. 'You're damned lucky to be allowed to speak to your superiors in this manner.'

Vince gave a derisive snort. 'Don't see yourselves as empire builders. Your forefathers might have been, but you're not. You didn't fight to make the country great. You didn't build the mills and the factories. You talk about the apathy of people like me – well, you've been missing for the last fifty years, when the country could have done with strong leadership. Now it's too late, and you no longer serve any useful purpose at all. You're certainly not my fucking superiors.' He drained his glass in one gulp and set it down gently.

'And here, gentlemen, we find it once more, the language of the gutter finally making its appearance.' His flash of anger faded to a look of disfiguring blankness. 'Now listen, lad, this is serious. The League of Prometheus was founded in the reign of George the Fifth. No non-member has ever been allowed to enter its halls . . .'

'They have now,' Vince offered.

'This is just one of our offices. You won't have found much here. What worries me more is your lack of repentance, and the need to teach you a resounding lesson.'

'You've already taught me a lot. Which cutlery to use with asparagus, how to ask for a toothpick in French. Surely you must have expected me to betray your trust?' *To think I picked his name out of a magazine*, thought Vince. *Jesus.*

'I can't believe you're the same boy who wanted so desperately to know how I lived. What a dreadful disappointment you are. Right now I feel like smacking that smug little smile from your face.'

'Lay a finger on me and I'll get you locked up somehow. I don't give a fuck who your friends are.' It was brave talk, but his heart was knocking against his ribs. What could they do? he asked himself. What could they *really* do? Sebastian beckoned to a couple of his pals and they moved off to a corner of the room. Everyone else stood around looking embarrassed, waiting for their leader to return. After speaking for little more than a minute, he dispersed the meeting. Several members started bundling files of paper-work into briefcases. Sebastian walked up to Vince and stood watching his face, his hands clasped behind his back.

'Listen to me carefully, Vincent. It would be easy for me to simply punish you, but you're clearly unrepentant about this, so go back to your grim little flat and continue writing, fuelled by the thought that you've uncovered something. You don't understand what any of this means. You think your actions will have no consequences. You have issued me with a challenge, and I – *we* – accept that challenge.' He looked to the others for approval.

'I pick up your gauntlet.' He waved a hand, gesturing Vince up from his seat. 'We'll behave like civilised men. Go on, return to your home. At some point in the weeks to come you will receive a summons, and then we shall see who is on the side of the angels. But before that, Prometheus will bring you a sign. It will be the sign of fire, Vincent, and I hope it will make you realise the gravity of the challenge. Go, go, go.'

The men at the entrance doors stepped aside to allow him through. The room was pin-drop silent as he took his leave. He felt sure they would set upon him and at least give him a good kicking, but no, moments later he was walking briskly along the fourth-floor corridor, then down the thickly-carpeted stairs and back out onto the streets of Holborn, half-wondering if he had imagined the entire episode.

He returned to his apartment more determined than ever to write about Prometheus. So far he had a plastic ring-binder full of notes, some pages of observations and research references, his Internet material, a stack of source books and seven and a half chapters of the first draft, all of which had somehow been pawed over by Sebastian's burglarising playmates. That night he searched the flat for signs of a break-in. Nothing was missing. Nothing appeared to have been moved. He asked the couple who lived in the flat across the landing if they had seen anyone calling, but they were unable to help.

The phone rang, but he did not answer it. Probably Louie, wanting to know what had happened.

That night he fitted a deadbolt on the front door. Drove screws into the window frames to keep them closed. Put Louie's old cricket bat under his bed. Made a copy of his notes, and sent them to his brother at his army base in Southampton. Then he began looking for evidence that would really take the wind out of Sebastian's sails.

CHAPTER SEVENTEEN

Approval

SEBASTIAN CALLED a special meeting of the Inner Council at his flat in Regent's Park and presented his idea for the challenge. Only Caton-James and St John Warner complained, considering the exercise to be a waste of time and money, but their objections were quickly overruled. In particular, Caton-James felt that Sebastian was using the situation to indulge his love of games, but he remained silent while the chairman outlined his proposal.

'From time to time throughout the century, the members of the League have been required to make a stand for the things in which they believe,' Sebastian pointed out. The eleven men gathered before him sat patiently listening. 'That occasion has arrived again, just as it did in my father's time. I think, gentlemen, that it will prove the solution to our internecine problems.' There were murmurs of agreement as he laid down the ground rules.

'The challenge must provide a genuine test of knowledge that teaches our young man a lesson. It must provide a fair opportunity to reach a solution. That means you cannot require him to visit, say, a club that refuses entrance to non-members, or a guildhall that bans public entry. Besides, I have a feeling Mr Reynolds would be able to handle problems like that. He got into the Holborn Chambers without too much trouble. Exercise more subtlety. Mess with his mind. He thinks he's closer to the street than you or I, and he's right, if the street includes the gutter. I want you to take the strut from his stride. Make him realise that he owns nothing of this city, and that his kind never will.'

'Fine,' said Caton-James, 'so long as you don't mind us adding a few rules of our own. After all, this isn't just about you and the boy, is it? There's the matter between ourselves to settle.'

'I understand, of course.' Sebastian was chastened. 'Tell me what you want.'

Caton-James proceeded to outline a handwritten page of additional points. It took another two hours for everyone to fully agree an order of events, but by the end of the meeting full approval from the other League members had been granted.

After the rest had taken their leave, Sebastian sat by the window thinking. It really could work. He could kill two birds with one stone, and enjoy the game along the way. There were hazards involved, of course, but where was the challenge without them? Best of all, there was something about Vincent Reynolds that he genuinely admired. His unrepentant questioning, his enthusiasm for tasks that offered little or no reward. Sebastian thought of him as a reconstructed cockney, a kind of junior Sid James, muddling through the post-war debris, making the best of things. He had earned his right to be an opponent. It helped to balance the odds, and made the risk all the more worth taking.

First of all, though, a gesture was required. Something that would prepare Reynolds for the seriousness of his situation, and goad him on. He set to work immediately.

CHAPTER EIGHTEEN

The Gesture

'IF YOU are prepared to accept Jesus into your heart, the keys to the Kingdom of Heaven shall be yours. HALLELUJAH!'

Carol Mendacre grimaced and dug about on the passenger seat until she found an unboxed cassette. She inserted the tape and adjusted the volume, then returned her concentration to the lane ahead. The rain had renewed its strength half an hour ago, and she had lowered her speed accordingly. At this time of night the wet roads were easier to negotiate, save for the spray from articulated trucks heading South West. Carol hated driving, and only undertook journeys of any length when she knew the traffic volume would be lighter. Why did they always have to hold publishers' conferences at hotels in the heart of the countryside?

There is something indefinably keen and wan about her anatomy; and she has a watchful way of looking out of the corners of her eyes without turning her head, which could be pleasantly dispensed with – especially when she is in an ill humour and near knives.'

Carol recognised Dickens's description of the maid from Chapter 12 of *Bleak House*, and recalled that she was a considerable way past that point in the novel. She glanced over at the seat; the 'Talking Book' tapes had slipped from their case and become muddled.

She was considering the best way to sort them out without leaving the road when the car behind switched its headlights to full beam. She was unable to make out the vehicle that loomed in her rear-view mirror. What was its problem? She was doing nearly sixty in the centre lane, and there were no other cars around. Was the driver mad? Her heart started thumping as her grip tightened on the wheel. Her mirror was a panel of white glass. The interior of the car was filled with light.

When the vehicle came so close that it gently touched her rear bumper, she panicked, allowing the wheel to slip through her hands as she swerved left into the slower lane. But the car was still with her, just as close, and she fought to control the sliding wheels beneath her and failed. The last thought to pass through her mind as her cigarettes slid from the dashboard and the vehicle began to slowly turn over, fighting the force of gravity, was the realisation that she would not hear the end of Dickens' epic tale of chancery.

On a freezing afternoon in early November Vince met with Esther Goldstone at her office in Covent Garden, and described what had happened in the Holborn chambers. Esther listened patiently, waiting for him to finish. She looked tired.

'I have some bad news,' she said finally. 'Your commissioning editor – my friend – was involved in an accident a few nights ago. Her car left the road and overturned just outside Bristol. It was burned out by the time the emergency services arrived. Nobody seems very sure how it happened. There were no other vehicles involved.'

'Prometheus brought her fire,' said Vincent.

'What do you mean?'

'Sebastian warned that Prometheus would bring me a fiery sign. It was meant to show me the seriousness of the challenge.'

'You think Carol's death was to do with you?' Disbelief creased Esther's face. 'Even if it were true, how could you prove such a thing?'

To Vince, this was obviously the handiwork of the League. They were stopping the book at its source. 'That's how they work, don't you see,' he said quietly, 'they leave no trace. You told me to use my heart, my instincts. Well, I know they did it, and I have absolutely no way of proving it. The fire cleanses. It destroys all the evidence, wipes out everything except your inner knowledge of the truth.'

Esther eyed him unsurely. The distant soprano was singing her scales in the Opera House's rehearsal room. On such a day as this it was hard for anyone to imagine that behind the normality of the streets, real, honest-to-God conspiracies were being hatched. Esther tried to shake his fears from her head. 'If these people really were responsible for such a terrible thing – which I have to say I doubt – they've failed to stop the project going ahead.'

'Why?'

'I offered to take her work over as a freelance assignment, and the publishers accepted. I came from the editorial ranks, after all. I'm familiar with the background and I'm aware of Carol's intentions for the series. I also know most of the authors involved. As far as I am concerned, the book will remain on schedule. And I hope to God your fears are ungrounded.'

'I'm positive the League was involved –'

'Carol was a terrible driver,' Esther cut in. 'It was late at night and raining hard, and she'd had a couple of glasses of wine. I know. I was with her when she drank them.'

'Oh God, I'm sorry.'

'Don't be. Just make this the best thing you've ever written, because her name is still going to be on the cover.' Esther slapped her palms on the table. 'Let's get back to what we were discussing. Are you sure about everything you've described to me? The way this League operates, for example? You're not exaggerating?'

Vince dug in his leather duffel bag and produced a fistful of crumpled photocopies. 'I think I've barely begun to scratch the surface.'

'You were on the premises illegally,' she pointed out. 'You were very lucky they didn't call the police. Telling people you're a writer guarantees you no immunity.'

'Do you think that's what I should do? Go to the police?'

'And say what? You're annoyed because your feathers were ruffled by members of a meeting to which you were not invited? Don't be so naive, Vince. If you really want to research the organisation – and while I find the subject interesting I don't think it's essential to your thesis – you need to approach it through more orthodox channels. Talk to associates, business colleagues, students who knew these people at Oxford. You have some contacts of your own. Your London articles showed that.'

'They're not the right sort. I don't get any sense from them about this kind of thing,' he said gloomily. 'Reliable sources won't talk about Prometheus because their knowledge is based on hearsay. It's all so hard to define. They're a bunch of blokes who hold private meetings – not an illegal thing to do – and they're used to getting their own way. People owe them favours. Friendships go back the best part of a century. No one's going to say anything bad. It's impossible to confirm or deny the simplest statement. There's nothing on paper anywhere.'

Esther set down her cup. 'Have you asked yourself why you need to find a conspiracy? This isn't just going to be a hatchet job on someone who's annoyed you, is it?'

'They broke into my flat –'

'You don't know that for sure. They might have obtained their information in other ways. Do you have a landlord?'

'A landlady, but she's not on the premises.'

'She has a key, though?'

Vince reluctantly nodded.

'There you are. You have to stop jumping to conclusions. If you're going to do that, you're no good to me. You need facts. If you have any doubts about the material you're using, if you're concerned about legal infringements, bring it to me and we'll sort it out together.'

'Thank you,' he said softly. Esther was right; the activities of the League were not essential to his piece. Her friend's death could have been a coincidence. Accidents happened all the time. He resolved to forget about his feud with Prometheus and concentrate instead on creating a piece of powerful journalism. He assured Esther of this, then left her office and returned to Tufnell Park.

A few days later his agent reported that a verdict of accidental death had been decided in the case of Carol Mendacre, there being no evidence to suspect otherwise.

For the next three weeks Vince worked late every night, often with Louie helping him.

At the end of the third week, just as he had completed his first draft, he arrived back at his flat and found a piece of hand-delivered mail on the mat beneath the letterbox. When he tore open the envelope a small steel key fell out, along with a letter from Sebastian Wells.

Part Two

'Prepare for death if here at night you roam,
And sign your will before you sup from home.'

– Samuel Johnson on London

CHAPTER NINETEEN

The Challenge

HE TOOK the letter over to the kitchen table, seated himself and began to read. When he had finished, he tried to decide if it was meant to be a joke. Outside, shopkeepers were hauling down the graffiti-sprayed steel carapaces that protected their stores, and commuters were quick-stepping from the tube station, casting apprehensive glances at the clouds above them. The day had been unseasonably warm, and a soft poisonous haze had hung in the air, blurring the edges of the buildings, modifying and improving the cityscape. Heavy rain was forecast for the evening, with the possibility of thunderstorms, and the overcast sky had grown ominously black with the departure of day, preparing to make good its threat.

Vince reread the letter, scarcely believing his eyes. This was not possible. It *had* to be a joke. He reached for the telephone, then stopped.

No phone calls. It was one of the rules, laid down right here in black and white. *It is necessary, not for the League of Prometheus to prove itself to you, but for you to prove yourself to it.*

The arrogance, writing in the third person! He studied the

letter once more, noting the heavy crested parchment and mock-Tudor penmanship, somewhere between an invitation to a golf club and a Pirates of the Caribbean treasure map.

THE CHALLENGE OF THE DECADIURNAL NOCTURNE

The League of Prometheus Charges Vincent Robert Reynolds With Acting In Defiance Of The League's Basic Tenets.

The Accused is required to make amends by performing a series of tasks to be set by the residing members of the League, said tasks to be undertaken during the period from the onset of darkness on December 6th until the arrival of daylight on the morning of December 7th.

This Challenge will take the form of a set of tests requiring ingenuity, energy and intellect to complete, for the purpose of measuring the Accused's supposed knowledge of his city and country, it being the belief of the League that the best form of punishment is the attainment of constructive knowledge.

Each part of the Challenge must be completed within its time allocation.

If the Accused refuses to accept the Challenge, he will be executed.

If the Accused fails to survive the Challenge, innocents will suffer.

If the Accused fails to carry out any part of the Challenge, those who are blameless will be punished.

If the Accused chooses to go to the authorities, said action will cause loss of life.

If the Accused attempts to speak to members of the

public in order to enlist their help or attempts to communicate in any way with anyone, that person will be taken prisoner and may possibly forfeit his or her life.

If the Accused fails to complete the entire Challenge within the allotted time, he will be executed in an appropriate manner and buried in unconsecrated ground by members of the League.

If the Accused fails to utilise the enclosed key before the hour of seven PM he will forfeit his life.

It is necessary not for the League of Prometheus to prove itself to you, but for you to prove yourself to it.

When the fight begins within himself, a man's worth something – Robert Browning

Vince chewed a thumbnail, watching as the first fat drops of rain spotted the pavements below. They were serious, they were goddamn fucking serious about this! Sebastian had to be feeling pretty threatened to issue such a challenge – not that he would have needed much encouragement to turn the whole thing into a game. He must have figured Vince knew something that would cause lasting damage to the League. The embarrassing part was that, despite the tough tone of what he had written so far, he had uncovered no hardcore evidence of any illegal activities.

But he knew.

He knew they had killed the journalist, Tyler, getting him drunk and shoving him down the steps. He knew they had run Carol Mendacre off the road and watched her car burn. Just as he knew that they would kill him if he failed to obey them, and hide the evidence just as successfully.

But this sheet in his hand was proof of their existence, solid testimony. And even as he studied it, the paper began to dry and crumble in his fingers, splintering first in half, then quarters. A faintly bitter chemical smell arose as the craquelure deepened across the broken page, and the flakes of paper drifted to the floor, disintegrating further. They would not even allow him such meagre proof as this.

He looked at his watch. Twenty-past six. He checked inside the envelope. There was nothing else except the key. How could they be watching him? The telephone was less than a metre away from his right hand. Suppose he lifted the receiver and called the police? Could Sebastian's men somehow see into the flat? What could they possibly do, anyway? They were just trying to scare him, having a laugh at his expense.

If only he believed that. He had seen the silent fury on their faces when they had discovered him in the chamber. They had the means to get rid of him, and now he had given them the motive. Fuck, fuck, fuck, what to do. It was coming up for six-thirty. If he accepted the challenge, he only had half-an-hour in which to find a use for the key.

They had to be able to see in somehow. Very slowly, he moved in front of the window and tried to look into the rooms on the other side of the street. The sudden racket of the telephone took a year off his life. He allowed it to ring three times before lifting the receiver.

'I hope you haven't forgotten about tonight,' said Pam.

'What?' Relief flooded through him.

'We're having dinner tonight, remember? You've blown me out twice recently, and I'm not standing for it a third time. Amazing as it may sound, I do have a scrap of pride left, you know.' Her tone was playful. The last thing he needed right now.

'Listen, Pam, I've got some kind of – thing – going on here and –'

'I have to win you away from that computer somehow, so I'm offering to pay for the meal. You're allowed dessert and everything.'

'I don't think I can –'

'No "no" for an answer this time, sonny boy, you promised, remember?'

'You're right,' he admitted, 'I promised.'

'So I'll see you at eight-thirty, as we arranged. Resistance is futile. I'm looking forward to it already. *A tout à l'heure,* saucepot.' She rang off.

He picked up the key once more and tried to think. The telephone rang again. This time he answered before the end of the first ring.

'I hope you slept well last night.' The voice was amused, male, almost playful. 'You received your instructions, I hope. This night will require all the intellectual and physical energy at your command if you are to survive it. You really should have started by now. You're going to miss your deadline. You've only until seven o'clock to use the key, or you're out of the game.'

'I'm not playing your stupid games, Sebastian, you can go fuck yourself –'

'There's that gutter language again. So limiting, when there are so many beautiful English words to choose from. In case you had trouble with the title of the challenge, by the way, Deca –'

'– diurnal means in a cycle of ten, ten challenges, yeah, I figured that part, I'm common but I'm not completely stupid.'

'You're not allowed to take anything with you that you

would not normally be carrying on the street. I think we forgot to mention that.'

'I'm not doing this, Sebastian, I already told you.'

'If you don't you will be killed, and others may be hurt too. We are deadly serious about this, Vincent. You're not the first to stand accused. But you could be the first to win. Where's your sense of gamesmanship?'

'And if I win, what does my victory entitle me to?'

'It grants you the title of "Grand Master Of The City". You get a badge, a hat and everything. More importantly, you win the right to publish. We'll be in touch again. Right now it's six-thirty-two precisely. You'd better get going. There's only a short time left for you to reach the base-point of your first challenge. The time limit for each section of the night will be given to you in due course. Now, if you're not out of that gruesome little flat in the next few minutes, we will claim our forfeit, invade your life and bury your pathetically miserable soul in pieces so far apart that no two people in the same time-zone will be able to find it.'

The line went dead.

It took him exactly two minutes fifty-five seconds to load his leather duffel bag and hit the street running.

First Clue

VINCE TURNED the tiny steel key over in the palm of his hand, tipping it to the light. There was something engraved on either side. On one, the number 12. On the other, a longer series of numerals. He tilted it back and forth until he could read the inscription. 18371901. Some kind of serial number, perhaps. There were no other markings.

Now what?

He was standing in the street, outside the Hallmark card shop three doors along from his flat. The hazy winter night was sharpening with sporadic gusts of rain, finer than sea spray. He found it hard to believe that they were really watching him. That evening in the Holborn chamber he had only seen a few of their faces; he would remember Barwick's moley features, but none of the others. And they were only the members of the inner circle. What was it Dr Masters had said about there being as many as fifty in the League? It was clear that he had to go along with this lunacy, at least until he figured out if they were just trying to scare him, or whether they really meant business.

He tried to recall his arrangement with Pam tonight. They were going to eat, then meet up with Louie, who was heading for a gig at the Jazz Café with some people from college. If he didn't show up she'd be annoyed with him, and might think it odd. Failure to appear was pretty normal behaviour within their group but Vince was known for reliability. He should have told her about the letter. Now it was too late. The rules forbade him from calling her back. He could feel the panic of indecision setting in.

Concentrate on the problem instead, he decided. Look at the key.

He studied the numbers again.

12 and 18371901.

They meant nothing to him. Serial numbers for a standard key, the key to anything from a bicycle lock to a petty-cash box. Big deal.

If he was going to get through this, he knew he would have to start thinking like Sebastian.

'Hey Vince, you okay, man?'

There was a crash behind him as Mr Javneesh pulled down the shutter of the card shop window. He had installed a new display of birthday cards that celebrated the recipient's year of birth. Each card had a montage of that year's events depicted on its cover, and featured the date in large black letters. 1953. 1965. 1972. He had been meaning to buy one for Pam.

'You should get inside, man. Looks like rain.' Mr Javneesh zipped up his jacket and headed off towards his car. Vince looked back at the numbers on the key. 18371901.

Could they be dates? 1837 – 1901?

Sixty-odd years. He looked back at the cards. Sixty *glorious* years. Queen Victoria's reign. Victoria. His fingers gripped the key. A locker key. The left-luggage lockers at Victoria station.

He was on his way.

The litter-filled ticket hall at Tufnell Park tube station was crowded with loitering drunks and wild-haired kids. As he punched coins into the ticket machine he wondered if members of the League were watching him.

'Oi, you got any spare change?' A sixteen-year-old white boy with dreadlocked yellow hair and a blue nylon sleeping bag wrapped around his shoulders was tapping him on the back. He stared at the boy in alarm. What would happen if he replied? Would they hurt the boy? He bolted for the escalator and the safety of the underground platform, unable to shake the feeling of being monitored. There were closed circuit security cameras mounted at either end of the platform. Who was studying their screens?

Mercifully, a southbound train arrived within a minute. At Victoria he made his way through the homebound commuters and reached the racks of grey metal lockers, locating number 12 at the end nearest the platforms. Four minutes to seven.

As he fumbled with the key, he checked about him, but it was hopeless. *Everyone* looked suspicious. Scanning the station forecourt, he noticed more tiny black lenses peering down at him from the steel superstructure, more robot periscopes jutting from shadowed corners. Now that he thought about it, the city was filled with cameras. Traffic, security, safety. Who was watching?

The key turned smoothly, raising tumblers. Inside the locker was another envelope, identical to the first – nothing else.

He tried to tear it open, but his bitten nails would not catch under the flap. *Slow down*, he told himself, *take it easy*. You made it here in time. The station clock read 6:58 p.m. He managed to rip open the envelope and partially tore the letter inside. *You've got about thirty seconds to memorise the letter before it starts falling apart.*

There were two sheets of paper inside, folded in half. The first read:

Dear Vincent,

The ten members of the Inner Circle of the League of Prometheus have been allowed to set you one problem each.

Welcome to your starter challenge, posed by our youngest member, the Hon. Barnabus Hewlett. I trust you will find it easy enough to afford you some small enjoyment, and you are allowed an *apéritif* upon reaching its solution.

Good luck, and may the best man win.

In God And Honour,

– Sebastian

He turned to the second sheet of paper. At the top were a few neatly printed lines, three quotes, and beneath them, a piece of poetry. *My God,* he thought, *I'll never be able to retain so much information before the paper starts to self-destruct.* He hastily scanned the page.

The Challenge Of Outraged Society

'I don't want any music. My husband has threatened to kill me tonight.'

'She made one great mistake, possibly the greatest mistake a woman of the West can make. She married an Oriental.'

'A person who honestly believes that his life is in danger is entitled to kill his assailant if it is the only way he honestly and reasonably believes he can protect himself.'

> 'Mine are horrible, social ghosts –
> Speeches and women and guests and hosts,
> Weddings and morning calls and toasts,
> In every bad variety:
> Ghosts who hover about the grave
> Of all that's manly, free and brave:
> You'll find their names on the architrave
> Of that charnel house, Society.'

Time Allocated: 1 Hour

There was nothing else.

He could smell the bitter chemicals rising from the pages. Clutching the envelope and its desiccating contents, he slammed the locker door shut and set off across the crowded concourse. His mind was swimming. He could not think lucidly, not in the way they expected him to. What if he did nothing? Would they really carry out their threats? He needed a place to sit, to clear his head.

He found an empty bench in a relatively quiet corner of the station and watched the commuters streaming past to their trains, their homes, their loved ones, oblivious to his ludicrous dilemma. They would think him deranged if he reached out to ask them for help. Everyone was guarded these days. It was absurd – how could he suddenly find himself so alone in such an immense city?

And that, Vince realised, was what Sebastian and the other

members of the League had intended for him. They aimed to render him as helpless as if he had been stranded on a barren moor without a map. They planned to make an example of him, to show him up for what they felt he was, vulgar, uneducated, stupid, blind, paralysed.

Obviously, he had no choice but to thrash them. Working-class men had more logical minds, better intuition, firmer resolve, everyone knew that. Perhaps the news hadn't filtered through to Sebastian and his friends yet.

If only he believed it. Vince turned his attention to the second sheet of paper and reread the quotes, reminding himself that he was seeking a location somewhere within the city. Sebastian's personal note had already crumbled through his fingers, but the clue sheet appeared to have been treated with a milder solution. It was drying out and starting to crack, but at a much slower rate. He concentrated on the words.

'My husband has threatened to kill me . . .' The site of a female victim, then, something prescient she might have said, just prior to her husband attacking her, perhaps.

No 'music'. Were they in a public place? Not talking to her husband, but about him to another. A lover?

'She made one great mistake . . . She married an Oriental.' A piece of hindsight, this one, uttered by whom, a judge, a lawyer, a biographer?

'She married an Oriental.' The language was pompous. Old. Victorian, perhaps? It was impossible to tell.

'Entitled to kill . . .' This had to be advice from a judge, a bit of a lecture after the conclusion of a case. It was no good, though, he had nothing more. He turned to the poetry, not his strong point, to say the least. The verse had to be tied to the quotes, but how? The ghosts of society. Outraged society.

Above him, the station announcements burbled incomprehensibly, blurring echoes. Indistinct people rushed past. A train was pulling out.

Could this female victim have been a lady of society? Speeches, weddings, hosts, toasts. She hadn't wanted any music. She was upset by her husband's threat. 'A person who honestly believes that his life is in danger is entitled to kill his assailant.' But it was a woman whose life had been in danger. So she hadn't been the victim, she had been the murderess, and she had been acquitted; she had honestly believed her life to be in danger. 'My husband has threatened to kill me . . .'

A society murder case, an act of violence that had possibly been committed in public. There had to be something more. Who had made the quotes, who had authored the poem? He started with the latter, speaking it aloud. An elderly woman standing nearby gave him a filthy stare and moved away.

It sounded like more of a song than a poem. A touch of iambic pentameter. There was an air of familiar jauntiness. Vince rose and crossed the concourse to the station bookshop, hoping to find something, anything that might point him in the right direction. He checked the time, 7:12 p.m.

He had no idea where to start in the small poetry section, so he turned to the crime books instead, and began checking the shelves.

True Crime and Criminals. Famous Cases of the Old Bailey . . . Great Crimes of the Twentieth Century.

He could hardly start buying books indiscriminately. He only had a few pounds in his pocket, and his current account was so empty that his cashcard would be no help, so he was forced to thumb through each volume looking for clues. A shop assistant with a face like an unpopular root vegetable stood watching with his arms folded, ready to weed out browsers. The shop was waiting to close. *The Murder Club Guide to London. The Trials of Marshall Hall. The Encyclopaedia of Modern Murder . . . Ghosts of the City.*

He had barely started thumbing through the indices when the assistant shuffled over to the entrance and pulled a steel shutter down with a bang.

It was impossible. He suddenly saw how difficult it would be uncovering information in the city after dark. There were no other bookstores likely to be open now, and most libraries would soon be closing their doors. One solution presented itself; he could gain access to the Internet. Sebastian had said nothing in the charter about that. He needed to find one of the cyber-cafés dotting the city like electronic beacons, and run some information searches. The man at the station information counter was mystified by his request, but the young girl refilling the brochure holders was not, and directed him to a street behind the coach station where a smart new cafeteria called Blutopia waited beneath a sign of flickering cobalt neon.

He wiped the rain from the scuffed sleeves of his black nylon jacket, purchased a coffee and threaded his way between shining aluminium tables to a free monitor with an up-and-running search engine.

How could he run a search without something specific to look for? The wording in the clue was so vague as to be useless. He could imagine how many thousands of matches a word like 'oriental' or 'society' would generate. He tried longer phrases, and finding no correspondents, entered the True Crime titles he had been prevented from perusing in the station bookstore, starting with 'Old Bailey', then weeding the information down to 'murder trials', but there were still so many that he knew it would take several hours to go through them all. He wanted to call Louie and ask his help, even though his esoteric knowledge extended no further than episode titles of obscure science fiction shows.

An extraordinary feeling of isolation had settled over him, a sense of secret urgency that no one who met his eyes would understand. He wondered if any of the other patrons seated around him harboured mysteries, but they mostly looked like the usual net-heads, filling up the hours of a dull, rainy winter evening.

Abandoning 'Old Bailey', he tried the title of another book he had seen in the store, 'The Trials of Marshall Hall' and was rewarded with an entry for the legendary Victorian lawyer. Almost without thinking, he opened it. The page was part of a bookstore's mail-order service. Under a heading marked 'Society's Greatest Scandals' he found the answer to his question – or at least, to part of it.

It appeared to be a chapter title from the book he had seen. *She made the greatest mistake a woman of the West can make. She married an Oriental.*' Below the caption was a photograph of Sir Edward Marshall Hall, defence lawyer for someone called Madame Marie-Marguerite Fahhim, a high-society Parisian beauty accused of shooting her Egyptian husband, Prince Ali Kamel Fahhim Bey, dead in 1923. A cause-célèbre, said the text, the greatest London scandal of the age. She was found innocent, provoked beyond endurance by the Prince's sexual habits and casual cruelties. But there was also a powerful undercurrent of racism here, just the sort of thing Sebastian and his pals would have taken delight in. The page of clues beside the console had finally disintegrated into a rough pale ash. He read on, scrolling down the page.

The Egyptian government had cabled the Attorney-

General to complain of derogatory remarks made about 'Orientals' during the trial. And the remark about not wanting music, it was made by Madame Fahhim to the band-leader of the Savoy, where they had a suite.

Where the murder had taken place.

And now the poem suddenly made sense, if one assumed that it owed its rumpty-tumpty style to someone with a strong Savoy connection, someone like W.S. Gilbert. But these were no lyrics for his composer, Sir Arthur Sullivan – or if they were, Vince was unfamiliar with them. As a child he had alarmed his mother by learning all the words to *HMS Pinafore* and singing them loudly in the bath when he should have been belting out the lyrics to current Top Ten hits like normal children. The poem had the feeling of an early Savoy song, as though from a simpler time. He ran a search on 'Gilbert and Sullivan' and connected through to their archive pages.

The stanza was contained in something called the Bab Ballads, a short anthology of verse penned by W.S. Gilbert and published before the duo went onto create their operas. The Savoy Operas, pretty, passionless pieces inspired by the extraordinary success of Jacques Offenbach, one of Sebastian's favourite composers.

Vince had twenty minutes left in which to reach the Savoy Hotel.

CHAPTER TWENTY-ONE

West End Farce

BUT OF course, they would never let him in. Not to any part of the hotel beyond the lobby, at any rate. He should have changed, worn something a bit more adaptable, but there had been no time.

How, then, to start? He approached the gleaming Rolls-Royce frontage of the Savoy with trepidation. It was a trick, of course, to make him feel aware of his station in life, to make him feel small. And it was working. Standing there in the chill air with a mist spilling in from the Embankment, he felt out of place, insignificant in his torn damp jeans and nylon padded jacket. Couples appeared before him in evening dress, drifting through the bronzed revolving doors into the night. Japanese, French and Italian conversations surrounded him, bossy Home-Counties' accents, the clipped tones of Henley gels, the Essex argy-bargy of bullish businessmen, every kind of voice except his own. He did not belong there. He belonged back in Peckham, in his mother's divided semi with its babies and aunts, with the blaring radio in the kitchen and the unrepaired motorbike in the hall.

Not true, he told himself, rubbing the blood back into his hands. He took another look at the guests. Tourists, conference speakers, business delegates, couples celebrating wedding anniversaries, just people. Hotel life had changed. Anyone could come here now. To hell with it, he thought, all they can do is kick me out.

Well, they could, and therein lay the problem. Vince knew he would certainly not be able to enter the hotel's American Bar dressed the way he was, nor the restaurant, the scene of Madame Marie-Marguerite Fahhim's 'music' remark. He had no idea in which room she had shot her husband, although perhaps one of the staff knew. But the League would not be so obvious as to leave his next assignment in the room. Too easy. He had to remember that this was a test. There was hidden trickery here.

Sebastian had advised his members about setting the challenges. How much instruction had he given them? How did his mind work? How much – or little – had the pair of them discovered about each other in the short time that they had been friends?

Another timecheck. 7:51 p.m. At the corner a gang of dead-eyed youths turned to watch him pass, checking for a sign of weakness. Scrawny-necked skinheads barking and spitting beside the half-excavated road, black boys in Armani knock-offs making sucky-sucky noises at passing girls. The safety of the Strand – a comparatively recent novelty – was already becoming a thing of the past. Unsure how to proceed, he walked back to the top of the short street and looked out into the traffic.

The street was busy. Theatres were beginning their evening performances. As he was wondering what to do next, the telephone in the call box nearest to him started to ring. He seized the receiver without a second thought.

'Well, why aren't you going in?' asked Sebastian. 'You'll

fall behind your schedule if you don't pick up the pace and solve the clue. You only have until 8:00 p.m. to find the answer.'

'Don't you have something better to do?' he asked, looking up at the dead office windows around him. 'Shouldn't you all be slipping into robes and fezzes, dancing about in circles, sacrificing goats?' *Where the hell were they? How could they see him?*

'How do you know we're not? Solve the clue, Vincent, solve it if you want to stay alive. You have about – oh, seven minutes.'

The line went dead. He threw down the receiver and paced angrily back to the corner. Think, damn you, he told himself. *Think.*

Something wasn't right. The poem. Details of the shooting scandal had been designed to lead him to the Savoy. So why bother to add the poem?

The W.S. Gilbert quote was meant to take him further. There could be no other reason to include it. He dug in his back pocket and pulled the remaining scraps of the disintegrated page from his jeans.

'– Horrible, social ghosts –'

It was no good. The streets were too boisterous. He couldn't think.

'– Speeches –'

'– Variety –'

He looked along the Strand again, to the Savoy Theatre – the original home of Gilbert and Sullivan, before they had moved up to the grandeur of Sir Richard D'Oyly Carte's Palace Theatre.

You'll find their names on the architrave . . . Not the Savoy Hotel at all, that was just a pointer. The architrave. Wasn't that the blank bit between a pillar and its roof? Theatres utilised such gaps to run favourable newspaper quotes along them.

He broke into a trot, pushing through the crowd that was filtering slowly into the Savoy Theatre. He tried to read what the critics had written about the play, something called *Whoops, There Go My Trousers*.

'A *Laugh-A-Minute Trouser-Dropping Farce*' – Sheridan Morley, *Evening Standard*. '*Does what Britain does best – makes a total fool of itself*' – Irving Wardle – *The Times*.

That was what it said above the doors, and there, on a dropping-stained ledge above the lightbulbs was what looked like a bottle of champagne with an envelope tied around its neck – but how on earth was he supposed to reach it? He stepped back and examined the front of the theatre. There was no way of scaling the wall. Nothing else for it; he would have to climb out from one of the first-floor windows.

Entering the crowded theatre foyer was easy enough. Two young ushers were tearing tickets at the foot of the main staircase. There was no other way up. He picked the dopier-looking of the pair, a spidery-haired youth in an ill-fitting jacket, and waited until he was tearing the tickets of a group. As he slipped behind the backs of the waiting patrons, the usher spotted him and raised a hand.

'It's all right, I just forgot something,' he said, pointing vaguely ahead, and kept moving forward with his head down, waiting for someone to come after him. But when he turned around, he saw that the usher's attention had been seized by a coach-party impatiently awaiting entrance.

He hurried on, checking his watch. 7:57 p.m. There was no time left for indecision. At the first floor was an open carpeted area, the arched windows beyond standing floor-to-ceiling. Attempting to look as officious as possible, he marched over to the one he judged to be nearest the bottle, pulled it open and looked out. The envelope stood in a blaze of light, still several feet from the window, but this was the nearest point of access. There was nothing for it but to go out on the ledge.

If only he didn't have this thing about heights. Well, not a thing, exactly. As a child he had been taken on a funicular railway, and had howled through the journey. Looking down brought that familiar sickening sense of the earth dropping away.

Remember the old adage, he thought, then dropped to all fours and began to edge himself out. At his back, several playgoers turned and shot him disapproving looks, something Londoners did when they were irrationally annoyed by someone but hadn't the guts to say anything. The angled narrow sill was thick with black dust and covered in tangles of electrical cable. It was virtually impossible to establish a firm foothold. As he edged out, his vision firmly fixed on the nearest wall, someone – incredibly – shut the window behind him and dropped the bolt. What the hell were they thinking of?

Light bounced from his watch-face; 7:59 p.m. He was out of time. There was nowhere to go but forward. He was sure he could be seen from the street, but few people ever looked up. His right foot slipped, scattering pieces of cracked paintwork out over the bulbs. His duffel bag slid from his shoulder and swung down to the crook of his right arm. If he had wanted to attract attention to himself, he was certainly going about it the right way.

The envelope was less than a metre from him now. In the light from the display bulbs he could clearly read his name on the front. He shifted his left knee forward across a clump of wiring, but the clump moved and his leg went with it. Within moments his centre of balance had shifted badly and he was fighting to maintain his equilibrium. But it was no good; he could feel himself going over. His left foot thumped down on one bulb and smashed it, then another popped as the lower half of his body slithered off the ledge and out into space. Below him, someone shouted up in alarm.

It was his last chance to seize the letter. He threw out his right arm and grabbed the bottle as he slithered into the air and dropped towards the pavement below. Why he couldn't have landed on a fat woman in a fur coat, he didn't know; instead he crashed down on top of what appeared to be an emaciated crustie leading a mongrel on a piece of string, which yelped and promptly bit him on the leg. The crustie slid over onto his back, and Vince landed astride his chest.

'Shit!'

'What the –'

He kicked out at the dog, which had its teeth sunk firmly in his left boot.

'Mind my dog!'

'Get him off me!'

Vince sat up and shoved his hair out of his eyes. It wasn't a crustie at all, but a sickly young man with a badly-shaved head and an oversized navy raincoat who, having fulfilled his role as a human airbag, was attempting to wriggle out from beneath his attacker and stand up. Patrons peered timidly out from the foyer of the theatre at them, convinced that some sort of crime had been committed. The dog was still refusing to relax its jaws, presumably out of loyalty to its master.

'Crippen, let go! It's just his way of making friends, mate. He likes to get a taste of you first.'

'He'll get a taste of my boot if he tries it again.' Vince belatedly remembered that he was not supposed to talk to anyone. Alarmed, he finally managed to push the dog away, rose and wiped himself down. The man who had broken his fall was patting his chest as if testing for broken ribs.

'What were you doing up there? That could have been nasty. Did you fall out? Who's the bubbly for? You celebrating something?'

He dared not answer. He could feel Sebastian's men watching him from some vantage point nearby.

'What's the matter? Don't you talk to street people? Fucking Tory! Sybaritic Saatchi sycophant!'

'Do you mind, I voted Labour in the last election,' Vince muttered, groggily setting off along the kerb. The fall had disturbed his equilibrium.

'Typical, bloody champagne socialist!'

He slipped into an alleyway at the side of the theatre, praying that Sebastian had not seen him talking to a stranger. He didn't want to be responsible for anyone's death. He shifted beneath the nearest streetlamp and detached the envelope from the champagne bottle. Tearing it open, he removed a single sheet of paper and read:

<u>The Challenge Of Inspiration</u>

Speedwell 711

There was nothing else typed on the paper apart from the time allowance: one hour. He held the sheet up to the light, and even as he did so it broke in two. What the hell was it supposed to mean? It would take a special kind of inspiration to figure this one out. Clairvoyance, more like. All he knew was that he had barely managed to solve the last clue in time, and now had exactly fifty-eight minutes left to solve this one.

As he looked up into the sky and forced his breathing to a slower rate, the rain began pumping down from the clouds in earnest.

CHAPTER TWENTY-TWO

Mr Pink

OKAY, THE hour had started, but was this all he had to go on? As far as he knew, there was no area of London called Speedwell. Perhaps there had been in the year 711. This had to be a history question. He picked up the bottle of champagne and examined the label. Non-vintage, no year or corresponding serial number. Möet & Chandon, nothing unusual there.

He was stumped. There were no libraries in the vicinity, and there was no point in trying to track down an open book-store – besides, what could he look up? The events of that year, perhaps.

There was one person who could help him – Harold Masters. From where Vince stood, he could see a red call box on the next corner. The narrow street led down to the Thames, and was quite deserted. The air from the river was further chilled by the falling rain. Sebastian had no men posted around here. How could they see him make a call? He dug in his pocket and pulled Masters's card from his wallet. He kept a phonecard somewhere. He checked again. The street was still empty. He loped to the call box and punched out the doctor's home number. A woman answered.

'Is Doctor Masters there, please?' He stood with his back

to the call box, watching the road. 'Hi, Doctor Masters? This is Vince Reynolds, I met you outside the British Museum. You gave me some advice? And your number?'

'Oh – um –'

'Listen, I wouldn't call like this but I really need your help.'

'Is this to do with – what we were talking about?'

'I'm afraid so, yes. Don't ask me to explain. I seem to be involved in some kind of a game.'

'Do be careful, for heaven's sake. I told you they could be dangerous.'

'I need help with a sort of clue thing, and don't know who else to ask. What happened in London in the year 711?'

The doctor, who infinitely preferred academic conversations to mundane calls about train-times and dinner arrangements, perked up no end and gave the question careful thought. '711? It's hard to say, just like that. The eighth century – that was before the country even had its first monarch.'

'I just wondered if anything particular occurred in that year.'

'I can't just tell you off the top of my head, you know. This is not my area of expertise. Can you hold on while I grab a book?'

He came back after a moment. 'Well, it was before the Great Slaughter.'

'What was that?'

'The Vikings attacked London, but that was in 842. St Paul's Cathedral was already built, not as we know it now, of course . . .'

'But is there nothing that's –'

A shadow crossed his peripheral vision. There was a man standing behind him. A hand fell onto his shoulder. Vince dropped his fist on the connection, cutting the call.

'Do you always go running off like that without apologising?' asked the pasty-faced young man he had fallen on outside the theatre.

Vince was furious. 'You moron!' he shouted, 'I've just cut him off!'

The young man threw up his hands. 'Great, fine. First you parachute onto my back from the sky, then you swear at me and vanish, then when I find you again you bloody insult me. Are you in PR, by any chance?'

'You don't know what you've done,' Vince said angrily, shoving him away and throwing the receiver down.

'Tell me.'

'That was a very important call!'

'If you're, like, so important, why haven't you got a mobile phone? Answer that, then. Everyone else has. Why isn't your e-mail faxing your voicemail?' He rattled out sentences, as talkative as only the very skinny can be.

'I didn't say – never mind, just get away from me.' Vince didn't need this, wasn't he under enough pressure already without – 'What now? What the fuck are you staring at?'

He was scrunching up his face, gurning a visual representation of intense thought. 'What were you doing up there in the first place? Fringe performance, was it? Acrobatics?'

'It's none of your business.' Vince swung his duffel bag onto his shoulder. 'I can handle it.' *Sure I can*, he thought.

'Is that yours?' He was pointing to the bottle of champagne standing on the shelf of the call box. 'Just gonna leave it there? Don't you want it?'

'I don't know how to say this politely but –'

The young man held up his hand. 'There is no polite way, trust me, I hear it every day. "Fuck off." "Get yourself a job." "Earn a living." "Just *fuck off*." Don't worry, I'm going. It's a pity, because Crippen took a shine to you.' He paused. 'I just want to check one thing. You're all right, you don't need any help at all.'

'No.'

'You're fine, then.'

'Yes.'

''Cause street people look after each other.'

'I am *not* a street –'

'And you're bleeding.'

'Am I?' He touched his face, and his fingers came away wet.

'It's a wicked cut. You need help? Life is short. Parks and paintings survive the centuries, not people. We're here and gone. Make friends, man.'

'There's nothing you can do, trust me.'

'You don't know that.'

Vince rooted about in his duffel bag for a notepad and pen, then wrote out what had been written on the League's latest page. 'All right, smartarse. Tell me what that means.'

The young man read it slowly, moving his lips. Made as if to speak. Crumpled his forehead deeper – three furrows. Closed his mouth, then opened it again.

'Mr Pink,' he said finally. 'Telephones.'

'What?' Vince gave him a strange look.

'You've asked the one person around here who can tell you. It's one of those odd little stories you find about London. How do I know? Weird, huh? Sit down for a sec.' He eased himself onto the sheltered step of a building and waved Vince down. 'Many years ago, the LTE –'

'The what?'

'The London Telephone Exchange – was responsible for naming all of the city's exchanges, and it had to come up with a name for the one at Golders Green. Its own name had been rejected because it was numerically identical to the first named automatic exchange, Holborn. The letters used to go around the dial in threes, so GOL and HOL were on the same fingerhole. A bloke called Mr Pink – sounds like a character from *Reservoir Dogs*, dunnit? – was the Deputy Director of the LTE. He rejected over fifty names, looking for the right one. Having a poetic turn of mind, he thought about the name Golders Green and translated it into the phrase 'gold as green'. Then he asked himself, what makes gold, or yellow, turn green? The answer is blue. One of the brightest shades of blue he could think of came from a flower called the Speedwell. So that's what he called the Golders Green telephone exchange.'

Vince was dumbfounded. 'So you think this is a Golders Green telephone number, then?'

'No,' he replied. 'The SPE of Speedwell only accounts for the first three digits, so with SPE 711 you're still one digit short. But I tell you what – there's a Seven-Eleven in Golders Green High Street.'

Vince mentally slapped himself. 'A *Seven-Eleven*?'

'That's what it says here.' He pointed to the pink price label on the champagne bottle. The answer had been in front of him all the time. 'Maybe you'll find what you're looking for in the drinks cabinet there, eh?'

His name was Strangeways. He refused to reveal whether it was because he'd been inside it, or simply had them. If he had a real name, he did not encourage its use. He was twenty-two and badly needed a bath. He had been living on and off the streets of London since he was seventeen. How and why he came to be there were not questions he cared to answer. Indeed, he replied to every enquiry in such an elliptical fashion that after a few minutes Vince gave up. His speech bore the faint trace of a Newcastle accent. He was too thin for his considerable height, like an excessively watered daisy overreaching itself. His clothes marked the style of true street wear; practical black jeans, perilously tattered leather jacket, immense, warm and probably flea-filled navy-surplus overcoat. His head looked as if it had been shaved by Sweeney Todd during a party. A moderately fashionable goatee sprouted on his chin. These were the only outward signs of the man within.

Vince considered taking him into his confidence. He needed an ally, and Strangeways looked moderately sane, alert, not entirely untrustworthy. It meant breaking the rules, though, unless he managed it surreptitiously. They were seated beside each other on the Tube as it swayed through northbound tunnels on its way to Golders Green. Strangeways had flatly insisted on accompanying him, only to then borrow the price of the ticket and pocket the change.

Crippen the dog was on the opposite side of the carriage, snuffling around the shoes of an irritated businessman. Strangeways had smuggled the Jack Russell into the station inside his jacket, but Vince had insisted on him standing some distance away, further along the platform. There was a closed circuit monitoring system placed near the tunnel entrances, and even though he was unsure of the technical capabilities of such equipment, he had begun to suspect that the members of the League were somehow utilising the traffic cameras, so why not the ones in there? Some of the new trains had cameras in their carriages, but this was ancient Northern Line rolling stock, unfitted with modern technology. He was pretty sure they were safe for the time being.

'So, do you do this a lot? Charging around town on treasure hunts?'

'It passes the time,' Vince replied. 'What do you do apart from wander the streets with a dog on a piece of string?' He waved his hand at the terrier, which had its head in a dozing woman's shopping basket. 'And why does it always have to be string? What statement are you trying to make?'

'The statement that I haven't got any money,' Strangeways said and shrugged. 'I would have thought that was fucking obvious.'

'Are you unambitious?'

'No,' he protested. 'I have ambitions. They just haven't been realised.'

'Why, what do you want to be?'

'Ideally, a shepherd. Actually, I could have got myself a graphics degree if I'd had the application.'

'Applying yourself is a matter of –'

'No, man, the form, I didn't get the application form posted in time. I have immense artistic ability. What I don't have is a job and somewhere to live.'

'Why can't you get a job?'

'Are you kidding? There's no call for illustrators any more. Everything's comped together on Macs. I'm a fine artist. I don't want to cobble adverts together. That's for the computer generation, cheap labour that does what it's told and to hell with artistry.'

'There must be some –' Crippen caught his eye. 'Your dog.' The Jack Russell had partially eaten a bar of soap and appeared to be frothing at the mouth.

'I don't know why he does that,' said Strangeways, hauling the dog towards him and removing shreds of soapy paper from his canescent jaws. 'People think he's got rabies. I wouldn't mind having a go at club flyers, CD art an' stuff, but the competition's too far ahead of me now.

Listen, why are you doing this? It's some kind of initiation test, is it?'

'Yeah, sort of. I'm doing it because I have to.'

Perhaps it would be better to confide in him. Now, before they reached the next station. Deciding that communication was power, Vince attempted to outline his role in the evening's events. Between Chalk Farm and Golders Green stations he described how he had come to be involved with such a group as the League of Prometheus. Telling a stranger eased the weight of the problem. Strangeways thought about it, scratching at his skinny goatee. He carefully realigned the folds of his overcoat and sat back. 'Do you always do what people tell you to do?'

'This is different, believe me.' As they exited the station, Strangeways pondered the problem.

'Run this by me again. Perhaps I'm being thick. Some nights I've got less brain cells than a footballer's wedding, know what I mean? What are these people going to do if you don't follow their instructions?'

'I don't know. Maybe nothing. They might just be trying to scare me, but I don't want to take that risk.'

'So they're not going to – like, kill anyone, then.'

'Erm, well, yes they are, if they're not obeyed.'

'Don't you want to know how I knew about Speedwell? I mean, that's like a one in a thousand chance, you asking me.'

'Go on, then.'

'It's something all the older BT engineers know about. I trained as a telephone engineer for a while, but the work was so fucking boring. Just another branch of digital technology. I went back to the street. I've tried my hand at most things, but I always seem to be in the wrong place at the wrong time. I should have been training to use Photoshop on a graphics computer, and now I can't afford to. Doesn't that sort of thing ever happen to you?'

Vince smiled. 'All the bloody time. Why do you live on the street?'

'Why not? There's no rhyme or reason to the world any more. Nothing is safe. Nothing is sure except that the rich will put out your ambitions by pissing on the fuse. Fuck'em. Why not live according to the demands of each day?'

'Because if everyone did that society would collapse.'

'Stone me, you think it isn't doing that already? Look around you. We're living in the remnants of the past, like scavengers. All of us. A hundred years ago, that train we were just sitting on ran more efficiently than it does now. If we keep progressing at this rate, we'll soon be back in the Stone Age. People sometimes call me a tramp, but I'm not a tramp, I'm just homeless. The street is my office. I'm on the phone, look.' He pulled a mobile phone from his overcoat pocket and waved it at him. 'That's really all I need to conduct business.'

'Business?'

'A little buying and selling.'

'Oh, right.' Vince threw him a dubious look, deciding not to ask for details. 'Is it charged up?'

'Sure.'

'Can I use it?' Vince thanked him and punched in Louie's number. Inspired by Strangeways's rebellious attitude, he had decided to dispense with the League's rule forbidding telephone contact. Louie's answering machine picked up the call. Damn.

'There's the Seven-Eleven.' Strangeways pointed over the rainswept road.

CHAPTER TWENTY-THREE

To The Tropics

ACROSS THE city, teenagers hung around outside Seven-Elevens in a state of expectant stasis, as if waiting to receive news of world-changing events, but the most that ever happened was a small exchange of drugs and money, a scuffle when the pubs turned out. Vince squeezed between two ominous youths sheltering beneath the awning and walked to the rear of the store. Strangeways remained outside with the dog. Crippen had been hawking up chunks of Imperial Leather ever since they left the tube station.

He found it easily enough, a small rectangular envelope sealed inside a misted plastic Jiffy-bag, taped behind the heavy plastic strips of the drinks cabinet. It made a *thwuuuup* noise as he removed it, and he was aware of the Chinese clerk behind the counter watching him in the convex mirror above the magazine racks. He purchased a suspicion-killing carton of orange juice and some nutrition-packed pepperoni sticks.

'So what's in it?' Strangeways tried to snatch the envelope from him as he emerged from the store.

'Move away from me, someone will see you.'

'There's no one around but kids, for God's sake. You're paranoid.'

'With good reason.' He pointed up at the traffic cameras on the corners of the buildings. 'Do you know who's watching? I don't.'

'Open the damned envelope.'

'Let's get off the main street.'

They turned left and walked into a quiet side road filled with pebble-dashed bay-fronted houses, stopping beneath the spattering aureole of a streetlamp. Vince tore the envelope from its plastic cover and ripped open its flap. Inside was the usual single page of chemically-treated vellum. He unfolded it and stared with a puzzled frown. At the top was the stated time allowance of an hour, and the title of the challenge:

The Challenge Of An Exotic Childhood

'Yeah, and? Well, what else does it say?'

'Nothing.'

'What do you mean, nothing?'

'See for yourself.' He passed the page to Strangeways. The rest of it was blank but for a large round blot of ink in the centre.

'What do you suppose that's meant to be?' Strangeways rubbed at the patch with his forefinger, then examined the tip. 'Plain black ink. Staines. Beauty spot. No, black spot.'

'Like an Accident Black Spot? How would we know which one? I remember seeing the signs when I was a kid. Do they still have them?'

'Shagged if I know. I'd like to help you out, but I don't think it's a telephone question. That's my specialist subject fucked. Check the envelope. There must be something else.'

Vince slid his hand back into the envelope. His fingers touched something gritty at the bottom. Carefully he turned it upside down and collected the residue. 'Crystals of some kind. Looks like salt.'

'Don't.' He pushed Vince's finger away from his tongue. 'Let me test it. If it's some kind of a drug I'll know.' He licked the tip of his finger and touched it to the sprinkle of white in the palm of his hand. Vince watched as he tasted the crystals and laughed. 'You're right, it's just plain rock salt. You know, sea salt. I don't get it. It's not a very good clue, is it? If that's the best they can come up with I'm most unimpressed.'

Vince looked up at the sky. From here, high above London's bright centre, the clouds had broken and he could see an abyss of stars. The air was clearing now, but the temperature was dropping fast. A ghost-galleon of a cloud rolled lazily towards the moon, its hull illuminated by the city lights. The wind was rising.

'Sebastian's losing his touch,' he said finally, taking the page back and crackling it into his pocket. 'I know where this is. Too easy.'

'Look who's cocky all of a sudden.' Strangeways was crouching by his dog, feeding it a pepperoni stick. 'Can we play too, or don't you need us any more?'

That's what Sebastian's doing, thought Vince, sitting in the warm somewhere playing a game. He looked back at the dog. 'I guess you can come along. I may need someone who can get their head around the mindset of a juvenile.'

'Thanks a lot. So.' He rose and darted his head around conspiratorially. 'So where are we going, then?'

'To the South Seas. Treasure Island, of course,' Vince replied, swinging his leather bag onto his shoulder and setting off for the tube station once more.

CHAPTER TWENTY-FOUR

Blood Island

'YOU'VE GOT to admire his gall if nothing else,' said Sebastian. 'Blatantly breaking the rules like that. The insolence is fucking incredible. Does he honestly think that we can't see him? That we don't know exactly where he is every damned minute of the night?' He rose, bringing his billiard cue back to an upright position. Somewhere to the rear of the gloomy room, Jessye Norman fulfilled the title role of Offenbach's *La Belle Hélène* on a portable cassette player. Sebastian was very, very disappointed. He had expected a better show of gamesmanship from Vincent. The boy was simply not taking any of this seriously. How many people would they have to kill to prove the gravity of their intentions?

'Come along, Barwick, you glutinous little tick, it's your shot. Let's finish this game. I'm starving.'

'What are you going to do with him? Perhaps we should call the whole thing off.'

He pretended to consider the option, although nobody took Barwick's opinions seriously. 'I was rather wondering about that. I suppose I could put it to a vote.'

'The others have already gone into dinner. They'll agree with whatever you suggest. But something must be done. It's a clear breach of the rules. And he's already running late for the next challenge.'

'I know, I know,' said Sebastian irritably. He watched as Barwick spectacularly failed to pot the red. 'This game's going to go on all night if you don't start showing some finesse, Barwick.' He looked around for the end of his cigar. 'As I see it, we have two choices. One, we abandon the challenge in order to conduct the whole thing democratically, as Caton-James suggested from the start. Or two, we allow Reynolds to continue, but we punish him in order to acknowledge his breach of the rules. I vote for two. And you do as well, don't you?'

'Well, er, yes.' Barwick always did exactly as he was told.

Sebastian set his cue back in the rack. 'Serious punishment is called for. Implement it, would you? Stir that unmetabolised sludge you call a body, go and talk to St John Warner. It'll mean interrupting him during his soup so he won't be very happy. And tell him not to leave connections, eh? Remember what happened last summer. You might try ringing Stevens direct.' Sebastian straightened his brocade waistcoat and checked his bow-tie in the tall gilt mirror that hung beside the table. 'I'll be down to dinner shortly. Now go about your task and don't be long about it.'

Barwick nodded anxiously. He was already punching out a number on his mobile phone as he hastened in the direction of the dining room.

It was only when he was alone that Sebastian was able to express his rage. He could not afford to let the others see him so vexed. Emotion of any kind was a sign of weakness, and they needed no encouragement to find fault with him.

The situation was controllable; it simply needed a firm hand. As in any game, penalties had to be exacted. It was important to deal with infringements swiftly and severely. Fucking little oik! No jumped-up, council-flat, white-trash wideboy was going to show him up before his peers and get away with it.

A glance in the mirror revealed that he was actually baring his teeth at the thought, growling rhythmically like some kind of inadequately caged panther.

'So,' he said aloud, 'you still think it's a game, do you? Let's see if you think that in an hour's time. Then, perhaps, you'll start doing what you're told.'

'Blind Pugh,' explained Vince. 'In Robert Louis Stevenson's *Treasure Island* Pugh holds out the piece of paper with the dreaded Black Spot on it.'

'The mark of disease,' said Strangeways. 'We could try a clap clinic. James Pringle House, I've been there a few times. I picked up a girl in their reception area once. We waited until we both had the all-clear, then went at it like goats.'

'There's supposed to be an ancient plague-site at Highbury Fields. They built windmills over it. It was said that the bread of London was ground on the bones of the city's dead. And plague victims were buried in the great pit at Cripplegate.'

'How come you know so much about it?'

'My specialist subject, this city,' Vince replied proudly. 'I've never had a chance to use the knowledge until now.'

'So where are we going?'

They were still waiting for a train on the empty platform at Golders Green station. The electronic board above them promised to deliver one in five minutes. London Transport minutes were longer than real-life minutes, and could be stretched infinitely.

'To Blackfriars.'

'Why there?'

'The Mermaid Theatre. Every year it stages *Treasure Island* at Christmas. Look.' A poster for the production had been pasted to the wall no more than ten metres from them. Previews were starting in a few days' time. 'Blind Pugh comes on stage waving the Black Spot about, frightening all the kids in the audience. The clincher was the sea salt, a bit of a give-away, that. So, we just go there, retrieve the envelope –'

'Hold on, how long do you have to keep this up?'

'The challenges? There are supposed to be ten of them. This is the third.'

'And say you don't get completely cream-crackered from all this running about and manage to find all ten envelopes, then what's supposed to happen?'

'I win the right to go public with my story, the whole bit.'

'And you honestly think you'll be allowed to do that?'

The same thought had not left Vince's mind. 'These people pride themselves on being gentlemen,' he explained uncon-vincingly. 'It's what they hang onto most in life. Honour and duty. Victorian values. I think they'll stand by their word.'

'It didn't bother Lord Lucan, mate. I guess we move in different circles. I trust myself and Crippen. And I don't even trust him because he'll go with whoever feeds him. And I especially don't trust this city. The richer you get the more private you become, the more private you become the more you disappear. And when you disappear, you can hide any-thing. London's so private it's almost invisible. A place of great secrets. I think you should protect yourself.'

'How?'

'You could give me a copy of what you've written. I'll put it somewhere safe.'

There was a distant booming as the train approached.

'It's on my computer. But I made copies on disks.'

'Where?'

'I have one on me.'

'Then let me look after it. Trust me. Just in case anything weird happens.' He hoisted Crippen into his arms and wrapped him inside his overcoat. Vince hesitated. He knew nothing about his companion, beyond the fact that he was willing to help a stranger. Suppose Sebastian had planted him, instructed him to help Vince out with one of the clues, just to show that he was genuine? For what purpose though, to make him hand over what he had written? There was no point in that, not when the League had shown how easily they could enter his flat. He could afford to trust no one, not tonight, perhaps never again.

'I think I'll hang onto this, if it's all the same to you.' As the train rushed in Vince reached for his bag and held it close to his chest.

The darkened theatre stood on Puddle Dock, at the edge of a blank new section of the city. Between the building that housed it and the sluggish grey waters of the Thames ran a four-lane road that passed alongside the gilt statues of Billingsgate on its way to the Tower of London. The area had been bombed flat during the Blitz, then rebuilt to accommodate a fast-lane society that was only beaten by the city's Barbican Centre in its spectacular failure to co-exist with pedestrians. There was nothing remotely theatrical about The Mermaid. It was modern, anonymous, red-brick, hardly a theatre at all, more like a bottling plant. There were no glass awnings, no strings of bulbs, no Art Nouveau balustrades behind which to hide an envelope.

'This *has* to be the place,' said Vince. 'Look, there's even a picture.' He pointed to an encased poster showing the character of Blind Pugh displaying his dread message. Strangeways hopped up and down, trying to see above the entrance. Crippen decided that this must be the signal for something interesting and threw himself about in circles, growing ferociously overexcited.

'I can't see anything. Maybe it's inside.'

'The building's locked up. He wouldn't leave it in a place that was completely inaccessible to me. Sebastian wouldn't be interested in playing if he thought I didn't have at least a sporting chance.'

'Sounds like you know a lot about him.'

'I'm learning, believe me.'

Beside the theatre an arch passed over a narrower road, a slipway to the brilliant yellow tunnel which led to the bypass. From here came the sudden loud clang of steel on steel. Vince and Strangeways exchanged looks. The noise emanated from the rear of the building. As they followed the wall around, they left the main streetlights behind for an area where pedestrians were trespassers.

At the back of the theatre an extraordinary sight confronted them. Tall, waving palm trees. Dozens of them stood in rows, their emerald plastic fronds eerily rustling in the cold night air. The polystyrene logs of Ben Gunn's island stockade stood against a wall, awaiting assembly. The vast steel doors to the stage stood wide, and the prow of a great wooden ship could be glimpsed within. Scenery shifters often worked at night, after performances. They must have been here only moments ago, but were nowhere in evidence now.

'It's there, look, that's got to be it.'

Strangeways waved excitedly at him, pointing to one of the trees.

'I don't see anything.'

'Here, take Crippen a sec.' He threw Vince the string lead and ran forward into the artificial forest. It took Vince a while to spot the envelope taped high up in the tallest palm. Strangeways began climbing the trunk. 'I'll bring you back a coconut.'

'You don't know if it'll take your weight. They're not made to –'

Strangeways had already reached the envelope and pulled it free when he seemed to lose his balance. 'Oh, fuck.'

The plastic foliage was rattling and shaking, then shaking still harder, shedding fronds. Something was flying through the trees – a tiny silver bird.

'Strangeways?' Vince could only imagine that he had slipped on the base of one of the trees, had fallen further into the *faux*-undergrowth and was attempting to pull himself back up. He ran forward, pushing through the cellulose tatters, trying to see in the faint light flickering from the arch. Strangeways was in the grass below him, and suddenly grabbed upwards at his jacket. He was like a winded footballer, too surprised by a foul to cry out. His hooked fingers were red and lustrous, as though they had been dipped in gloss paint. Vince saw the sickly oval of his face, his puzzled eyes. Heard him try to speak, only to spatter his chin and neck with blood. A black arc twisted his throat into a deathly grimace; the skin had been opened with a razor. Dark liquid poured over the lower rim of flesh like a flooding bath. As his head fell back, the parted wall of his trachea revealed itself in pornographic detail. The cascade abruptly ceased, and his body dropped down.

Strangeways passed from life to death in just a few seconds.

There was someone else in the prop-jungle, the blurred figure of a man in retreat, clambering over the papier-mâché rocks and hillocks. He felt Strangeways's hand still digging at his stomach, and looked down to see the envelope crushed in his fist.

Then Vince was stumbling, slipping into the road, nearly swiped by a passing car, dodging across the entrance to the dazzling tunnel, vaulting over the railings, swerving across the bypass, brought up short by the wall of the Embankment. Hacking, gasping, vomiting into the river, frantically wiping the blood from his hands and jacket as he relived the strange speed of the attack. A man he had known for little more than an hour, a body bleeding to death among tropical palms . . .

And in his jacket the mobile phone, the phone he had failed to return, was buzzing against his chest. As he punched open the line, he fought to keep the bile from once more rising in his throat.

'Perhaps now you'll learn to keep this affair private, and to take me a little more seriously,' said a sickeningly familiar voice. 'It's getting late, Vincent. There's no time to mourn. You'll never make it to the next deadline.'

CHAPTER TWENTY-FIVE

Chasing Ghosts

SHE CHECKED her watch again. 10:27 p.m. Pam could not understand it. Vince never missed out on a meal, ever. She switched her gaze from the empty chair opposite to the window and the traffic-filled street beyond. She'd been waiting in the café-bar for nearly half an hour, overdosing on garlic bread while fending off the disgruntled Italian waiter. At ten-thirty she called Vince's flat, but there was no answer. He couldn't have forgotten that they were having supper together tonight. She had been looking forward to hearing about his progress on the book. Unlike Louie, Vince was almost boringly reliable about such arrangements. He didn't like to let people down. Where could he be?

She was aware that Vince had been warned away from Sebastian Wells and the League of Prometheus. He had told her that it would be dangerous to upset them. Perhaps they'd kidnapped him? She rang Louie and caught him just as he was leaving for the gig.

'For God's sake, these people belong to a glorified debating society, not the Hellfire Club,' Louie told her. 'They're bored rich kids. Don't you think you're overreacting a little?'

'Probably. I don't know. Vince has been digging into their

background a lot lately, and they know it. I'm worried that something might have happened to him. You know how he gets.'

'Then why don't you go around to his apartment, if you're so worried?'

'You're right, I should do that. Perhaps he's sick.'

'And he might have gone on a date,' said Louie with unnecessary cruelty. 'People have lives to lead, you know.'

'Come *on*,' Pam said, refusing to take offence, 'I spoke to him earlier tonight. Besides, this is Vince we're talking about. There's a reason why nearly all of his friends are men; he finds it very hard to talk to females. He would have let me know if he'd changed his plans.'

'Maybe the offer came up suddenly and was too good to refuse. You're going to have to work this one out for yourself, Pam. I'll see you there, okay? I'm really running late.'

She apologised for bothering Louie, rang off, paid her bill and left the restaurant. Outside, on Camden High Street, the temperature was still falling. There was even a smattering of wet snow in the air. In the entrance to a punkish shoe store near the bus stop, two young men were bedding down for the night in orange nylon sleeping bags. It always amazed her how customers were able to step over such people in order to window-shop for luxuries. She seemed to be forever surrendering her small change to sickly-looking kids. Surely that was the decent, the right thing to do, yet the very act of trying to help out got you into trouble half the time. She had no faith in public servants who acted as if they knew what was best for her. Highly organised groups unnerved her. They were like ambitious politicians who seemed so sure of themselves, so determined to prove their theories that they couldn't possibly have the welfare of the public at heart. Wait until she found herself in a position of power; she'd show them all a thing or two . . .

Pam no longer felt like going to the gig tonight. She wasn't a gig sort of person, anyway. That was much more in Louie's line. As she boarded the bus, she told herself that she would find Vince sitting quietly at home, having forgotten all about supper. Perhaps his phone had developed a fault.

She had never met this Sebastian but he sounded like a bit of a creep, and Vince was easily led. He was so . . . not trusting, exactly, but in awe of people who liked him, as if he found it hard to believe that anyone could. And of course, he was utterly blind to the people who really loved him. Or rather, the person.

She checked her eye make-up in the tiny silver compact Vince had given her last Christmas, and decided to wait five more minutes outside the café-bar before heading in the direction of his flat.

Vince had torn open the envelope and unfolded the page, but could not absorb the words. If he shut his eyes all he saw was Strangeways lying among the plastic palms with that gaping crimson gash in his throat. What would they do if he went to the police now? There was no point in trying to direct someone to the site of his death, foolish to think Sebastian and his pals hadn't already taken care of the body. He was sure they would get a kick from having him perform that great movie cliché, 'But he was right here, officer, I swear I saw him with my own eyes.'

If the League had wanted to remind him that this was not a game, surely they could have found some less destructive way of doing it. But Strangeways had proven the ideal victim. By his own admission he had no friends or relatives who would come looking for him. He had become just another Home Office statistic, convenient and invisible, beyond care or community.

The streets and alleyways leading away from the Embankment appeared far more menacing than they had an hour earlier. The last commuters were returning to their mainline stations. As they vacated the city a sharp chill deepened in the air, the offices, gyms, restaurants and bars shedding the heat of so many bodies. A laughing, arguing mass of humanity was in retreat, abandoning the city to a handful of night inhabitants.

After midnight, a new set of rules would apply. Already the landscape had a different look. The main thoroughfares shone a dead, unyielding yellow. The backstreets were just dark enough to cause anxious glances over the shoulder. But to know that there were others here, men hiding in the shadows, watching and waiting, was enough to break his stride into a run.

He darted into the road, back towards the hard white lights of the West End, running until his throat was filled with burning scraps of breath. Forced himself to stop, knowing that somehow, somewhere they could be studying his every move. Was it possible to be in the centre of a city of nine million people and yet be entirely alone?

Although the wind from the river was freezing against his face, rivulets of sweat trickled down his spine. He looked at his watch. 10:55 p.m. He'd miss the next deadline and that would be it; he would end up like Strangeways, lying in a gutter with his throat slit, bundled into garbage bags by a couple of rented thugs. It would be so easy to disappear. A wild malevolence swept through him as he snatched the letter containing the next challenge from his jacket and opened it.

Three dead men, tried in court as if alive.
Slaughtered and tortured beyond the grave.
Buried once more.
Only to rise and continue their damnable conversation.
How can this be? They have no mouths but still must speak.
Obtusus obtusiorum ingenii monumentum. Quid me respicis, viator? Vade.

Time allowed: 120 Minutes

What? He stared at the page in horror, knowing that this time he had been stonewalled. The text was gibberish, obscure, impossible. He had nowhere even to begin, no one to help him, no time to solve the damned stupid puzzle or to reach the destination hidden within the text. How long did he have before the paper it was written on fractured into dust?

Vince sat down on the wet kerb, heedless of the icy slush seeping into his jeans, and rested his head in his hands. There was nothing more he could do but await the arrival of the League.

Pam pulled a piece of gum from the pink stiletto of her left shoe and stepped back in the road. She looked up at the first-floor windows. No lights showed. If Vince was in he must have gone to bed, but the curtains were undrawn. She rang the bell again and waited. He was her closest friend, someone who could be trusted with nearly all of her most important secrets, and she really wanted to be with him tonight. When she set her mind to a task, she rarely stopped until she had completed it. Where the hell had he gone?

It would have to be a process of elimination. She slipped into the doorway of the laundromat next door to shelter from the biting wind, dug into her bag for her mobile phone and began making calls.

'He's not going to crack this one, Bunter,' complained Sebastian. 'You've made it too difficult.'

'Well, there's no point in the clues being too easy, is there?' said Ross Caton-James, who allowed no one to call him Bunter but Sebastian. 'You said so yourself. And he's got about fifteen minutes to figure it out before the chemicals eat through the paper. Look, is it too much to ask for the port to be passed in the correct direction?'

He reached out to accept the decanter and poured himself a generous measure. The wind was sweeping across the river's reach to moan and bat at the mullioned windows like Marley's ghost. Caton-James had thinning sandy hair, a florid complexion, a corpulent girth and the torpid demeanour of a fifty-year-old who had made his pile and was now resting. The fact that he was only twenty-four made his profound sense of self-satisfaction all the more alarming. But then his father was one of the richest men in England, and the elderly knight's children had never been contradicted or disobeyed in their lives. It lent one's most frivolous remarks a certain gravitas.

'Do you propose giving him a clue? I should be rather disappointed. It would count as cheating.'

'I have no desire to aid him in any way, as you can imagine.' Sebastian pulled his bow-tie undone and loosened his shirt collar. 'Give St John Warner a call and find out what he's doing now. Don't use that thing at the table; show some fucking decorum.'

Caton-James rose and moved to the rear of the dining room. He pulled the black plastic button from his jacket top pocket and clicked it, addressing the tiny transmitter. 'This is Mount Caucasus. What's happening down there?'

A thin crackle of static preceded the reply. 'He was sitting by the river a few minutes ago, close to giving up by the look of it. Now he's moved out of range.' St John Warner had access to the Embankment's closed-circuit traffic cameras. Indeed, via his father's connections with New Scotland Yard he had access to virtually every transmission received by the electronic crimewatch and traffic surveillance equipment in the city. The rest of the monitors, those situated on private property and operated by independent security firms, were pretty much covered by colleagues in the private sector who had access to the larger CCTV systems in use around the city. In the course of nearly a hundred years, the League had managed to lay in place a comprehensive network of grace and favour. The roots ran deeper than even Sebastian himself realised.

'You'll let us know when he comes back in vision?'

'Of course. Although I think he's blown it this time.'

'We'll do the thinking, okay? All you have to do is bloody report.' He returned the transmitter to his pocket. 'Stevens has dropped the homeless boy off in the Thames, although the dog ran away before he could catch it.'

'Dogs can't talk, Bunter.'

'He wanted an extra hundred for getting rid of the body but we're persuading him to settle for sixty.'

'He's pushing his luck,' said Sebastian, refilling his glass with port. 'Stevens hardly had to do anything. We're doing all the real work. How can he call himself a hit man when he only half-finishes the job? Anybody can drop someone in their tracks. You have to clear up afterwards. It's all part of the deal.'

'He complained about getting blood over his clothes. Wanted us to foot his cleaning bill.'

'Bloody cheek.'

'Said he feels bad about having to kill the boy.'

'Classic liberal stance; go along with everyone else, accept handsome payment, then start bleating. Take no notice; Xavier Stevens has killed plenty of times before. You're not telling me he didn't get out of his car and watch that editor burn behind her steering wheel. You know he gets off on it, don't you? I mean, it's a sexual thing with him.'

'I'd heard that.'

'Well. He's just trying it on.'

'I think we got our money's worth,' said Caton-James. 'Reynolds is running shit-scared now. You should be enjoying yourself. This whole charade is costing enough.'

Bunter was right, of course. Crucially, though, the League's 'investment' in this evening's events had passed through such a convoluted network of international financial institutions that it would not be traced back in this lifetime.

'So, no clues then,' muttered Caton-James, reseating himself and draining his port. 'He may come through yet, of course. If he uses his head. Get it?' He sniggered at Sebastian and reached for the decanter once more.

The buzz of the mobile phone startled him. Vince had intended to throw the damned thing in the river. He didn't like using them, anyway; they were talismen, part of the new shamanism, like web sites and swipe-cards. The boy had probably spoken into it so often that it contained part of his spirit. Besides, it was unusable now that he knew they were listening in. He withdrew it from his jacket and opened the line, dreading the sound of Sebastian's voice.

'Vince? Are you there?'

'Pam? How on earth did you get this number?'

'Welcome to the twentieth century, darling. I collected my messages and picked up the last number redial. It works with mobiles now, didn't you know? Where on earth are you? Do you remember you were supposed to be eating with me tonight?'

'Listen, Pam, you can't stay on this line, it's not secure. Let me call you back in two minutes.' He folded the phone away and ran up the slope towards Blackfriars. In the street that curved behind the statue-bedecked parthenon of Lever House he found a phone box covered in call-girl stickers, and rang Pam's number. He lost precious minutes explaining his predicament, still more trying to decide a plan of action with her.

'Please, Vince,' pleaded Pam, 'let me go to the police.'

'If you do, the League will know about it.'

'How can they? Ask yourself, how would that be possible?'

'I don't know, I just know they would. I've seen what they can do. I don't want to put anyone else at risk.'

'Then what can I do to help?'

'I have to see it through. If you want to be of use, you can find me a fast answer to this damned puzzle.'

'This is crazy . . .'

'You asked if you could do anything, here's your chance. I can't solve it by myself.' Pam could help him without placing herself in danger. Even if they could see him, they could not possibly know who he was calling.

'Well, if there's no other way –'

He read the instructions slowly enough for her to write them out. The paper was drying, but had not yet started to dissolve.

'Christ, you'll have to spell out the Latin stuff.'

'I don't have the time.' Vince glanced back, half expecting to see figures running through the shadows. 'Just put it down as it sounds. You'll have to concentrate on the first part.'

'But how can I? I failed history and I was never any good at languages, I don't know –'

'Wait. Call this guy, explain who you are and ask him to help you. I'll ring you back in ten minutes.' He gave Pam the home number of Dr Harold Masters and replaced the receiver. Then he pushed himself back against the wall of the building, waiting for his pulse to slow. He studied the letter again.

Three dead men.

They were setting him tasks whose solutions reinforced their own beliefs, in order that he might learn lessons; the solution to the first challenge had shown a disapproval of mixed marriages, the second and third suggested a nostalgia for times past, solid right-wing notions. What on earth could this be?

A historical puzzle. Corpses tried in court, buried only to rise and continue talking – as what, ghosts? That had to be it, the spirits of dead men, but whose? A fine damp mist had settled at the end of the crescent, causing penumbral light-cones to form around the streetlamps. His feet were growing numb. He stamped and checked his watch. Just gone eleven o'clock. They had generously given him two hours to solve the puzzle this time, but he had already lost the first hour. Even if he somehow came up with a correct solution, he still had to allow for travelling time.

He reinserted his phonecard and called Pam again. The line was still engaged. He tried Harold Masters's number. This time the call was answered.

'Hullo there, Vincent. I think your friend is just about to ring you.' Far from being annoyed, the doctor sounded pleased to have been asked to participate in the evening's events. 'I've got something. I was just checking the exact location in my A–Z. I think this is to do with the revenge taken on Oliver Cromwell.'

That made sense. The League would have heartily disapproved of such a man. They saw a symbolic threat to the monarchy, plain and simple. No sense of Charles I's absolutism or Cromwell's puritanism. World history in black and white. 'What about him?' he asked. 'Wasn't there some confusion about where Cromwell was buried?'

'That's just it. Cromwell and his parliamentarian colleagues Ireton and Bradshaw were originally interred in Westminster Abbey, but after the Restoration their bodies were exhumed and brought to trial at Westminster Hall.'

. . . tried in court as if alive . . .

'They were found guilty of regicide and sentenced to be hung, drawn and quartered. As a mark of public humiliation they were dragged on sledges to Tyburn . . .'

'The Tyburn route is now Oxford Street, isn't it?'

'Yes, but the actual site of Tyburn tree, the name of the triangular gallows, is at the junction of the Edgware Road and Bayswater Road, although Charles Dickens pointed out that the exact location was still under dispute in his time. There's supposed to be a stone marking the purported spot on the traffic island there.'

'You're both geniuses, thanks,' said Vince.

'Well, not really because –'

'I've no time to spare, Doctor. I'm on my way.'

'You misunderstand me,' said Masters, 'that's not where the clue is sending you at all.'

But Vince had already returned the receiver to its cradle. Even now he was running into the mist enveloping the end of the road.

CHAPTER TWENTY-SIX

Trick Question

HAROLD MASTERS stood in the kitchen with his hands in his pockets watching his wife making a cup of tea. Jane had been working at the Victoria and Albert Museum when they'd met. A shy, almost reclusive woman, one of the world's leading experts on Peter Carl Fabergé, she had asked his advice about the supposed rediscovery of a jewelled casket, a legendary 'lost' piece that had vanished during the Russian Revolution, and in doing so had unexpectedly awoken a deep and abiding passion within herself. Finding a strength she had not known she possessed, she had asked him to marry her, and Harold had gratefully accepted. They never did manage to locate the missing Fabergé casket. Jane was his voice of reason, his calm centre. He had already decided that he would take her advice on the matter that was troubling him.

'It's a bit late to start getting people together,' she pointed out, placing the kettle on the stove.

'It's *supposed* to be for insomniacs, for God's sake!'

'We're not due to meet up until next week, and that's meant to be at Maggie's place, not here. I've hardly got anything for them to eat.' She removed two cups from the cupboard and set them out. 'I suppose you could call around and see who's available. Ring Arthur, he'll definitely be up for it. The poor man never seems to sleep at all.'

Masters slipped his arms around Jane and gave her a quick hug. Anyone else would have considered his idea preposterous. 'I don't just love you because you indulge me, you know,' he said.

'I know.' Jane smiled and began digging about in the refrigerator. 'Go on, then. Get out of my way. Go and make your calls.'

Vince was going to miss his deadline for the fourth challenge, he knew it. Nobody would be safe then. Alighting from the half-empty tube at Marble Arch he made his way up to ground level and exited on the north side of Oxford Street. Any day now the stores would start staying open late for Christmas shoppers, but tonight they were dark and silent. Absurdly postured mannequins bore blank witness as he passed. The great floodlit block of Marble Arch, designed as the main entrance to Buckingham Palace and moved because it was too narrow for coaches to pass through, rose above the traffic, a remnant from a grander time. And there, running through a revolving phalanx of black cabs in the centre of the intersection was – Pam, dressed in a navy-blue two-piece with gold buttons and pink high-heels, looking like a cosmetics representative late for a date.

But he didn't want to see Pam – couldn't see her. There were traffic cameras staring down at every section of the road. She had placed herself in terrible danger coming here. Vince turned away and began hastily walking in the opposite direction, back towards the searing neon lights of the Kentucky Fried Chicken restaurant further along the street.

'Wait, Vince, it's me!' Pam had spotted him. There were few other pedestrians left on the streets. The cameras were bound to pick her up. There was nowhere to hide. He searched the cornices of the buildings; nearly every single one had a small black box at its apex. He imagined the two of them, soft grey figures colliding and talking as their electronic images sprawled across banks of TV monitors. Pam was running full pelt towards him, stilettos tick-tacking across the tarmac, her candy-blonde hair flying about her face. Vince fell back into the unlit doorway of a shoe store, praying she would pass by.

'What are you doing, it's me!' Pam came to a halt in front of him.

'We can't be seen talking,' hissed Vince. 'Do you want to get killed?'

'No one's expecting to see us here, Vince, you're safe.'

'You don't believe me, do you? That I saw somebody murdered tonight? That anyone who talks to me is at risk? They're watching each of the challenge sites.'

'But this isn't one of them,' said Pam breathlessly, 'they're not expecting to see you here. That's what I'm trying to explain, if you'll only have some patience and listen for a minute. You hung up on the doctor too quickly. You're in the wrong place. I came to tell you –'

'Tyburn tree . . .'

'It's nothing to do with Tyburn! I spoke to Doctor Masters, he was giving you the full story when you jumped to conclusions and cut him short. Hang on.' She pressed a hand against her chest, drawing breath. 'It's recorded that Cromwell and the others were hung up here until sunset, then beheaded. Their remains were supposedly chucked into a pit under the gallows, and their heads were stuck on poles on the roof of Westminster Hall. But Masters reckons it's a trick question. He says that the night before the bodies were taken to Tyburn they were kept at the Red Lion Inn in Holborn, and that a "Tyburn" can mean any place of execution.'

'So they may not have come here?'

'Think about it. Why would they have been dragged east to Holborn when this Tyburn lies to the north-west of Westminster? There were other Tyburns, one where Centrepoint now stands, and another in Fetter Lane. The bodies were kept at Red Lion Square and here's the important part – there used to be an obelisk with your Latin inscription on it, standing in a paddock near the square.'

'So the last lines of the riddle refer to what, their ghosts?'

'They've been seen through the centuries, walking diagonally across the square deep in conversation, which is weird because their heads weren't buried there with them.'

. . . They have no mouths but still must speak . . .

'Do you have any money on you? I'm nearly out. I'll pay you back if I get out of this alive.'

Pam dug in her shoulder bag. 'I just got paid. Let me come with you, Vince.'

'Absolutely not. I won't be responsible for something bad happening to you. You can't risk being seen with me.'

Pam stopped and stared at him awkwardly. 'You are sure about all of this, aren't you?'

'What do you mean?'

'I mean you're sure you really saw someone – killed?'

'Well for God's sake you don't think I'm making it all up, do you?'

'Well no, it's just that –'

Vince tore the riddle-page from his jacket and waved it in front of Pam's alarmed eyes. 'You think I sat at home writing these damned things out, do you?' He became aware that he was holding a scrap of paper no bigger than a postage stamp. The rest had fallen to pieces in his pocket. Pam had edged out into the street and was now standing within range of the traffic cameras. 'Get back in here!'

'No, let's test out your theory.' She looked about at the passing traffic, then walked towards the nearest intersection. 'Let's see if we can make this secret society show itself.'

She really didn't believe in any of it, not deep down. His best friend didn't believe him. Perhaps it was better this way. Thank God she hadn't brought Louie with her; they would really have stood out in a crowd.

The moment Pam's back was turned, he slipped from the safety of the store entrance and ran off down the street. He hated to do it to her, but by the time she missed him he wanted to have vanished from her sight.

CHAPTER TWENTY-SEVEN

Walking Into Trouble

ARTHUR BRYANT halted in the middle of Battersea Bridge and gripped the handle of his umbrella tightly as the wind tried to snatch it away. He looked along the line of the river, but his vision was obscured by squalls of gale-driven rain and sleet. The city was well-protected from the elements, but here above the Thames, away from the sheltering mansion blocks, a man could catch pneumonia. Why Harold Masters had persuaded him to move their monthly meetings a week forward wasn't entirely clear. The doctor had mumbled something about 'being on hand' to help a friend in trouble, and had promised to call the others, so Bryant had set off to visit his friend unmindful of the late hour. Which was fine by him, because after all, they were jokingly known as the Insomnia Squad.

The elderly detective was not enjoying his sabbatical one bit. His partner John May was busy making a fool of himself over a woman in a closed-for-the-season hotel somewhere in the Greek islands, and would not be back until the new year arrived or his passion departed. The damage caused by the fire that had virtually destroyed their offices six weeks earlier was supposed to have been fully repaired by now, but thanks to a remarkable number of malingering carpenters and decorators claiming that they couldn't get the parts, their vans had broken down in Wandsworth, their wives had left them and so on, the work had yet to be finished. May had swanned off leaving his partner in an office without a roof, and so far he had not even sent a postcard detailing his absurd affair with the former Miss Ghana, or somewhere like that, who was young enough to be his niece. It really wasn't good enough. May knew what he was like when he couldn't work, how wound up he became. Not even a phone call.

So when Harold Masters had called twenty minutes ago, Bryant had jumped at the chance to get out of his flat and start solving something. 'I think you'll be intrigued by this,' the doctor had told him, whetting his appetite. What could he have meant? Still, it would help to find a cab right now. What did they all do in the rain, melt away?

Damn and blast, thought Bryant, setting off with renewed vigour, I must be half-mad to come out in weather like this. And of course, there were many in the metropolitan force who believed he was.

There was someone walking behind her, she was sure of it. There had been for the past five minutes or so. Pam quickened her pace, cutting down into Bond Street and checking the reflections from the street in each window she passed. There were three people following her route, a woman laden with Christmas shopping bags, a young Asian man in a track suit, an older man in a long black raincoat. None of them seemed to be paying her special attention. Releasing a cautious breath of relief, Pam doubled back to the tube station. She was furious with Vince for running off and leaving her, but she had decided to go to Red Lion Square and keep a watchful eye on him anyway. Display her initiative. Show some leadership qualities. Besides, she was curious to see if any members of this mythical League would put in an appearance.

Vince studied the buildings as he passed, endless terraces of Victorian homes, carved into tiers of offices. It was close to midnight now, but even at this late hour there were a few lights in the windows, legal and medical secretaries still at their desks, chatting on phones, talking to colleagues. These days a lot of people felt that they could only get their work into some kind of manageable shape by waiting until their switchboards had closed for the night. Pleasant, ordinary people, seated in cream-coloured rooms with great closed fireplaces, toiling quietly, sipping coffee, as unapproachable as if he was viewing them from a telescope a thousand miles away.

He walked through Queen Square, where a few doctors, nurses and students would still pass each other through the night on their way to Great Ormond Street Hospital, and the great dark weight of London surrounded him. Layers of history compressed like geological formations were here beneath his feet, ancient countryside lying in disguise. These roads were older than history, their paths twisting to preserve routes around long-dried marshes, their walls following the borderlines of land once defined by hedgerows. A two-thousand-year-old city that had stood in darkness for all but the last century. So many murderous deeds had occurred here beneath the heavy cloak of night, and yet he felt protected, as though the metropolis would ultimately prove itself to be on his side.

The air was sharper here than in the traffic-choked West

End. Red Lion Square stood dark and empty before him, the bare branches of its trees entwined in symbiotic dependency. The new buildings stuck out among the old, square and plain, of lighter brick. They marked the sites of the Blitz's bombs more clearly than if the land had been left razed.

He was not scared now. Melancholy and a little tired, hungry even, but no longer frightened by the prospect of what the night still held in store, even though – incredibly, it seemed – there were still seven full hours of darkness ahead. It felt strange to be so completely alone, even though there were friends and family out there in the dark. And Pam – what had she said about the ghosts walking diagonally across the little park?

He reached the main entrance to the square and found the gate padlocked, but it was an easy matter to climb over the low railing and follow the path inwards. He moved beyond the reach of street light to a point where he could barely see the way ahead, but could already make out the sharp white rectangle of the envelope propped up in the circular central flowerbed, waiting for him.

Pam briskly cut into the backstreets beyond Holborn tube station. She remembered most of the roads around here from her temping days. Having been forced to wait nearly fifteen minutes for a train, she felt sure that she would arrive too late to find Vince.

She entered the southern side of Red Lion Square, keeping against the walls wherever possible, and watched. There was someone in the little park; she could see a bluish shape moving between the bushes. From her vantage point it was difficult to identify the figure, but just at that moment it turned, and her friend stood revealed in profile. He stooped, disappearing for a moment. Then reappeared, holding something in his hands and studying it.

There was someone else in the park with him, the dark shape of a man standing motionless behind a hollybush. Marooned where she was, Pam could do nothing but watch and wait. Presently Vince left the park, vaulting over the railings and setting off at speed. The remaining figure shifted off through the undergrowth, making for the top side of the square. It was impossible to tell if this was one of Vince's phantom tormentors or simply a loony locked out of his shelter.

She slipped from the protection of the office doorway, keeping him in her sights. He was a hundred yards from her, then eighty, then fifty. He was wrapped in a heavy, expensive-looking overcoat, murmuring into a mobile phone.

She needed to be nearer still, but the pavement between them was broad and empty, too brightly lit, and her shoes made too much noise. Vince had gone, and for all she knew she could be stalking some poor innocent businessman. But he had been in the park, hidden and watchful. It was worth the risk. As he shut the phone and moved off, Pam moved with him.

CHAPTER TWENTY-EIGHT

The Reaches

AS VINCE walked wearily into High Holborn, sooty snow-flakes began slanting through the sweeping grey skies like television static. His breath drifted before his face in clouds. He brought out the latest letter and examined the envelope. Tearing open the dampened vellum, he found, as usual, a single square of chemically treated white paper. Three lines of type adorned the sheet:

The Challenge Of The Crenellated Pachyderm

Nine Trees In The Nineteenth Reach
Opposite The Secret Five
Pray Remember The 25th Of July
To Three Of Four Doors
And Up To Steel And Stars

Time allowed: 120 Minutes

More gibberish that he was expected to unravel into something tangible. Not much to go on here, but it would have to do. Two hours allowed again. It was almost as if they were regulating the timing of his movements to some specific undisclosed agenda. He checked the batteries on the mobile phone; they were standing up at the moment, but he would have to choose his calls wisely. His boots were starting to let in water. The slush-puddled street in which he stood was empty in either direction. He hoped Pam had gone home and was safely tucked beneath her duvet. It was best to face the rest of this night alone.

. . . Nine Trees In The Nineteenth Reach . . .

The Thames was divided into reaches, but he had no idea how many there were. Who would know? His Uncle Mack might. His father's younger brothers had both worked on the river until one of them had fallen from the stern of a tug and drowned. Mack had filled his head with lurid stories as a child, always showing him the kindness his father had never managed. Vince opened the phone, thought for a moment and punched out a number.

Dinner had been disappointing. Barwick really was the most frightful cook. Anything more complex than a steak was beyond him. Thank God the cellar was still well-stocked. Sebastian reached for another bottle of Montrachet while Ross Caton-James, seated at the far end of the table, adjusted his portable TV screen.

'He's on the bloody phone again,' he exclaimed, tapping the blurry monochrome image on the monitor. 'It really is too much. You're going to have to take it away from him.'

'No doubt he prides himself on being a part of the modern world. We shouldn't have made the questions so academic, Bunter, then he wouldn't need to consult people all the time.'

'The next one is hardly academic.'

Sebastian snorted in disgust. 'It's quite the least appropriate of them all, but it was the best that poor old Barwick could come up with. The fellow's hardly a mental giant, but he demanded to have his turn.'

'Oh, I don't know,' said Caton-James airily, 'I think it has a certain panache. I'm surprised he figured it out by himself.'

'But will Reynolds, though?'

Sebastian gestured vaguely into the air. 'He's working class, he's supposed to know about that sort of thing.'

'He's taking longer than you thought, isn't he?' said Caton-James, needling.

Sebastian was agitated. In truth he had expected a faster response from Vince, a little more ingenuity. He was merely plodding from one problem to the next, whining to his friends until they solved each challenge for him. He was supposed to be running in terror for his life. You'd have thought that seeing someone killed before his eyes might gee him up a bit. He needed more of a spark from his key player. It was inconceivable to think of failure now.

'There's no sport in this, Bunter. We have to do something. I don't think the demise of Mr Street-Trash was enough to shake him.'

'If this one proves too easy to crack, we can change the running order.'

'Good show.'

'One thing bothers me,' said Caton-James, fiddling with the TV controls. 'The weather's having an adverse effect on our signal. It's hard to make out who's in some of these shots, and quite a few of the cameras are getting snow on their lenses. There's nothing we can do about that.'

Sebastian rose and wandered over to the mullioned window where Barwick sat, miserably staring down into the deserted streets. 'Snow in London before Christmas – a rare thing. No wonder it's so sodding cold. Stir yourself, Barwick, you gormless protozoid, stoke up the fire, get me a drink, make toast or something. Don't just sit there like the sad corpulent lump you are. We still have a long night ahead of us.'

'Gravesend, Northfleet Hope, St Clements, Long, Erith Rands . . .' Mack Reynolds read from the maritime manual he had not opened in years, 'you count the reaches of the Thames from the sea inwards.'

'I need to know what the nineteenth is called.'

'Hold your horses, young man. I don't hear from you for nearly three months, then when you do call it's after midnight, and you can only stay on for a minute.'

'I told you, this is an emergency situation. I'm taking a terrible risk just talking to you.'

'You're not taking drugs, are you? You know, after your father died I promised your mother to try and ...'

Vince sighed. 'Mack, I don't have time for this right now, mate. I promise I'll visit you.' *If I'm still alive in the morning*, he added under his breath.

'All right, let's see. Give me a minute. Halfway. Barking. Gallions. Must be further along.' He heard Mack rustling the pages, trying to hurry for his sake. 'Ah, here. Limehouse, Lower Pool, Upper Pool, London Bridge. No, can't do it.'

'What do you mean, you can't do it?'

'The nineteenth has no official name.'

'Are you sure?'

'Absolutely. From London Bridge to Westminster and from Westminster to Vauxhall Bridge are the only two reaches that are unnamed.'

'What if you don't count the unnamed ones?'

'Hang on.' The line started crackling. He prayed it would hold. 'That would make the nineteenth – Nine Elms.'

Nine Elms, near Lambeth Palace, where the Covent Garden market had relocated. He should have known. It was clear to him now. 'Thanks, Mack, you're a wonder.'

'Call me soon. Keep your promise, you hear?' His voice was cutting out.

'I will.'

'You've said that before, Vincent.'

'I mean it this time. I have to go.'

'You always have to go.' The old man chuckled, then the line failed. It was probably a bad reception area. The mobile's battery had enough life in it for a few more calls. He would try to rely on call boxes wherever possible. Vince checked his watch. 12:23 a.m. It would take him at least half an hour to get to Nine Elms. His deadline was up at 2:00 a.m. The snow was trying to settle. Turning up the collar of his soaked jacket, he set off in the direction of the tube station once more, hoping to catch the last train south.

Cities bisected by rivers often develop distinct characteristics in their separated halves, and London was no exception. South was low ground, traditionally poorer, now patchily gentrified, but with a unique nature of its own. Here a car was called a 'motor', problems were 'sorted', people would 'see you all right'. Vince knew that a rough guide to an area's wealth was provided by McDonald's outlets; the larger the yellow arches, the poorer the neighbourhood. Hampstead would only allow a discreet McDonald's symbol outside its much fought-against outlet. South London had giant drive-through branches.

On the southern side of Vauxhall Bridge stood the next part of the clue – *Opposite The Secret Five*. This was obviously a reference to the Secret Five of Nine Elms, the headquarters of the British Secret Service, MI5, housed in an extraordinary cream-coloured wedding cake of a building that looked more like a latter-day redesign of St Clement Dane's, with cyprus trees added to the Thameside upper levels, rather than a government office. The architecture of the edifice was absurdly high-profile for an organisation dedicated to the creation of covert operations. Everyone knew what it housed. It was a very public secret.

On the other side of the road there was nothing, just a piece of wasteground and rows of blackened railway arches leading south out of the city. Here a number of raucous night-clubs were buried, and lines of clubbers, oblivious to the freezing night air, shuffled patiently forward in their black nylon puffa-jackets like war babies queuing for rations.

There had to be something else here.

. . . Pray Remember The 25th Of July . . .

What could that mean? Pray remember? Something to do with a church? The only other structure in sight was the cabbies' tea-stall he had sometimes used coming back from the clubs. That couldn't be it, could it? He carefully crossed the six-lane road, passing beneath the traffic cameras, and checked the walls of the shuttered plywood tea-cabin, but found nothing. The stall was closed for the night and there was little else of interest around. At least, nothing opposite the government building. The snow was growing heavier, speckling yellow in the lamps of Vauxhall Bridge. Vince looked at his shaking hands and knew that he would have to find a warm shelter soon. He dug into his duffel bag and pulled out a small diary. Flicking to July the 25th, he checked beneath the date. St James's Day. He knew nothing about the saints; his family were Church of England, and Vince considered himself an agnostic.

He would have to make another phone call. Part of him considered it cheating. On the other hand, if he was supposed to be, as Sebastian put it, 'a child of the streets versus the people who own the houses', he was free to decide that their rules were not his, and take the course he felt necessary. He reached the public call boxes beside Vauxhall station and punched out Harold Masters's number once more. The doctor answered on the third ring, almost as if he was expecting him.

'I'm sorry, Doc, I need your help again.' His breath formed over the mouthpiece. 'I hope I didn't wake you.'

'Oh, no chance of that. When you get to my age you sleep less. You don't want to risk missing anything. I felt you might ring again, and made according arrangements. We're going to be up all night.'

Thank God for that, he thought. 'It's a date – the 25th of July. Does that mean anything to you?'

'Well, it could mean all sorts of things. It really depends on which year.'

He hoped the doctor would keep his answers succinct. After this call, he only had twenty pence left in telephone change and would have to rely entirely on the mobile. 'St James's Day,' he prompted. 'Ring any bells?'

'No, not really. I have a *Book of Days* here, somewhere, perhaps that can –'

'Doctor, I don't have much time left on this phone. The clue says: "Pray remember the 25th of July".'

'That's the whole thing?'

'I'm afraid so.'

'Pray remember – wait a minute, would you?' There followed the sound of him setting the receiver down.

Shit, he thought, he's wandered off to ask somebody else and I don't have time for this. He heard the receiver being raised once more.

'You're in luck. I've brought in some friends. We're all in different academic fields, we just meet informally in a group, for the fun of it really. I thought they might be useful –'

'Doctor,' he cautioned. 'Time.'

'Yes, sorry. There's a tendency to ramble when one grows older. We think it was a street cry.'

'What was?'

'The "Pray remember" part, someone here says, hang on –' Vince could hear someone speaking in the background.

'Hello? Young man?' A new voice now, the voice of a middle-aged woman. The doctor was putting his friends on the line for a chat, for God's sake.

'Yes, I'm here.'

'I don't know if this is of any help at all, but in Victorian times, if you couldn't afford a pilgrimage to the shrine of St James on July the 25th, you built your own.'

'Hang on a sec,' said Vince, dropping his last coin into the phone slot. 'Sorry.'

'Are you still there? On St James's Day the poor children collected pebbles, flowers, shells and bits of pottery, and built little grottoes. They'd sit beside them collecting coins in their caps, and they'd call out "Pray remember the grotto". You heard the cry in the poorer parts of London as late as the 1920s. My grandmother can remember . . .'

Vince leaned out from the station alcove and peered back at the clubs tucked beneath the railway arches. The twisted rope of crimson letters jumped out of the gloom even at this distance. There must have been a hundred and fifty people queuing to get into The Grotto.

'Young man? Can you hear me?'

'Yes, I can, you've been a great help, thank you. And thank Doctor Masters for me.'

'He says you must call whenever you need him, no matter how late it is. He suffers from insomnia. We all do.'

'Thanks. I may well have to call again.' The Grotto. Very funny. Another of the League's little jokes. The club shared its name with one of the largest social organisations associated with the Freemasons. He returned the receiver to its perch and ran off towards the club.

Pam had followed her quarry to Cheyne Walk. This was quite the bravest and most foolhardy thing she had ever done. Behind her, the lights of Chelsea Bridge wavered in the falling snow, glittering in the icy river like the illuminations of an abandoned carnival. At the end of the street, the striding figure turned and crossed the junction into another road. She followed as quickly and quietly as she could. She was fairly certain that he had not spotted her; she had been careful to keep her distance for the last half-hour.

Pam presumed they were moving parallel to the river, but within minutes she was lost in the labyrinth of neat little streets. The buildings here sported an air of wealthy discretion. It was the sort of area where Members of Parliament were caught for drunk driving after visiting their mistresses.

The figure before her suddenly left the street, pushing open a high gate of black wrought iron. She was surprised to see a tall gothic building with mullioned windows set back from the pavement beyond a grass-covered quadrangle. She caught the gate with her foot just before it shut and slipped inside. He was stamping the snow from his shoes on the steps of the main entrance, muttering to himself. She waited on the far side of the flagstone courtyard while he twisted the door-ring and vanished within.

Pam waited a full five minutes before wobbling across the courtyard on her heels and standing before the bevelled iron ring. There was nothing she had covered in her business courses to account for this situation. She wished Vince was here. After a moment of hesitation she turned the handle and felt the door shift inwards, unlocked. Pushing it further open she saw a gloomy flagstone hall, a great oak staircase lined with unfurled flags – and half a dozen men in dinner jackets waiting for her to step inside.

Before she could back out, Barwick stepped forward and pushed the door shut.

'I'm glad you finally decided to join us,' said Sebastian. 'We were freezing our parts off waiting for you to make up your bloody mind.'

CHAPTER TWENTY-NINE

Steel And Stars

VINCE KNEW he had one advantage over the League. He could talk to people out here in the queue beneath the freezing arches and get some honest answers. Sebastian and his pals had no street sense. They had made a mistake with this challenge, playing into his hands for once.

'How big is this place?' he asked a hypertense young black man in a fake-Armani jacket at the back of the line.

The young man bounced up and down on the balls of his feet, his face scrunched up in puzzlement.

'Yah-what, man?'

'How many bars are there inside?'

'Bars? Lessee, now. Upstairs. Downstairs. Balcony. Dive-bar. Restaurant. Club Lounge. Chill-out Room. VIP Suite. Terrace.'

'They're all different?'

'There's four different entrances, man. They're all numbered. This the third.'

. . . *To Three of Four Doors* . . . at least he was in the right line.

'Sounds big.'

'Different club nights. House. Garage. Jungle. Banghra.

Hardbag, Techno. Funk. Thrash metal. Trance-Dance. Retro. Pop. Jazz. Loungecore. Straight. Gay. Bi. Can hold three thousand people on a good night. Not at the rate these guys admitting us, though.'

'They have a strict door policy?'

'Strictest-ever.'

Given the number of stabbings that occurred in such places, most of the clubs in the area were extremely choosy about whom they admitted. Vince was able to work his way further along the queue, jumping a few places by telling a complex but convincing lie about a lost jacket. When he reached the front, the doorman finally admitted him to a tiny foyer of sweating white-painted bricks, where he could decide Vince's fate at leisure.

'How much is it?' asked Vince, digging into his duffel bag.

'How much is what?' the bouncer asked back, smiling quizzically. Music thudded heavily beneath their feet.

Oh, it's going to be like that, he thought. *Just what I need.* 'I'm meeting someone inside, actually.'

'Only if you get in – actually.' His smirk turned to a grin. 'Where do you want to go?'

'What's at the top?'

'You don't want to go upstairs. Upstairs is rubber. You got any rubber?'

Vince shook his head. The bouncer persisted. 'Latex? PVC? Padded vinyl? Nylon? Plastic? Spandex?'

''Fraid not.'

'Yeah, well. Makes people sweat,' he replied consolingly.

'What's downstairs?'

'Twenty-two pounds fifty.'

'That's expensive.'

'It includes the price of having your nipple pierced.'

'Just the one? There must be something else.'

'Garage.'

'I like garage music.'

'No, it's just a garage. Full of cross-dressers tonight.'

'You mean angry –'

'No, transvestites. I get muddled up, meself. It's like stalactites and the ones that come up from the floor. You wouldn't like it in there. A lot of bonding going on.'

'How close?'

'*Very* close. You'll be better off in the alternative lounge, middle floor. Eight quid.'

Vince figured it was the minimum he'd get away with spending. He paid his money, had the back of his wrist branded with a purple day-glo stamp and stepped into darkness, slowly climbing beer-slick concrete steps to the centre of the building.

. . . *The Challenge of The Crenellated Pachyderm* . . . So he was looking for some kind of elephant? In here? The walls vibrated as a train rumbled past, seemingly through each of the crowded dance floors. He was hungry, thirsty and dead-dog-tired as he reached down to a red styrofoam sofa covered in cigarette burns and collapsed into it.

'Hey, wake up, man.' A cadaverous creature with cheese-and-onion-crisp breath was leaning over him. Vince had nodded off for a moment, and awoke with a start to be confronted by what appeared to be a Mott The Hoople-era hippie. He had hair extensions and cropped patches like bleached corn-stubble. 'You look knackered.'

'And you look like a dealer,' Vince replied.

'Who made you clairvoyant?'

'Making sure the house is sorted for es and whizz, are you? I don't want any.'

'Hey, don't be so aggressive, man. Gern, take your pick, every one's a winner.'

He pulled open his black nylon bomber jacket to reveal an array of brown plastic medicine bottles fixed to buttons in the lining with rubber bands. 'Doves, Hearts, Downs, Whippets, Jellies, Wobbly Eggs, Purple Screamers, Heebie Jeebies, Blue Poison, Black Death –'

Vince made a face. 'Christ, they sound awful.'

'Oh I don't know, it does you good to get out and have fun occasionally. I'm providing a service.' He pulled a bottle from his jacket and held it out. 'Here, they used to give these to injured soldiers just before they had amputations. Two quid apiece.'

'That's cheap.'

'I mix them with something from my shed and pass the savings onto you.'

'You got something to keep me up all night?' He leaned out of the strobing lights and shielded his eyes. 'Come here a second.'

The dealer realised his mistake and started to back away, but Vince caught him by the sleeve of his jacket and pulled. 'Mr Wentworth? Jason? It *is* you! Christ, I can't believe you're doing this. You used to be our art teacher.'

The dealer moved sheepishly towards him. 'I didn't recognise you. Vincent Reynolds, isn't it?' He sat down beside him on the sofa. 'How are you getting on? I hope your figure drawing's improved.'

Vince was aghast. 'You were going to get back to nature, go off and live in the Algarve. You said the light would be better for painting.'

'Yeah, well, I went there for a while but it wasn't like I thought it would be. All golf clubs and holiday parks. Really expensive. I ran out of money after six weeks. Teamed up with some bloke who was planning to open a beach disco, persuaded me to draw out all my savings to invest in it. Bastard only spunked out the first half of his dosh before clearing off. He was supposed to put in the same amount as me, only he never turned up to the bank when we went to secure the loan. The British embassy had to pay for me to get home. I'm married now. I've got responsibilities.' He pulled a vial of white tablets from his coat pocket. 'You still want something to keep you awake?'

'Only if it works all night long.' Vince wearily pulled himself up from the seat. 'I'm on the search for the "Crenellated Pachyderm". You can help me find it if you like, but don't blame me if someone tries to kill you.'

'It's your go, Maggie,' said Harold Masters. 'Stop daydreaming.'

'I can't help thinking of that poor boy out there all by himself,' said Mrs Armitage. The flame-haired occult specialist of Camden Town was not concentrating on her hand. 'We should be doing something to help him.'

'The best thing we can do is be on the other end of the telephone line when he calls,' said Masters, checking his cards once more.

'Perhaps we should ring the police.' Mrs Armitage ran nervous fingers through the brightly varnished shell necklace that looped her neck. 'Explain what's going on. I have connections. I know people who could psychically assist them in their investigations.'

'That would slow them down a bit,' said Stanley Purbrick, a curator at the British Museum whose usual field of expertise was Victorian ornithology. He had no time for Maggie

Armitage's new age brand of vaguely holistic spiritualism. He was a rationalist, and a conspiracy theorist. He could find a conspiracy inside his morning cereal packet or behind the lateness of the train that bore him to work, and frequently did so. 'They have no idea what goes on in this city. Besides, talk to the police and it stays on your files for ever. For God's sake play your hand, Maggie, you're driving us all mad.'

'What files? They have files on us?' Mrs Armitage distractedly laid out her cards in a hand that made so little sense it seemed impossible to imagine that she had been paying attention for the last half-hour.

'What on earth have you been keeping there, you silly woman?' Purbrick tossed his cards aside in disgust. 'If you'd spent less time arguing about spontaneous combustion and more remembering what cards you were holding we could have finished playing ages ago. These are spades. Those are clubs. Christ on a bike.'

Harold Masters and his wife were used to this sort of behaviour. Virtually every meeting of the Insomnia Squad featured a card game disrupted by the most arcane arguments imaginable, but the five of them continued to meet, which, he supposed, proved that they still had something in common.

'I can't concentrate,' said Mrs Armitage, walking to the window and staring down into the darkened street. 'That poor boy needs spiritual fortification.'

'So do I,' said Purbrick. 'Harold, I seem to recall that you have a decent twelve-year-old malt whisky over there, don't you?'

'I might have,' Masters replied carefully. Once the last member of their group arrived and got his hands on it, the bottle would be lost. 'Jane, have a look in the sideboard and give our guests a drink.' His wife gave him a gentle knowing smile as she crossed the room.

'So it's agreed,' said Masters. 'Mr Reynolds needs our help, and I for one don't think it's cheating. After all, the League has at least twelve members working against him, and we are only five.'

'Four at the moment,' Mrs Armitage pointed out.

'The least we can do is stay up with the poor fellow until dawn,' said Masters, 'and try to guide him through. What are you doing?'

The occultist pulled something from the unruly red mop of her hair and set it down before her. 'It's a divining rod.'

'It's a pencil.'

'You can use anything so long as the wood is right.'

'I don't see how that helps us at all,' complained Purbrick. 'What use is that?'

'I use it to write with,' she explained. 'Harold, why don't you start by telling us everything you know about these people? Perhaps we can do something more positive than just sitting beside the phone.'

Pam watched in annoyance as they argued around her.

'What I don't understand,' Caton-James complained, 'is why you couldn't find some ordinary rope.'

'How many people do you know who can lay their hands on a coil of rope at short notice?' shouted St John Warner. 'It's all very well for you to say "tie her up" as if it was the most natural thing in the world to do. You don't even carry a penknife on you.'

'I'm not a fucking boy scout. If I have any dirty work to do, I'll get someone congenitally stupid to do it for me, right, Barwick?'

Barwick gave them both a long hard stare as he knotted Pam's hands behind her back. In the absence of rope he had been forced to make do with an old 16mm print of *Carousel* someone had once borrowed from the BFI and not returned. Knotting strips of plastic proved problematic, though, and Pam had complained that it was cutting into her wrists right up until Sebastian gagged her with his handkerchief and the end of a roll of parcel tape.

They arranged her astride a bentwood chair with her arms tied around the central supporting column of the reading room. Still clad in her navy-blue suit and *faux*-pearls, she looked like a flight attendant getting into bondage.

'What are we going to do with her, anyway?' asked Caton-James. 'She can't stay here.'

'She can for the remainder of the night,' said Sebastian. 'She was helping the enemy.' He looked over at Pam, who was glaring at them in forced silence. 'I think she's putting gypsy curses on us all. It makes one wonder if all unattractive women are really witches.' Pam threw him a look that almost struck him dead.

'I think we should go upstairs and check the subject's progress on the big monitor. We're wasting time down here.' St John Warner made for the spiral wooden staircase in the corner.

'For once I agree with you,' said Sebastian. 'Barwick, you stay here and guard.'

'Good dog,' said St John Warner, barking and laughing as they trooped upstairs, leaving the miserable student with his captive.

'My first thought was the Elephant and Castle,' Vince explained as they climbed towards the roof. Below them, the cacophony of several different sound systems competed for dancers in different parts of the warren-like building. 'Crenellations are those dips in battlements that troops fire from, so Pachyderm Castle – it seemed a reasonable assumption. But the instructions brought me here instead.'

'And quite rightly too,' said Jason. 'I'll show you your elephant and castle in a minute. There's an emergency exit up here. It isn't alarmed or anything.'

'How do you know?' Vince struggled to keep up with him. For a man whose tabescent appearance suggested that he might keel over at any second, Mr Wentworth was surprisingly agile.

'Listen, in my line of business you always make sure you know where the exits are, know what I'm saying? Here.' He hammered a fist down on the steel exit bar before him and shoved back the great red fire door. A blast of icy air blew in over them, snowflakes satellising in the sudden square of light. 'Blimey, fresh air in Nine Elms, there's a novelty.' He barked out a phlegmy cough, then held out his hand and hauled Vince onto the roof. 'Come on, squire, you can do it.'

Vince carefully levered himself onto the narrow concrete ledge that ran past the fire door. At his back an odd four-foot brick wall ran off into darkness. In front of him lay the sluggish ebbing river, and on its north bank the hazy floodlights of the Tate Gallery.

'Follow my finger.' He held his scrawny arm out, pointing across the yellow grid of the intersection to a battered edifice caught in the traffic's crossfire. 'Observe the name of the building,' Jason instructed.

Vince could vaguely make out some stone lettering around the edge of the first floor. 'I can't read it from here.'

'Then look at the roof.'

He found himself staring at a large gaudily-painted stone elephant. On its back was a giant chesspiece, a rook. 'That's the other elephant and castle,' he explained. 'A boozer, a right old trouble-spot. People don't notice the statue from the road, but from up here . . .'

'Up to steel and stars,' said Vince, puzzled. Just then, the bricks behind him started to vibrate ominously. He turned in alarm to see a great dark mass curving towards him with a rumble and a screech, and suddenly understood where they were. The club was hollowed out inside the structure of Vauxhall's vast red-brick railway bridges, with its sweeping roof underneath the track.

He looked back to see the moon momentarily clear the clouds. The arcing steel lines formed a night smile, silver in the drifting snow. It looked as if the railway line was launching its cargo to the stars. Moments later the track was gone, obliterated by endless thundering carriages on their way to the terminus at Waterloo.

Inside The Hive

'ARE YOU just going to sit there and let him repeatedly flout the rules?' asked Caton-James, 'because if that drug dealer he's talking to starts putting two and two together, he could wreck everything.'

'You're joking, of course,' said Sebastian. 'We know all about him. He's just a stupid junkie. He's not in a position to help Vincent.'

'Right, he's so stupid he just worked out the answer to the last clue. I don't understand you, Sebastian. He's bound to find the next letter and read its contents now that they're up on the roof together. You promised us Reynolds would be the only one to gain full knowledge of the challenge. After tonight no one else would know a thing, that was the beauty of it, you said. Instead he's telling anyone who'll listen. Now you have these – loose cannons –'

'What do you want me to do?' asked Sebastian quietly.

'I want you to start behaving a little more like a general. We should be cleaning up our house. We need to get rid of the junkie,' said Caton-James heatedly. 'Show some balls about it. Our forefathers had to take care of their mistakes. When your own father set up the WBI –'

A sub-zero glance from Sebastian told him he had over-stepped the mark. 'I'm fully aware that my father's plans for the WBI were not based on libertarian concerns.'

'We have to tidy up as we go,' Caton-James pleaded. 'I can arrange it if you don't want to.'

'No, I'll do it. Where's Xavier Stevens now?'

'You'll have to ask Barwick.'

'All right, but this is the last time I'm prepared to let out-siders interfere with the game,' said Sebastian, draining his glass and setting it down. Caton-James scowled contemp-tuously as their leader made a great show of rising to his feet and heading for the stairs to the reading room.

'It's not a game,' he said under his breath. That was Sebastian's trouble. He indulged his personal tastes to the detriment of the others. It was time he started looking to his laurels. There were others coming up behind him – faster, stronger men who had little interest in outdated games, and even less in fair play.

Pam could not breathe. The gag was not tied tightly, but it prevented her from taking air through her mouth, and her nose was becoming blocked. She signalled to Barwick, who finally noticed her discomfort, set down the SAS training manual Caton-James had given him to read and came over.

'I can't take it off,' he whispered at her, pointing to the ceiling. 'They're upstairs. If you make a noise they'll hear you and then we'll both be in trouble.'

Pam rolled her eyes pleadingly at him for a few minutes, enjoying his tortured indecision, then turned on the water-works. That did the trick. Barwick slunk back to her and loosened the gag. He wasn't too familiar with the ways of women. Pam was too smart to start yelling. She realised she was inside the hive, as it were, and that her shouts were only likely to bring her enemies.

'Thank you for doing that,' she told Barwick gratefully, 'I couldn't breathe. Sinuses. And my hands are going numb.'

'I can't untie your hands, you know that.' He dragged his chair over to her and sat disconcertingly close, watching her face. He appeared genuinely concerned for her welfare, but she had no way of gauging his sincerity.

'I'm not going to try and get away.'

'I should hope not. Get me into trouble.'

One look at his weak eyes told her he had absolutely no authority here. She had heard how his colleagues treated him. Her best hope was to use him to glean information. 'Forgive me, I can't help noticing,' she said gently, 'the others seem very hard on you. Why do you let them push you around so much?'

'Oh, they're not bad fellows really,' he said, glancing nervously at the ceiling. In that moment she saw how frightened of them, and how desperate for their approval, he was. For the first time she began to wonder what they were really up to. This was far too elaborate to merely be some form of *divertissement* for bored aristos. She looked around at the reading-room floor, trying to see what they'd done with her shoulder bag. Her mobile phone was in it.

'I don't know your first name,' she said, trying out what she hoped was a nervous smile.

'I don't tell many people.' He looked at her shyly. 'It's Horace.'

Christ, no wonder you keep it to yourself, she thought. She was a little insulted to have been left with the stooge of the gang, the traditional court-jester-butt-of-everyone's-jokes that groups of men always seemed to designate. Clearly she was not deemed to be a major player in the night's events. Well, she would find a way to change their minds about that. They were dealing with a professional business management trainee now.

'Horace, could you get me a glass of water?' she asked sweetly, thinking hard. 'My mouth is really dry.'

This constituted a major decision for Barwick, whose pained look presumably indicated some kind of tortured thought process involving responsibility within the power hierarchy. Eventually he left her side and brought a half-full plastic bottle of Evian from the table.

'I got into trouble for buying this,' he told her, removing the cap and allowing the water to run into her upturned mouth. 'Sebastian was furious. He doesn't allow plastic at the table. How's that?' He had tipped the bottle too high. Water splashed down her chin and dripped inside her blouse. He was staring hard at her wet throat. Perhaps he'd never been this close to a female before. He wasn't doing too well now, she thought, not when you considered she was tied to a post.

'Why aren't you upstairs with the others?'

'They needed someone to guard you.'

'And they always give you the crap jobs, don't they?'

'No, I like doing this, really. I can be useful to them.'

But never really part of the team, she thought, just the dogsbody. She remembered in her business management classes how to search out the opposition leader and mark a rival, one on one. 'How do they always know where Vince is?' she asked, 'if it's not giving away trade secrets.'

Barwick seemed quite happy to talk, almost desperately so. He rubbed his florid chops, thinking. 'The League has friends everywhere,' he explained. 'We all went to university together. And we know lots of people, of course, through – the families,' he added obscurely.

'What about the traffic cameras? Vincent says you've been using them to keep tabs on him.'

'They operate on closed circuit systems, but they have feeds running from them to central monitor stations. The more important ones are dumped down onto IBM hard drives or CD-Roms at peak hours. And the private infra-red cameras installed by shopping precincts, business developments and public buildings that have to monitor occupancy to comply with fire regulations can be downloaded into a number of West End video suites, where the tapes are collated within a digitalised computer system and stored as back-up copies. We have somebody monitoring your friend's movements, following him from system to system, and he just ISDNs the appropriate monitor scenes from the suites up to St John Warner's computer system. Simple, really, although the varying download times can sometimes cause surveillance discrepancies. That's when we switch to video grabs taken from Quicktime footage on the Internet.'

Oh God, a techno-nerd, she thought. 'You like computers, do you?'

'Oh yes, my chosen field, actually.'

So that was why they'd made him an outcast. She was willing to bet that the others had all taken classical studies. Poor old Barwick had probably been forced to go to Oxford when he had really belonged in a technical college, happily constructing web-sites.

'What's going to happen to Vince? They're not going to hurt him just because he wanted to write about your club, are they?'

'Oh no, not at all, he's in no real harm.'

'I'd argue with that. He's having a pretty tough time out there by all accounts. I'd be frightened out of my wits, not knowing who to trust.'

'Frightened, yes, but not actually harmed,' her guard explained. 'Quite the reverse, actually –'

'What do you mean?'

'Well, he has to be all right for the morning.'

'Why, what happens then?'

Barwick froze, realising he had already said too much. Damn, the little prick had nearly given something away. And now there was somebody thumping down the stairs. She would have to wait until the two of them were alone again. But hey, if Vince could survive this night, so could she.

CHAPTER THIRTY-ONE

The Escort

'YOU WERE a good pupil, you know?'

'Yeah, well, you were a good teacher. Really different, the way you saw things.'

'I know. I must have been different to get in so much trouble, not sticking to the educational guidelines. All that "Anarchy In The UK" stuff when I was supposed to be showing you how to make pots. Over there, can you see it?'

The letter was sealed in a clear plastic bag, taped to one of the sleepers on the railway track behind them. Wentworth vaulted the low wall and began stepping between the rails. 'Don't worry,' he called back, 'it's nowhere near the third rail.' For a sickening moment Vince remembered what had happened to the last person who had offered to collect a letter for him, and stepped forward to stop his former teacher, but it was too late. Wentworth had snapped the plastic packet free from the sleeper and was holding it up. 'Want me to see what it says?'

'Let's wait until we get downstairs first.' Vince held out a hand and helped his accomplice climb back over the wall. There was a mournful echo of metal as another freight train shunted closer.

'What time do you make it?' Wentworth resealed the fire-escape door behind them.

'Seven minutes to two. Beat the deadline, thanks to you. I don't think I can handle much more of this.' His feet were hurting, and a shivery flu-bug sensation had settled in the pit of his stomach. He could not remember the last time he had eaten, or felt so desperately tired.

'Let's get you a cup of coffee,' said Wentworth, pushing back the double doors leading to one of the club's black-light chill-out areas. 'I don't know what you've got yourself into, but it sounds like you've some sorting out to do, some deciding in your head.'

'I'm not so sure it's a matter of choice. Christ, Jason, look at all the preparations they've made. I think I'm intended to see this through to the bitter end.'

'Well,' said Wentworth, confused, 'remember you don't have to do anything you don't want to do, man.' He dug sugar packets from the bowl on the bar and emptied three each into their coffees. 'I mean, it's elaborate, but it's only a game, isn't it? Here, you need plenty of glucose if you're gonna take some of these. They'll keep you awake until morning. Actually, you probably won't sleep for about three days.' He shook two of the white tablets he had taken from the vial in his jacket into a plastic teaspoon and stirred it into his ex-pupil's drink.

'If this was just something to teach me a lesson,' muttered Vince, barely hearing, 'something to keep me in my place and provide them with amusement, they wouldn't kill anyone, would they?'

'People kill foxes for the sport of it.'

'I mean, all it does is expose them to risk. Unless I win, of course. What happens then?'

'I don't know, man,' said Wentworth, who was adept at shoring up nonsensical late-night conversations. 'Who does, you know?'

'They've planned for everything else. What will they do if I beat them at their own game?' Vince stirred his coffee thoughtfully and drank. The chemical taste made him wince. He searched around for more sugar. 'See, that's what I don't understand. Even if I fail one of the challenges and they try to have me killed, I could still have the manuscript published. I'm not bound by their rules. Sebastian knows that.'

'Yeah. It sounds very complicated.' Wentworth's interest began to wane as he dug around in his pockets for a chunk of dope and started rolling himself a joint. 'Sometimes you just have to go ahead and do, uh, what you have to do. You know?'

'Okay, let me see what the game is offering this time. Pass over Pandora's Box.'

'What?'

'The envelope.'

Wentworth handed him the clear plastic packet. Inside, he found the usual single sheet of white vellum, folded twice.

The Challenge Of The Disgraced Wife

'Oh death rock me to sleep
Bring on my quiet rest
Let pass my very guiltless ghost
Out of my careful brest'
– May 19th 1536 at noon

Lorraine
Fylfot
Pomme

Botonne
Moline
Patte Fiche
Fleury
Aimee

'For how myght sweetness ever hav be known
For hym that never tastyd bitterness'

Time Limit: 120 Minutes

'Poetry's not my strong point, either,' said Wentworth, ordering himself a Glenfiddich to accompany his joint. Vince noticed that, as the club's resident drug dealer, he didn't have to pay for anything at the bar. So much for the club's ostensible 'no drugs' policy.

'I know the answer to the top part,' said Vince. 'It's not poetry – at least, not intentionally. It's very well known, though. Anne Boleyn's last words, spoken on the morning of her execution on Tower Green, right in the middle of the Tower of London. Surely they don't expect me to break into the place. It would be impossible to get in at this time of night, anyway. Nobody goes in or out after the Ceremony of the Keys takes place.'

'I guess they want to make you try scaling the walls or something.' Wentworth's laugh became a hacking cough.

'No,' said Vince, 'it's not right. If they wanted to send me to the Bloody Tower, why not set the challenge earlier, while there was still a realistic chance of getting inside? Sebastian likes misdirecting me. This has to be somewhere else.' He turned his attention to the second part. 'I don't have the faintest idea what those are. Painting techniques, regional languages, vintage wines, could be anything. I'll have to call someone.' But not from here. He needed to find somewhere a little less noisy.

'So you're gonna go back out there on the streets?' He sucked hard at the joint. 'London, man. All those centuries of civilisation, for what? We tried to raise ourselves to heaven, but something snapped and we just fell back to earth. We were in sight of the gods, now we're grubbing about in the ruins. London. From a celestial city of dreams to an urban dystopia. That's what it is now. Urban dystopia. Disturbia.'

'Jason? You okay?'

'Yeah. Fuck.' He wiped his eyes. 'Let me see that page.' Vince handed him the letter. Wentworth studied it with his brow furrowed. He nodded slowly as he read, finally emitting a grunt of comprehension.

'Well?'

'Haven't a fucking clue, man. It's a puzzle of some kind, isn't it?'

Vince had forgotten how infuriating dopeheads could be. He made a mental note not to forget again.

'Listen, I have a business transaction to conclude in the bar downstairs,' said Wentworth, rising. 'I'll meet you outside in a few minutes, give you a hand with this. 'Cause you need someone with a clear head.'

'That's not such a great idea, Jason. I appreciate your help but I think you're better off in here.'

'Believe me, man, I could do with the fresh air. My brain doesn't work properly in this heat. Stay cool.' He squeezed Vince's arm and threaded his way through the chromium stools to the first of the stairways leading to the dance floors. Wentworth grinned happily to himself. If the man was there he would clear five or six hundred tonight, even after the club's cut.

The DJ's choice pounded in his head as he stepped onto the flashing, heaving dance floor, some kind of crossover NU-NRG/trance/hardcore stuff that sounded identical to last week's hot new crossover. He could not tell which particular end-slice of the social spectrum occupied the floor tonight, but there was an abundance of fetish-wear, rubber vests and microskirts, one of the nicer Saturday night crowds, less aggressive than the snarling image portrayed on The Grotto's flyers.

According to the bargirl, the man was called Denny and had bleached-white hair shaved in a No 2 crop, but Wentworth could not see him in the crowd. What he saw instead was a slim pale guy gesturing at him. He registered dark deep-set eyes, a smirking bony face and an old-fashioned public school side-parting. Wentworth looked around, pointed at his chest in a *Do you mean me?* gesture, and the guy smiled back and nodded, which was odd, because he looked more like a plain-clothes cop than someone who wanted to purchase a stash of pick-me-ups, especially as he was obviously wearing a wire. The damned thing was sticking out of his shirt.

Shit, he thought, panicky now, this is a set-up. Time to get out and get lost fast. The club was supposed to have a deal going. They dealt with The Man. They were supposed to protect him.

'He's standing in front of me right now,' said Xavier Stevens, dipping his head to avoid being seen speaking. 'I just want to confirm that I have authorisation for this at the price we've just agreed.'

'I'm in a position to confirm that,' replied Sebastian.

Stevens had once been destined for great things in the Territorials, but his attempts to intellectualise the Greek warrior spirit and instill it in his men cut against the grain of an army that saw itself strictly in terms of a peacekeeping force. His uneasy superiors had finally discharged him. Now he was the unacceptable face of the League of Prometheus, carrying out their dirty work, a Gordon Liddy to Sebastian's Nixon. But if Sebastian thought he controlled his violent footsoldier, the reverse was actually true; Stevens had compiled quite a lengthy file on their beloved leader. Who knew when it would come in useful?

'The general consensus here is that there should be no loose cannons,' buzzed his earpiece, 'so I guess that's a green light to proceed.'

'All I needed to know. Out.'

Stevens pushed aside the spaced-out waif in lime Lycra who was blocking his path, and closed in on the nervous-looking dealer. Wentworth threw out his arms and began to say something, but before he could be heard above the pounding beat Stevens drew a pencil-slim blade from his jacket and slid it smoothly into his target's gut, cutting through the padded jacket that he hoped would absorb much of the blood, and hooking the edge up, up, until he was sure he had cut so deep and so far that life would entirely depart the drug-wasted body before it fell to the floor.

Wentworth's mouth was still wide with his first words, but already the light in his eyes was changing. Stevens withdrew the steel as easily as he had brandished it, and allowed his cruciform victim to be borne onto the dance floor by the backs and shoulders of the hypnotised crowd.

'Hang on, there's a train going past.' Vince put a finger in one ear and looked back up at the arch as the carriages clattered by. 'Sorry about that.'

'Okay,' said Harold Masters, 'this time we're ready. We have pens, dictionaries, thesauruses, encyclopediae, volumes of forgotten lore and reproductions of historical maps, not to mention Maggie's collection of ancient burial sites. We're ready for anything you can throw at us. Read out the clue.'

It wasn't until Vince felt in his pocket to locate the letter that he remembered where he had last seen it. In Jason's hands, being refolded as he absently placed it in his coat. How long did he have before it turned itself into chemical dust?

'Ah, there's a bit of a problem with that,' he explained. 'I'll call you right back.'

He stamped his soaked boots in the slush and studied the illuminated entrance of the club. The admission queue snaked halfway around the block now, but no one was coming out. In clubbing terms, the night was still very young. He would never be able to blag his way back in. Wentworth had probably forgotten his promise to meet him outside. Come to that, he had probably forgotten his own name and which planet he inhabited.

Vince looked back at the garish doorway, the bitter sleet-laden air dragging at his bones. He did not have time to return and look for the art teacher-turned-dealer. He felt like going home, packing a bag and leaving the country for a few days, but flights required money, and he had none. At least the draft of his piece on the League was safe with Esther, and the other copy –

'I only came here for a bit of a night out, you know? It's not fair.'

Vince turned to find himself facing an attractive

dark-haired woman of about twenty-two who appeared to be dressed in a soul singer's concert outfit. She was wearing elbow-length purple satin gloves.

'I'm sorry?'

'Didn't you see it?' she asked incredulously, looking back at the club.

'See what?'

'They've turned the music off and put the lights up and everything. If people want to get into punch-ups they should do it outside so it doesn't interfere with us.' She addressed him at great speed, speaking as if she had known him all her life.

'What do you mean?'

'Somebody just stabbed this bloke I know. Right in the guts. I mean, right through, like lethal and everything. Blood up the walls, everywhere. They called an ambulance but they'd have been better off ordering a hearse. So he's probably gonna die, right, so there's no point in spoiling everyone else's evening, right?'

He had a horrible precognition of the victim's identity. The coincidence was too great. 'You saw this happen?'

'Only from the other side of the room. I was up on the stage, dancing and that.' She indicated her outfit with a resigned shrug. 'You know, showing off a bit. It's that time of the night. You know. After two.'

'I know what you mean.'

'After two's a state of mind. Anything can happen between two and dawn, can't it? I mean, it's the only time when everyone is equal. Look out on the street, whores, junkies, career girls, rich businessmen. If they're out after two, there's no difference between any of them. It's my favourite time. You can say what you like, do what you like, make your own rules. The barriers don't go back up until daylight. Until then you're like, a free spirit.'

Great, thought Vince, do some more drugs. He returned to the club entrance but the doorman was refusing to let anyone inside. Knife wounds had to be reported to the police, and they were the last people he needed to see right now. He had no choice but to get away.

'Hey, listen,' called the stoned dancer, pushing through the crowd towards him, 'don't look so worried. He's not a mate of yours, is he?'

'You haven't told me who got stabbed yet,' he said, exasperated.

'His name's Jason, he does some work for the club, always hangs around there, skinny bloke, long blond hair in clumps.'

Vince's stomach twisted in a sudden plunging cramp. Someone else had been hurt, and once again it was his fault. He stared back into the crowd milling outside the club. What if Sebastian's assassin was still here?

'It's not unusual, you know, stabbings and that. Happens all the time. There's some pretty bad people in there.'

'Dealing drugs?'

She gave him an old-fashioned look. 'No, dancing round their handbags.'

'Do you know which hospital they'll take him to?'

She rolled her eyes at him. 'They're not gonna take him to a hospital, you moron. He's carryin' for the club, isn't he? See the pub at the end of the next street?' She raised a satin finger and pointed to a corner tavern lit with strings of grubby, coloured bulbs. 'The bouncers'll drop him off over there.'

'In a *pub?*'

'Well, he's got mates there who'll sort him out. If he goes to hospital it's the start of a long chain of events ending with the club closed, the licence fucked and him inside, so what do you reckon's the best solution? Here, my name's Betty. Let me give you my number.' She pulled a business card from her purple satin cleavage and pushed it into his hand. Vince read the card in his palm.

'Hostess/Escort Service and Ace Van Hire?'

'They're sidelines. I also do bereavement counselling and candle-art. Turn it over, that's my home number. No, I'll tell you what, you look like you need a drink inside you. You wanna buy me one? Go on, be a sport, it's the best offer you'll get around here.'

'I don't know,' said Vince. 'You're a bit aggressive.'

'You've got to be,' she replied. 'Didn't you notice? Girls outnumber blokes two to one in there. You need to find an original angle just to get a bit of chat out of someone.'

Striking up a conversation about who's been stabbed lately should do it, thought Vince. Betty was an extremely attractive woman, although she seemed to be suffering from battle-fatigue. It was hard work meeting new people these days.

'Look, I've got to say goodbye to my friends. Go on, go over there and wait for me. I'll have a large Black Death vodka and grapefruit. I'll see you in two minutes. Honest. God, I'm freezing my tits off.' She pulled at her décolletage, but goose-pimples were stippling her pale breasts. 'I knew this would be one of those fucking trouble-nights.'

Vince watched in wonder as she tottered away through the slush on three-inch heels. Then, helpless until he could locate the envelope containing the sixth challenge, he set off in the direction of the tavern.

CHAPTER THIRTY-TWO

The Source Of Barbarism

'I WONDER if you understand what has happened to your country,' said Sebastian, pulling out a pine chair and reversing the seat so that he could sit astride it, facing Pam. He had sent St John Warner, Caton-James and the others up to the top of the house to monitor Vince's progress more carefully. Accorded the status of a dog, Barwick was allowed to remain.

Christ, thought Pam, he's got a captive audience. I'm going to get a speech.

'I believe the start of this city's decline into barbarism occurred between 1941 and 1943. Up until then we were a disciplined race. Did you know, they set up psychiatric clinics to deal with Londoners' neurotic illnesses during the Blitz, but hardly anybody attended? People stayed calm, drank tea and chatted about their problems with friends. No, it wasn't the bombing raids that broke our will, it was the silences between them.'

Sebastian shifted his chair closer. 'Three years of just

getting by, surviving on rations, clearing rubble, making and mending. Londoners grew fractious, tired by the shoddiness of it all. The Regency buildings that typified this city – and there were a great number of them – decayed and disappeared. They couldn't ring church bells for fear the belfries would collapse. Soldiers were everywhere, trampling the parks. The only thing that rose from these ashes was London Rocket, the flower that sprang up on bombsites.' His eyes lost their focus. He looked past her to the night beyond the mullioned windows.

'And gradually, it changed. People lost their cheeriness, sleepwalking through their lives, no longer surprised by any deprivation. Delivered into chaos, their young became difficult to control. Vandalism was born. Women rebelled, worked alongside men, entered public houses unescorted. The LCC-controlled British Restaurant chain that provided cheap meals for those remaining in the city gave rise to a national reputation for poor cuisine. Temporary housing became permanent. A shabby wrecked city and its exhausted populace were poorly patched up and packed off into the next decade. Which leaves us where we are today, not seeking out inner peace and spiritual improvement but "competing in the world marketplace". In short, dear lady, we won the war and lost ourselves.'

Pam had been released from her post for Sebastian's visit, and was still rubbing her chafed wrists. She felt like a character from a prisoner-of-war movie, except that prisoner-of-war movies didn't usually make you sit through lectures about the good old days. She sensed a change of mood occurring; Sebastian had snapped out of his reverie.

'Time for you to answer some questions, I think,' he told her, rubbing at his eyes. He looked tired. 'Why were you following your friend?'

Pam thought it was obvious. 'I wanted to make sure he wouldn't get into trouble.'

'Excuse me?' Sebastian was incredulous. 'He got into trouble when he decided to break into our premises and access private information. He has no further rights of his own, and he's certainly violated ours. I think we've been very fair under the circumstances.'

'By scaring the life out of him with this ridiculous game?' Pam snapped back. 'What do you want from him?'

'I thought I'd made that pretty clear. Your friend needs to be shown that the city is not his personal playground. There are parts he is simply not qualified to enter.' He held up his hand and ticked off each point on his fingers. 'He is not free to publish whatever he feels like writing. We could simply wait for him to try and then sue his publisher for libel, but that's not the Promethean way. We intend this challenge to be instructive. I hope that eventually it will teach him how to behave in a once-civilised society such as ours. I was prepared to give him a fighting chance of publishing his book. I told him that if he completed all ten challenges successfully, he would be released from his contract with us –'

'Vince signed no contract.'

'Released from his contract,' he said, talking over her, 'and allowed to enter a modified version of his report for publication.'

'What do you mean a modified version? One that you've censored and rewritten?'

'I intend to fact-check it, yes,' he agreed. 'Which brings me to the main purpose of this meeting. We know he made two hard copies of his manuscript. Where are they? Who has them?'

'Why don't you ask him?'

'I'm asking you, Pamela. Is one of them in your charming Primrose Hill apartment?'

She had not told them her name, or where she lived. How the hell did they know?

'Look, I don't know what you think you're playing at –' she began.

'Oh for fuck's sake just tell me where I can find the fucking manuscripts!' he shouted in her face. 'Do you have either of them, and if you don't, where do you suppose they are? I can't be any plainer than that.'

His sudden change of mood alarmed her. Pam tried to think clearly. She knew the location of both manuscripts, but there might be even more than two. Vince had meticulously covered his tracks. Esther Goldstone had one copy. There could conceivably be another at the college or in Vince's apartment. Anyway, there was bound to be a version of it on disk somewhere. She doubted there was much point in trying to bluff Sebastian. His diatribe against declining standards had failed to explain the night's entertainment or his pleasure in finding a worthy opponent, and there was something in his defensive attitude that suggested another more mysterious purpose behind his bursts of self-righteous anger. If this was just a diversion for bored rich kids, it was an absurdly baroque one.

'I thought you valued your sense of fair play,' said Pam. 'If you destroy Vince's manuscript, you'll have cheated him.'

'I have no intention of destroying it. He will still be allowed to publish, but the version we'll produce together will be more balanced. I wish to prevent his earlier version from being released, that's all.'

Pam eyed him balefully. 'I don't believe you.'

'I'm hardly fascinated by your beliefs, Pamela. Earlier this evening my men took Vince's apartment to pieces. We found the manuscript on the hard-drive of his computer and wiped it, then destroyed all his disks. We searched his college locker and wiped both of the back-up copies we found there. I'm afraid all his course-work was destroyed in the process. All his research. All his previous writings.'

'Oh no –'

'You forget that I know how he thinks, Pamela. I know his mind. He trusted me. I know how he works, how he researches, how many copies he keeps, and I'm sure he struck two hard copies from the disks. He told me he always does. Now, there were no copies in his apartment, so what has he done with them? Given one to his agent, presumably, so we can get hold of that easily enough. But the other one, there's the mystery. Perhaps that's something you can shed some light on.' Poor Carol Mendacre hadn't been in possession of it. Or if she had, it had burned with her.

'You have no right to involve other people in this,' she said.

'Vince's agent helped to plan these half-baked books, Pamela. She encouraged Vince to spy on us. I think she has every right to be involved. But perhaps you can dissuade the members of the League from upsetting her too badly.' He leaned forward, his generous smile filling her vision. 'All you have to do is tell us where the remaining copy is.'

'I don't know where Vince would have put it.'

'Then I suggest you start thinking fast.' A door at the rear of the room opened and closed. Sebastian rose to his feet. 'Ah, good. There's someone I want you to meet.'

Pam looked up at Barwick, who was performing a hasty shamefaced shuffle out of the way. The pale, hollow-cheeked man who came and stood before her was clad from neck to toe in black, and although he was physically large seemed insubstantial, as if a beam of bright light might be able to penetrate him like a wraith.

'This gentleman is Mr Xavier Stevens, Pamela, and it pays to be his friend. He's here to help find out if you're telling us less than you know. And, I think it's time –' he checked his Cartier Panthere '– to raise the stakes a little. Vincent is still breaking the rules. He's enlisting outside help. So we're going to do the same. And if he fails to meet any one of the remaining challenges, there's going to be a forfeit. You, Pamela.' Sebastian gave Stevens a gentle pat on the shoulder. 'Xavier will forfeit you.'

CHAPTER THIRTY-THREE

Stitches, Sequins And Sex

JASON WENTWORTH raised his throbbing head and looked around. He found himself in a tiny room constructed of sweating bare bricks, propped up in a wicker armchair, surrounded by what appeared to be sequinned sixties' cocktail frocks and wigs. Hanging on the wall was a tattered pantomime cow's head. A broad white bandage was swathed across his bare stomach. When he tried to sit up properly, it felt as if someone was pouring boiling water over his gut.

'Where am I?' he asked weakly. 'Eric? What are you doing here? What the hell's going on?'

'You'll split your stitches if you don't stay still, fidgetty-bot,' complained an ugly elderly man seated at a make-up mirror across from his chair. He was patting the fleshy oval of his face with pink powder, testing bee-sting lips. 'Drink your tea while it's still hot.' He wore a bulging string vest and a lime green ballet tutu. 'You've been in a fight, dear, but you're going to be fine so long as you keep very still.'

'What time is it?'

Eric checked a minuscule gold watch hanging from a pair of rubber breasts above the mirror. 'Ten to three. The security at The Grotto had to make a full report to the police about your 'incident' and of course they lied through their teeth. None of those boys will ever go to heaven. You was stabbed, dear,' he said loudly, as if having a conversation with someone who was profoundly deaf. 'The cops wanted to ask you questions, but the boys got you out. Do you remember what happened, or don't you want to tell me?'

'There's nothing to tell,' he replied, nervously wondering where his multi-coloured dreamcoat had disappeared to. 'Some geezer didn't like the look of my face.'

'It wasn't your face we was worried about. The blade of that knife only just missed your stomach wall. It's a good job you was wearing that jacket of yours. Buggered up the kapok lining.'

'Where is my coat?' He was sure it had been ripped off for the drugs before he had even hit the floor.

'Behind you on the door. I had Malibu Sidney take it off you before the cops turned up. Don't worry, everything's still in it.' Thank God, thought Wentworth. His entire investment was tied up in that mind-altering garment. He realised with a shock that his former pupil had not paid him for the uppers, either.

'What do you reckon on them bandages? I did a nice job, didn't I?'

'You did this? What, stitches and everything?'

'Well, we couldn't let you be taken to hospital while you had God knows what tucked about your person, could we?' Eric explained, lighting a cigarette from the butt of his last. He was performing at the pub tonight for the benefit of a local AIDS charity. The bar would remain open until

5:00 a.m. and the last bleary-eyed patron would stagger out at 7:00 a.m. Not like the old days, when last orders were called at twenty-past ten. He preferred the old days. Ah well.

By day Eric worked as a nurse at Charing Cross Hospital, where he also held a position as a bereavement counsellor working in the same team as Betty, but it was the nightwork he undertook performing with his drag troupe that really made the money. This was not the first time he'd agreed to help Wentworth out, but who could resist him? There was a sense of lost innocence and something worth saving about the boy, even though the 'boy' had to be in his early thirties by now. Eric always told his friends that the drag routine helped him to relax, but the simple truth was that he loved doing it. He had been applying his make-up and hoping that Betty would come over to see his act when news reached him that Wentworth had been attacked.

'Did they catch the bloke who did it?'

'Darling, that building has too many exits to stop people from leaving sharpish. You get a kip – I've got to go on in a minute. You're not in any danger. I gave you a couple of pain-killers and a strong antibiotic to prevent infection, so I hope you haven't taken anything else tonight. Now it's down to you to rest and stay out of trouble. That means no dealing for a while, Jase, you understand?'

But that, he knew, was impossible, because the second Eric left him he would be up and attempting to head back to the club.

'I've got to get back, Eric. Maudsley will need feeding.'

'The boys brought her over so she could be with you. She's by the door.'

Wentworth winced in pain as he pulled the reluctant terrier forward. He'd named it Maudsley after the famous schizophrenics' home in Denmark Hill where his mother had spent the later years of her life.

'Dog-minder, wound dresser, Jill Of All Trades, that's me, and don't keep calling me Eric, only you and my dear sainted mother know that name and I'd like to keep it that way thank you.'

Maudsley seemed determined not to enter the star's dressing room. Wentworth had to admit that the smell of cheap perfume and hair lacquer knocked the breath from most people.

They were in a converted storage room at the back of a pub in Vauxhall, a few feet from the pungent half-flooded toilets and a cramped bar area where a mixed crowd of two hundred locals, regulars, tourists and slumming yuppies waited for Eric and his well-drilled team to hurl themselves about the stage in shameless abandon. The dressing room was part of the old beer cellar, and was decked in gaudy harlequin rags the colours of a Battenburg cake. Eric gave up his attempt to glue a sapphire-studded caterpillar of eyelash onto his right lid, and studied Jason's stomach in his make-up mirror.

'Seriously, I don't want you going back there no matter how good you reckon your constitution is.'

'Heaven must be missing an angel, Eric.'

'Fuck heaven, dear. They've got quite enough of my friends already. Listen, I'm going on now, so what do you need?'

'I was supposed to meet this bloke just before it happened, and I need to find him again. It was a big deal.'

'Oh you and your deals, you're always just "meeting a bloke". You know I don't approve. I wonder what your missus thinks. Well, he won't be there now, not with the lights up and the plods swarming. Is there anything else?'

'I've got no cash on me. Can you lend us a tenner?'

Eric shoved a coatstand of sequinned gowns and feather boas to one side and blew away a dune of face powder in order to make some space on his desk top. On this he upturned the contents of his evening bag. Among the mound of seventies' colour cosmetics he found a ten-pound note, clamped it between coral nails and passed it across.

'You haven't got a coat I can borrow, have you?'

'Fucking hell, take the shirt off my back, you will,' complained Eric. 'Have a look in the alcove. You might find something that fits you. Don't put any pressure on that wound or you'll end up in hospital. Wait till you see the gorgeous cross-stitching I've done on your tummy. It's not surgery, it's art. Hang on.' He emptied some small white pills from a tin on the desk. 'If you insist on staying up all night you'd better take a couple of these every three hours. The stitches will hurt like buffalo after the pain-killers wear off, but these'll get you through.'

Outside the crowd were starting to slow-clap in unison. Eric dug out a heavy navy-blue Schott jacket that had belonged to a former lover and had somehow migrated into the troupe's wardrobe hamper.

'Go on, then, take it, but I want it back. Got sentimental value, has that, seeing as the owner, a man very dear to my heart, is no longer with us.'

'Did he die?' asked Wentworth, checking the sleeves for length.

'Good God, no, he's in jail in Singapore for soliciting. Go on, bugger off and let me do my act.'

'What is it tonight?'

'Tarts medley, Madonna and Child sketch, bad disco medley, drunk Liza Minelli sketch, anti-Tory medley, Michael

Portillo in drag. They'll love us. This crowd is so pissed David Mellor could come on and strip down to a g-string and still get a round of applause. Oh, hello, who's this nice young man?'

Vince stood uncomfortably in the doorway, his fist poised to knock on the half-open door.

'Come inside, dear, don't be strange.'

Vince entered the cramped dressing room and nearly choked on the overpowering scent of hairspray. Wentworth looked terrible. His face was the colour of stale dough.

'Vince, how'd you find me, man?'

'I brought him over.' Betty stepped around them and found a place to perch. She had changed into a short black skirt, boots and a white T-shirt. Vince felt an alarming stirring in his jeans as he studied her.

'Here, I've still got your letter, man.' He tried to twist around in the wicker chair, but the stitches in his stomach tightened and stung. Vince reached behind him and felt inside the jacket, extracting the crumpled page. It had only broken into quarters. He could tell by the discoloration of the paper that some sheets had been less chemically treated than others.

'Just don't burst them stitches or Mother will be very fucking angry with you,' admonished Eric. He tucked a ratty blanket around Wentworth and eyed Vince lasciviously. 'Now you must let this poor boy get some rest. Surely there's something Betty can find for you to do upstairs. Come on, get your arses out of the fucking way and let an artiste get to the stage before they start chucking beer bottles.' Eric had disappeared, his character superseded by a more waspish persona, an alter-ego that regarded the punters through cynical spangled eyes for a moment before slipping between the mouldy red velvet curtains and acknowledging the entrance music to the roar of an appreciative crowd.

Vince looked back at Wentworth, curled in the wicker chair, to find that he had already fallen asleep.

'We should do as he says,' said Betty. 'Eric's suggestions are usually for the best.' She took his hand and led him from the claustrophobic cell to a narrow staircase covered in a dozen layers of black paint. It led behind the stage to a dingy linoleum-floored corridor above the bar.

'Follow me.'

'Where are we going?' he asked, although he already had a pretty good idea. She pushed open the first of the doors they reached and led him inside, backing him against the far wall of a tiny bedroom lit by a single red bulb. The sleet that drifted against the cracked window above the bed was turning into rain. Water leaked through the bottom of the casement and dripped from a black fungal patch in the corner of the ceiling, yet the room felt inviting and warm, like a gypsy caravan. Coloured scarves of every hue hung from the walls and formed a crumpled quilt on the bed.

Betty placed her hands against the wall, on either side of his head.

'People say I'm too aggressive. Do you think I'm too aggressive?'

'No.' Vince swallowed. 'If you want something, you should go out and get it.'

'Well, I don't normally have to do that. It usually comes here, sent up those stairs. But there are nights. Bad weather slows some people down. Not me.'

Her tongue flickered hotly in his mouth, her citrus-scented hair enveloping his neck. She undressed him quickly, clipping open the belt of his jeans with practised ease, and sat him naked on the corner of the bed while she disrobed. Vince had no illusions about the profession of his new-found friend. As she freed her breasts from her T-shirt and shivered out of her panties to lay beside him, he could only marvel at her libidinous grin, her shameless touch, her miraculous body and her spectacularly inappropriate sense of timing.

CHAPTER THIRTY-FOUR

Clue, Cat And Tortoise

NIGHT-TIME LONDON had entered a new phase now, a temporal no-man's-land between departing clubbers and arriving cleaners. The sky, if not exactly dark, was becoming less reflective. By five it would be as deep as ink. There was still plenty of life on the streets, in coffee bars, at night-bus stops, but it was more subdued, less optimistic, less reputable, wearier and warier. Down by the river, the plangent tone of Big Ben tolled the half-hour. On the other side of the turpid waters, Vince was back on the street and the phone, sheltering from an elemental downpour. Ahead of him, the last of the night's traffic straggled across the rain-misted bridge towards the city.

'What was the next one on the list?' Harold Masters asked.

'*Fleury*,' said Vince, trying to read the decimated shards of paper in his hand. 'I've only got about three quarters of an hour left before my cut-off time,' he added guiltily.

'Bear with us – we're writing them down. How are your batteries holding up?'

'Oh, they're great now,' he was about to say, until he realised that the doctor was referring to his mobile phone. Physically he felt – what was the word – re-energised, with freshly pumped-up voltage, prepared to face the vicissitudes of the remaining dark hours. After their lovemaking, Betty had dried the sweat on his chest and smiled a crooked, knowing smile at him. Holding a silencing finger to her crescent lips, she had slipped back into her clothes and vanished into the crowded pub downstairs. She wasn't the kind of girl who said goodbye, because she knew he'd come calling again; he still had her card, memories of her thighs, the small of her back, her opal eyes.

Vince checked the power level on the phone. 'They're all right at the moment, but I've not much change for public boxes. I'm low on money and nowhere near a cashpoint, and there are still four challenges to complete.'

'Okay, we're working on it, don't panic.'

'I know what they are,' said Maggie Armitage excitedly, flapping a ringed hand at the doctor, 'why won't anyone listen to me?'

'Sssh, I can't hear him very well.' Masters held his receiver closer.

'People don't listen to you, Margaret, because you get everything wrong,' Stanley Purbrick complained. 'You new age people are all the same with your lovely warm wibbly-wobbly vibrations and purple auras, but when it comes down to hard facts and figures you ignore the evidence. New age? Symptoms of old age, more like.'

'Oh, for the love of Mithras don't give us your government infiltration theories again,' complained Maggie. 'Call me narrow-minded but I think there's a bit of a difference between you insisting that Margaret Thatcher was involved in the cloning of Ronald Reagan's sperm to create a new breed of super-politicians, and my beliefs about astral alignment.'

'The main difference is that my theories are rooted in

scientific reality and yours involve waving a bit of crystal about on a thong.'

'Your aura turns a very unpleasant shade of heliotrope when you start being rude, did you know that?'

'I wonder if you two could give it a rest for five minutes and help out here?' asked Jane Masters, pointing to her husband holding the telephone receiver.

Maggie pushed herself forward, elbowing Stanley away. 'They're crosses. Tell him they're all types of crosses. Heraldic ones, all kinds. There are drawings in this book, look.' She held the pages open for all to see. 'They're not just Christian, you know. The ancient Egyptians used them as sacred symbols. And the Aztecs.'

'There used to be a chocolate bar called an Aztec,' said Purbrick, morosely hoisting a bottle of red wine over his empty glass.

'Vince, we think they're crosses,' said Masters. 'Though I don't see a connection between such artefacts and the Anne Boleyn lines.'

'Suppose the lines were just there to point Vince towards Anne Boleyn,' said Jane.

'So what?' asked Purbrick. 'She's connected with all sorts of places.'

'Think about the crosses. Is there a particular church associated with her? What about the chapel at Hever Castle?'

'But that's not London, is it?' said Jane.

'Isn't there an exhibition at the National Portrait Gallery, something about the Treasures of Hever Castle? Paintings on loan.'

'Does anybody have a newspaper?' asked Arthur Bryant.

'There's one in the rack over there.'

Maggie tore open a copy of the *Independent* with a

theatrical flourish and began intently scouring the pages, which was a waste of time because she was looking at the sports section, having left her reading glasses in a vegetarian restaurant in Tooting the night before. 'Nothing in here,' she concluded. 'Pass me the *Guardian*.'

But Masters had already found the appropriate advertisement. 'Here you are, "Treasures of Hever Castle", opening tomorrow at the National Portrait Gallery, and there's a reproduction of one of the pictures.'

'Oh, it's the famous one,' said Jane, 'the portrait of Anne Boleyn by Hans Holbein. That would fit the bill.'

'That's where you have to go,' Masters told Vince. 'Then I guess you need to find something with a lot of crucifixes.'

'It had better be on the outside of the building, or nearby. I certainly won't be able to get in.'

'Saint Martin in the Fields is opposite. Could that mean something?'

'No,' said Vince. 'This is something in or on a painting, I'm sure of it.' He knew how much Sebastian admired monarchist art. Holbein's portrait of Boleyn would have struck a chord with him. Perhaps he simply expected Vince to break a window and find the next letter before anyone could catch him, but such an attempt would be suicidal.

'Hang on a second.' The doctor turned to Purbrick. 'Who do we know at the National?'

'George Stokes has been there for over thirty years,' said the elderly gentleman who had just let himself in from the hall. 'A good man. Helped me sort out some nasty business with a vandalised Pre-Raphaelite a couple of years ago.'

'Do you have his home number?' Masters turned his attention back to the telephone. 'Listen Vince, this is going to take some organisation. If what you're being sent to retrieve is inside the gallery, we'd have to get the keys and the alarm codes for the entry system.'

'Is that possible?' asked Vince, his voice fuzzing as a truck passed.

'I wouldn't have thought so, but it's worth checking out. Head in that direction and we'll call you back.'

'Wait, you don't have my number.'

'Last number redial!' they exclaimed in unison.

'That's the trouble with young people today,' said Maggie Armitage, still trying to read the newspaper. 'They've a very poor grasp of modern technology.'

'Have I been missing something?' asked the frail elderly gentleman, unwinding a length of ratty red scarf from his throat. To those who did not know him well, Arthur Bryant was a cantankerous old tortoise who crept about the city in a rusty blue Mini Minor. He was two years past retirement age and capable of only the most rudimentary politeness to a handful of close acquaintances. Shunning technology, buried beneath scarves, forever complaining, he lived only for his investigative work at the North London Serious Crimes Division, housed above the tube station at Mornington Crescent.

As his commissions grew more prosaic and less taxing, he kept his agile brain alive by arguing with his partner John May, and by paying regular visits to Masters and his charming wife. For twenty years Bryant and May had shared an office at Bow Street police station before moving north, working the cases no one else wanted, and evolving some highly unorthodox methods. Their knowledge of London and its fringe elements was unique and indispensable, and gave them an advantage over younger officers.

'Arthur, you're late again,' the doctor pointed out. 'You were supposed to be here ages ago.'

'Oh, I had some difficulty with Bunthorne,' explained Bryant, rummaging around in the pockets of his voluminous tweed overcoat. A puzzled look crossed his wrinkled features for a moment, then he pulled a ginger cat from one of the pockets.

'What on earth have you got there?'

'Well, that was the problem with Bunthorne, you see. All this time I thought he was a tom, but tonight he wandered into my bedroom and rather unexpectedly produced four kittens. I had to leave Alma with them.'

'But that's not a new-born kitten,' said Maggie, pointing to the ginger cat that was now contentedly threading its way through the legs of the assembly.

'No, you're right there,' said Bryant vaguely. 'It's a stray I picked up on the way over. I had cats on the mind, and the snow was starting to turn to rain, and the little thing was shivering inside a scrap of binliner on Battersea Bridge. A bowl of warmed milk would probably please it, Jane. Then perhaps someone could explain what all the excitement's about.'

CHAPTER THIRTY-FIVE

Persuading George

XAVIER STEVENS studied his quarry carefully. He knew this type, the empty-headed secretary aspiring to nothing more than a mortgage in the suburbs and a husband who didn't fuck around on her. She'd be hard-nosed for a while, then start wanting to go home when she realised he wasn't joking, and that was when he could start looking forward to making her cry.

'What are you going to do, stick bamboo shoots under my fingernails?' Pam shut her eyes wearily. 'You're all silly little boys. None of you know when to stop playing games.'

'You're the only one who thinks it's a game.' He resited the kitchen chair and perched himself before her, legs apart, hands on knees. 'If my colleague Mr Wells doesn't get all of the copies of this damaging document, there is a chance – wouldn't you say – that it might be published after all. And if it is published, with all of its inaccuracies and character smears, Mr Wells and his colleagues will be publicly embarrassed. Are you with me so far?'

'People can say what they like. It's a free country.'

'But freedom itself is a prison. Does no one read Sartre any more?' He stared at her with poorly concealed contempt.

'Think it through. What good will it do anyone to publish? It will simply help to destroy a respected institution, and upset a lot of people who really should not be upset. The best thing you could do – for us and yourself – is speak with Reynolds and get him to surrender the other copy to you. You're his best friend. Who else can he trust at this precise moment?'

'You want me to betray him?'

Stevens looked around at the walls, incredulous. 'Well obviously!' He raised a hand. 'I know, I know all about you people and your fierce working-class loyalties.' *Cheek*, she thought, having always considered herself at least aspirationally middle class. 'But if I don't get hold of the remaining document before dawn, I'm going to start cutting off your toes.' He fished about in the pocket of his black leather jacket and produced a pair of ominously heavy-duty wire cutters. 'I'll do it cleanly at the joint – I always do – but I won't give you the piece I remove, so you won't be able to have it sewn back on. Without it, you'll find that your sense of balance is adversely affected. So if you don't want to spend the rest of your life falling over, go ahead and make that call.' He raised her right foot and gently eased off the tight pink pump, caressing her toes through her tights.

Sweat broke out on Pam's forehead. This, from a managerial point of view, was the worst possible thing that could happen to her. The thought of facing a corporate career with missing appendages was too much to contemplate. Even so, she had no intention of telling them where the other manuscript was, even if she could be absolutely sure of what Louie had done with it.

'It will do you no good threatening me with violence,' she said bravely. 'I can't fear you because I understand your motives. This cruel streak is to do with the inadequacy you feel about the size of your penis, isn't it?'

'George Stokes will not be thrilled about being woken at this time of the morning, and even less so by the idea of leaving his cosy house in East Finchley to travel back into the city,' said Bryant. 'Besides, reopening the museum after hours is inconceivable. The board of governors would have him removed from his post for committing such a breach of the rules. The gallery is a treasurehouse of works held in trust for the nation. He can do nothing that might put so many priceless paintings at risk.' He took a sip of tea. 'Sod it, let's call him anyway.'

But George Stokes was not at home, his wife sleepily informed them. As luck would have it, he was working late at the gallery itself, making final preparations for the Hever Castle exhibition which was due to open in just a few hours' time. They could call him there. These days he spent more time at the gallery than he did at home. She gave them the number of his direct line.

'It's completely out of the question, Harold,' Stokes explained, answering after an age (he had been lost in the pages of the *Model Car Collectors 1996 Price Guide*, trying to work out the value of his boxed 'Goldfinger' Aston Martin DB5 while his assistant was off in the toilet). 'There would be all hell to pay if something got damaged.'

'But can you physically do it?' asked Masters.

'Of course. There are a number of senior keyholders, but only three of us know the disarming code for the alarm at any one time. It changes –' he had been about to tell Masters how often it changed, and thought better of it '– all the time. And every setting is recorded by computer. There's just me and

Albert here, watching the monitors.'

'Oh George, stop being so damnably clavigerous.'

'I'm not, I'm – what does that mean?'

'Custodial,' said Masters, 'key-bearing.'

'But that's what I am, Harold, the bearer of the keys to a national institution.'

'It's not the Bank of England.'

'No, but its contents are probably worth more.'

Masters decided it was time for a little blackmail. 'George, how long have we known each other?' he asked gently. 'I'll tell you. We first met in 1967. That's how long. I've never given you bad advice since then, have I?'

'No, of course not, but what you're asking is beyond reason –'

'Is it unreasonable to want to protect what's right and good against the forces of evil?' he asked. 'If the boy fails to complete the tasks set for him this night, his work will be repressed, his very life will be in danger. This is not a third-world dictatorship, George, it's not Communist China, it's England, and if you're prepared to see everything you stand for eroded by those who abuse their power and use intimidation to gain their ends, then you're not the man I thought you were.'

'And you think this jingoistic bollocks will win me over, do you?'

'I have someone here who wants to talk to you,' said Masters, passing the receiver to the elderly detective.

'Now, George, I hope you're not going to be squeamish about this,' said Bryant. 'I can't make you help us, even though the NLSCD has helped you before, because I don't believe in making folk feel guilty by holding favours over their heads, but I do think you should get downstairs to the gallery floor and open it before my clumsy great lads set off up there and kick in a few windows answering a tip-off about intruders.'

'Arthur, you're talking about admitting an outsider into one of the nation's most prestigious institutions. I have a duty –'

'And I have a duty to uphold the law,' interrupted Bryant. 'These men are killers, and they may well strike again tonight. It seems likely from what I'm hearing here that we won't have a hope in hell of stopping them through the regular channels. Now George, you know there must be a point at which our duties intersect.'

'None of you are listening to me. I simply *cannot* place national treasures at risk. In the first place I don't have this kind of authorisation. Secondly, the video cameras record everything that happens here –'

'I didn't want to have to do this,' said Bryant with a sad sigh. 'George, forgive my retrogression, but do you remember the fishing expedition to Kerry, where you lost your head over that pretty little colleen at the hotel and arrived home a day late, and how you persuaded me to explain to your poor dear lady wife that the fog had prevented us from reaching the airport?'

'That was fifteen years ago –'

'The pain of infidelity is undimmed by time.'

'You're a right bastard, Bryant, you know that?' He thought for a moment. 'How long would the alarm system have to be off for?'

Got him, thought Bryant.

'Five minutes at the most,' he replied.

'I suppose if it appeared that there was a line fault with the system, I could have the entry circuits and the motion detectors switched off for two or three minutes, but no more than that. I don't know what I'd tell Albert.'

'Send him off to make tea or something.'

'The closed circuit monitors would have to be shut down, too. This boy has to find a letter, you say?'

'That's right.'

'Do you know which gallery it's in?'

Masters reclaimed the receiver. 'Perhaps you could help with that. We're looking for a painting in the Hever exhibition that features lots of crucifixes. There may be some kind of Chaucerian quote on the frame.'

'God, Harold, do you have any idea how many paintings there are in here? Your lad would have to know exactly where he was going. There'd be no time to mess about. If I know which gallery he's heading for I'll only have to disarm one sector, and it'll look less suspicious.'

'Tell him we'll work out where Vince has to go by the time he gets there,' hissed Maggie, tugging Masters's sleeve. 'There's less than thirty minutes left.' She looked questioningly at the rest of the group. 'Well, we can work it out in that time, can't we?'

CHAPTER THIRTY-SIX

The Fail-Safe

THE ENTRANCE to the National Portrait Gallery was in darkness as Vince crossed Charing Cross Road by the rain-darkened statue of Edith Cavell, and the rotund little man who suddenly stepped from the shadows made him jump.

'Mr Stokes?' he asked.

'Quick, come inside, out of the light.' He beckoned frantically, then pointed up at the wall. The gallery's security cameras were aimed down at the glistening pavement before them. 'I'm given to understand that it's a matter of national urgency for you to get in here,' he said, shaking his hand. 'Now you listen to me. I don't hold with breaking the law, but it's lucky for you that you're dealing with old friends of mine. I can sympathise with what they've told me, about these toffs holding you to ransom, like. I'm self-taught, me, from Burnley. Came to London in the fifties to make meself a living, and I've done all right. So, as I said, I sympathise. Dr Masters assures me that nothing illegal is to take place, but the fact is that you will be trespassing once we pass beyond this point. I must exact a solemn promise from you, therefore, not to touch any of the exhibits.'

'You have my word on that,' said Vince. Stokes saw how

wet and tired the boy was, and a wave of pity swept over him. 'You look done in, lad,' he said, his Lancashire accent broadening in sympathy. 'Bet it's been a pretty rough night for you. Let's get you inside.'

'That's just it,' he replied miserably. 'They haven't called back with the location yet. I don't know where I'm going once I'm in.'

'I don't have a catalogue of all the paintings,' complained Masters. 'How are we supposed to know exactly which picture has lots of crucifixes in it? It's absurd.'

'Can't he just head for the area with the most religious paintings,' asked Stanley Purbrick, kicking Bryant's stray cat out from under his feet, 'triptychs, altar-pieces, that sort of thing?'

'It's a bit hit and miss, isn't it?' said the doctor's wife. 'Maggie, don't you have any bright ideas?'

'Don't encourage her,' complained Purbrick, 'she'll want to hold another séance, and I'm still recovering from the last one. All those talking cats frightened the life out of me.'

'There's something odd about the list,' said Mrs Armitage, her voice muffled as she struggled into a voluminous yellow sweater. 'Surely the bottom name isn't a type of cross, is it? *Aimee*? Harold, don't you know?'

'I've never heard of one if there is.'

'What about the final line of poetry?' asked Arthur Bryant, removing his bifocals and screwing up his eyes at the sheet of paper Maggie had passed to him. 'You said it was Chaucerian?'

'I think so. I mean, the spelling is mediaeval and the sentiment feels right . . .'

'*Aimee*. French for loved?' Bryant tapped a pencil against his teeth. 'Aimee . . .'

The book Maggie slammed shut made them all jump. 'That settles it. The others are all definitely crosses. "Aimee" is not a cross.'

'Aimee. A crucifix. Anne Boleyn. What an odd group.'

They made an odd group too, seated in a circle at the dining-room table, hunched beneath twin cones of light thrown by the pair of bronze-green Victorian lamps, books, teacups and wineglasses scattered all about the rumpled tablecloth. Jane Masters rose to her feet. 'I'm going to make some more coffee,' she said with an air of finality. 'Someone should call poor George and let him know that we're stumped. Having got him to agree to this, you can't leave him in the dark.'

It was a bad line, not helped by the fact that Vince answered in a whisper. 'What have you got for me?' he asked, trying to keep their conversation brief.

'Put Mr Stokes on, would you?'

'They want to speak to you.' Vince handed him the phone. Stokes eyed it warily, then gingerly lowered his cheek near it, as though scared of being bitten. 'Hello?'

Masters carefully explained the problem.

'Amy?' asked Stokes, confused. 'Who's Amy?'

'No – Aimee. Wait – the Holbein exhibition, where is it situated?'

'On the lower ground floor at the back. Why?'

'I want you to go there and see if you can see a cross or crosses of some sort. Then call me back.'

'Don't you have any idea where this thing is, then?'

'If I did, I'd tell you, wouldn't I?' said Masters sourly.

The interior of the gallery was as cool and silent as any

garden of remembrance. Marble columns tapered into blackness, but it was not possible to switch the lights on without tripping one of the alarms for which Stokes did not have a code. The custodian reached up on tiptoe and opened the steel case of a box behind the reception desk, then punched in a series of numbers that caused a dozen rows of red LEDs to pulse.

'Four minutes,' he explained, 'that's how long we've got before the system overrides my manual command and turns itself back on. It's a fail-safe.' Stokes flicked on his torch and shone the beam ahead. 'Let's go.'

They ran as quietly as they could across sheets of squeaking marble to the rear of the building, then down the staircase to the lower ground level. Merely crossing the floors took over a minute. Vince's boots squealed as he slid to a stop. Stokes raised his torch and a startling image confronted them.

There stood Holbein's portrait of 'Anna Bullen', a tragic English noblewoman dead for over four and a half centuries, immortalised in paint by a German genius. The trusting innocence of her eyes was matched by the simple elegance of her dress. Three thin chains of gold adorned her neck. The hindsight of her tragedy steeped her portrait in an aura of unbearable melancholy.

Stokes shone his light around the walls, illuminating the courtiers and courtesans of a long-forgotten world. The beam skittered across portrait after portrait, briefly subjecting each to scrutiny.

'What about over there?' Stokes suggested.

Vince ran up to the banks of paintings. 'Crosses,' he whispered back. 'Hundreds of the bastards.' There were priests and cardinals, nuns, deacons, bishops, tortured sinners, penitents, martyred saints, crucifixes in almost every painting. 'Damn. How long have we got left?'

'Two and a half minutes. There won't be time to get back –'

'Wait a minute.'

Stokes was puzzled to see him punching out a number on the illuminated buttons of the phone.

'No service.' Vince snapped the mobile shut. 'Payphone?'

'Just over there.' Stokes flicked the torch beam to the far wall. 'You've got to hurry.'

'I think I've found the right cross,' he announced as the call connected. Stokes came over frowning and mouthing the word 'Where?'

He pointed at the ground. Stokes looked down, then his eyeline returned to the Holbein painting. The broad violet carpet runners laid across the white marble floor bisected one another directly in front of the painting, forming one gigantic ianthine crucifix, with two smaller ones on either side.

'Well I'll be damned,' said Stokes.

'Where does the top of it point?' asked Masters.

Vince shone the torch up on a Pre-Raphaelite painting of two lovers standing beside a tree.

'That's not normally there,' Stokes explained. 'It belongs in Birmingham City Art Gallery. It's on loan.'

'What is it?' asked Vince.

'Not to my taste at all,' said Stokes. 'All that preachy Victorian stuff is like stuffing yourself with iced buns, too sickly. I prefer something more robust. Tintoretto's more my style –'

'The painting, man, what is it?' Masters fairly shouted over the line.

While Vince stretched the telephone cord as far as it would reach, Stokes peered close at the painting with his torch held high. 'It's called *The Long Engagement,* by Arthur Hughes.'

'I've got it,' cried Maggie, proudly holding the picture up for everyone to see.

'Well, what does it say?'

'It was originally called *Orlando in the Forest of Arden.* The artist replaced the central figure with lovers after the picture was rejected by the Royal Academy.' She read aloud. ' "The woman waits for her lover to marry her, even though she has been waiting so long that ivy has grown over her name, carved into the tree's bark." Amy,' she said, closing the book. 'The girl's name is Amy.'

CHAPTER THIRTY-SEVEN

No Witnesses

'I REALLY have to make a phone call,' said Pam, shifting uncomfortably in the armchair where Xavier Stevens had unceremoniously dumped her. 'They have no right to keep me here like this.'

'Sebastian doesn't see it like that,' said Barwick apologetically. 'I can't untie your hands again. He'd be furious with both of us.'

'One call, Horace. I promise I won't get you into trouble. It's not as if I'm going to ring the police or anything.' She wriggled and grimaced, pantomiming pain. 'At least find some proper rope.'

She had turned on the waterworks and admitted to Xavier Stevens that the other disk containing Vince's manuscript was carefully hidden in the bottom drawer of her office desk, failing to mention that, having suffered a series of break-ins, the estate agency was abnormally well alarmed, and the disk wasn't there anyway. She prayed he would get caught astride the window ledge in a blaze of light, but doubted her luck would hold out that far; if he didn't, he might well return in a less amenable frame of mind.

Vince had hand-delivered one of the disks to Esther

Goldstone a few days ago, and, she knew, had planned to give Louie the other. She had no idea where it had gone from there, but knowing Louie, he had probably left it in the pub.

At least she was holding her own against these arrogant young men, standing up to them. She could be just as bloody-minded as they were. She felt that the lessons she had learned in her most recent business management course (*'Hidden Persuasion at the Negotiating Table: The Art of Striking a Deal'*) were starting to pay off, and decided to put more of them into practice. Mark your man, they taught her, mark and mirror him. 'Now listen to me, Horace,' she wheedled, making eyes at the alarmed Barwick, 'come and sit over here beside me. I have an interesting proposition for you.'

The envelope was sellotaped to the base of the painting's frame. George Stokes had just finished easing it free when his wristwatch started emitting a reedy beep.

'That's it, lad, our time's up. We're too late. The alarm sensors are going back on right throughout the building. I don't know how I'm going to get you out of here now.' He shone his torch back along the corridor.

'What happens if we don't make it?' asked Vince.

'Every light in and around this place goes on, and sirens start up the likes of which won't have been heard in the capital since the Second World War,' he explained grimly. 'Make for that doorway over there. Stay off the carpet, but don't go any nearer than five feet to the wall. Don't touch *anything*.'

Thirty years of prowling the museum had caused the custodian to develop a delicate, silent run that made him appear to move on invisible wires. He sped through each eerie sepulchre like a tardy ghost. Vince could see thin pencil-beams of light flicking on all around them at a height of about eighteen inches from the floor. The sparkling red latticework was like a computerised spiderweb. Breaking any one of the gossamer lines would be enough to trip the entire alarm system.

A quadrant of beams pulsed on at his feet, forcing him to slow and step between them. 'Christ,' he whispered, 'they're everywhere.'

He was about to run through the archway leading to the main entrance when a row of beams appeared like a glittering ladder across the opening. Dropping to his knees and sliding the last few feet, he was able to avoid touching them by a matter of centimetres.

They reached the hall through which Vince had entered, and Stokes dived behind the reception desk just as the last of the override switches in the steel alarm box switched itself back on.

He looked up at Vince through a sweating bushy brow. 'That was too bloody close for comfort, lad,' he panted, pulling Vince towards a small side door. 'Well, you've got your precious envelope. Arthur Bryant has used up his last favour with me. I'm going back upstairs to fabricate some story for Albert. If you get into any further difficulties tonight you're on your own, understand?'

Vince clutched the unopened letter in his hand and looked out across Trafalgar Square. He was relieved to be out of the gallery without tripping the alarms. The rain had momentarily eased, and the roads were almost empty. An odd, contemplative stillness filled the air, as if the goddess of the city had momentarily fallen asleep.

Vince dug the phone from his jacket and rang Pam, but her answering machine switched itself on. The message she had left was a week old. He wondered if Louie had returned yet. It was unlikely, but worth a try. Vince punched out his number and waited, only to find himself connected to another answering machine. He gave the recording device his present location and Harold Masters' number before ringing off. A call to Esther connected him to a third tape machine. This time he hung up.

Where were all his friends? He had never felt so completely alone. His only link to the city's warm-and-normal interior world was via the lifeline to Harold Masters. He felt like chucking in the whole thing. What was the point of continuing, anyway? Let them bury the damned book, let them shut him up and anyone else that got in their way, what difference did it really make? He could find something else to write about for Esther. If they were that clever and all-powerful, they probably possessed both copies of the manuscript by now. He should have put them somewhere safer instead of placing Esther and Louie at risk.

He was exhausted. His arms and legs were turning into dead timber. He had twisted his right knee in the gallery. If he abandoned the game now and threw away the League's damned envelope, just turned on his boot-heel and caught the first night bus home, what would Sebastian do? Kill him? Where the hell were the League anyway? Did they really have nothing better to do than watch him stumbling blindly through the night? He wanted to be back in Betty's inviting arms, not stuck here in the city he had only thought he loved. He looked across the wet road to St Martin in the Fields, at the blank eyes of the security cameras peering down from the eaves like so many metallic ravens. The question nagged at him; what would they do if he stopped?

Well, there was one way to find out. He walked over to the nearest litter bin and with a grand flourish directed at the lenses monitoring his actions, dropped the envelope in. Fuck 'em, he thought. Let's see what happens now.

'Sebastian! He's quit!' Caton-James came running up the stairs. 'He's thrown away the seventh challenge and walked off!'

Sebastian had been dozing on the couch when Caton-James came bursting in. Elgar's *Nimrod* was playing softly in the background. 'Are you sure?' he asked, rubbing his hands briskly over his face.

'St John Warner just located him on the monitor. I told you this whole thing was a stupid idea. You had to turn it into a game, didn't you? What the hell are we going to do now?'

'Shut up for a minute and let me think.' He pulled himself upright and tried to awaken his brain. The room temperature had dropped in the last hour, and the Chelsea streets had grown silent as the night deepened. 'How many more has he got to cover?'

'Four. The most important ones. You shouldn't have grouped them all together. This whole enterprise is so bloody fraught with risk it's a wonder we haven't been caught yet. If the WBI gets wind of this –'

'How could they? Show some fortitude, Bunter. There's very little actual risk involved. Reynolds needs to be frightened into completing his tasks. Does he know about his little helper being taken out of the picture?'

'We lost him for a while in Vauxhall, but I don't see how, no.'

'So, he's not in fear of his life, or anyone else's. We have to change that.'

'The girl downstairs?'

Sebastian considered the option. 'It's the most obvious

solution, but my gut reaction is to get rid of someone else. She's on the premises, which makes it risky. Someone might have spotted her coming up here. You can see the house clearly from the road. Besides, we don't know enough about her, who her family is, who she knows. I'm short of facts. Barwick could at least have interrogated her but of course he didn't, and Stevens isn't much better.'

He rose and tensed the muscles in his tired arms. 'Still, we might threaten him with her demise, not that I trust hostage situations. They always seem to end in tears. There's something irredeemably vulgar about kidnap. And I have a feeling it would encourage him to come here rather than concentrate on finishing the game. Where is Xavier, by the way?'

'Right now he's busy tearing up some estate agent's office, searching for Reynolds's copy of his text. The girl told him she'd hidden it there.'

'Get him on the phone and tell him not to bother looking.'

'You don't think he'll find it? He already turned over her flat and found nothing.'

'Just do as I say, will you? Don't try to think.'

It seemed obvious to him that Reynolds would not have risked the life of his best friend by asking her to hide the manuscript in her apartment. Having monitored Goldstone's mobile calls, Sebastian knew that one disk had been left with the agent, who was used to handling such documents, and the other with 'someone who could take care of himself'. Which narrowed it down to the last member of their trio, the one they called Louie.

'What are we going to do about Reynolds?'

Sebastian gave a theatrical sigh. His original plan had been worked out meticulously. He was nervous about extemporising now. He knew that improvisation led to mistakes.

This was what happened when he took a nap for twenty minutes – everything went to pot.

'Just leave it to me, all right?' He looked about for his jacket. 'Tell Xavier to stop wasting his time and get over to Covent Garden. Where is he at the moment, Kentish Town? At this time of night he can be there in ten minutes on that monstrous motorcycle of his. And don't take your eye from Reynolds. I want to be kept informed about where he goes and who he talks to. I don't expect anyone to come up and tell me that he's gone missing again, do you understand?'

'Where in Covent Garden do you want Stevens to go?'

Sebastian raised his eyes. 'Where do you think? To the Goldstone agency. We already gave him a key to the place. He's to bring back the other copy of Reynolds's manuscript.' He had planned to retrieve it from the agent one day when she was out of the office, but while Xavier was in a ransacking mood, he could break in and remove the disk tonight. Sebastian had a nebulous idea that news of its theft might encourage Reynolds to continue, in order to protect his last remaining copy. Well, it was worth a try. He had no other stand-by plans.

In truth, he was tired of having to sort out everything by himself. Caton-James and St John Warner were the brightest of the bunch, and that wasn't saying much. They had no initiative. They were full of fine talk, but not one of them was capable of making a decision by himself. It was his own fault for setting this whole night up in the first place. What the League really needed was someone like that soaked kid out there, running through the rainswept city.

Dinner had not been quite the success Esther had hoped for. As an experienced writer-groupie she rarely expected much beyond entertainment from her dates, but her hopes for this one had been a little higher. A sexy thirty-something writer with an axe to grind and the ability to articulate his case was a rare thing these days, but unfortunately it was coupled with an immaturity that coloured his behaviour. He had suffered a mood-swing in the restaurant, sending back his meal and picking a fight with an innocent waiter, and Esther had been forced to reconsider her motives for taking him out, quite apart from the consideration that he was married and shouldn't have been there in the first place. Compounding her first mistake, she went back to his apartment and spent several hours listening to him rant about his absent wife, whom she clearly hated for invading his heart so completely. She wondered if he had even noticed her leave.

It was almost 4:15 a.m. when she placed her key in the lock and heard what sounded like a lamp being clicked off inside her office. Sometimes, when it was this late and the weather was bad, Esther preferred to sleep at the office. It was cosy here, more familiar than the apartment that just reminded her of Morris, her ex-husband. There was a kitchen and a bathroom, and the couch folded out into a comfortable bed, although the garbage trucks ended any chance of sleeping in late.

Esther put her ear to the wall and listened. Her daughter was the only other person who had access to the suite. Warily, she pushed the door wide and found the hall in darkness. Had she left the lights on earlier? She could not remember. Lisa must have called by, she decided. But as she approached the open door of the lounge area and saw the shutters fall back in place a second too late, she knew that a stranger was there with her, and that he had heard her enter.

For a moment she was frozen in the doorway, unable to

think of her next move. Then the figure broke free from its hiding place and rushed at her, catching her in the stomach with a projected elbow and knocking her from her feet. She fell back against the jamb of the door, thumping her skull with a wallop that flooded her head with sparkles of pain. The man careened drunkenly towards the front door and was gone. Esther waited until her heart-rate had slowed before hauling herself to her feet and checking what was missing.

Her first thought proved to be correct. Vince's manuscript, labelled and transferred to a Maxell disk, had been taken from the bottom drawer of her desk. She cursed herself for touching the handle of the drawer – it would have to be fingerprinted – and noticed that her hands were shaking.

The next noise she heard puzzled her until she realised that her attacker was still in the flat. It sounded like he was opening and closing a drawer, over and over. Perhaps he thought he had knocked her out. The telephone was on the coffee table, at the other side of the room. She slowly began edging towards it.

Xavier Stevens was looking for a decent knife. He had thrown the one he had used on the dealer into the Thames, and had meant to collect another from Barwick at Sebastian's Chelsea manor. He systematically searched the kitchen and finally found a decent set of Sabatiers. Wickedly sharp, these. You could cut through the breastbone of a twenty-pound turkey with the larger ones. He selected the biggest and walked back towards the lounge.

Anyone looking into the office from the street below would have seen Esther fall, and heard the grisly thump of Stevens hammering the knife through his victim until it pinned her to the floorboards beneath the carpet. But the street was deserted save for a man so drunk that he would remember nothing in the morning. Sensing the frequency of such atrocities and not wishing to become personally involved, the city turned a blind eye to Esther Goldstone's lonely death.

CHAPTER THIRTY-EIGHT

Nonconformists

THE CALL was marred by static and the voice kept cutting out, but its identity was unmistakable. Sebastian's louche drawl had tightened with urgency. Vince wondered why it had taken him this long. He checked his watch. 4:22 a.m.

'To give up now is the same as admitting you've been wrong all along,' he wheedled.

'You can do what you like,' Vince answered wearily, 'I'm going home for a hot bath and a large whisky, and I'm going to ask a nice thick Camden plod to stand on guard outside the flat, just in case you get any bright ideas.'

'Then you should know before you decide to abandon the challenge –'

'I've already decided. I should be doing your job, mate, I'd be much better at it.'

'– that your agent will no longer be handling that pernicious diatribe you call responsible journalism. She was killed at her apartment a few minutes ago. Surprised an intruder and was brutally stabbed to death. An awful lot of blood, apparently. Sprayed gouts of it across the ceiling, would you believe. Knifed in the neck, the lungs and the kidneys. Ruined the hardwood floor. A very thorough job, though. She squealed like a pig being slaughtered. The main thing is, we got your copy from her, which just leaves the one you gave your darkie pal.'

'Fuck you, Sebastian. You're lying.'

Despite the temperature, Vince broke out in a hot sweat. Christ, not Esther, not her. What had she ever done to hurt anyone? His hatred of Sebastian swelled into something insane and almost tangible.

'I wish I was, Vincent. None of us wanted this to happen, but there you are, it has and it will again unless you continue the challenge.'

'If you're telling the truth, why should I? There's no one left to publish the damned thing now.'

'How delightfully callous and self-serving of you. I had no idea you possessed such a streak. The game, dear oafish lad, the game cannot be abandoned. We've quite a wager going this end.'

The phone line wasn't secure. Didn't he care about the call being monitored or recorded? Vince prayed he was starting to get careless. 'No. I won't do it for your amusement.'

'Then do it in the memory of your publisher and your dear dead agent. Do it for the homeless boy you befriended, and the dealer in the nightclub. Do it for Louie. Do it for *Pam*.'

He expected they'd try for Louie; he could handle himself, but Pam? How did they know about her?

'What do you mean, Sebastian?'

'She followed us home. Can we keep her?' The receiver clicked down. The call had been made from a public telephone, he could tell. He prayed that Sebastian was bluffing about Esther, but Pam – without a moment of hesitation, he turned back to the strengthening rain and the litter bin where he had discarded the envelope of the seventh challenge.

It seemed obvious that the mobile telephone had been designed by a white man; the little velcro flap he had to open on the carrying case before he could put his ear to it stuck itself to dreadlocked hair and pulled a piece away every time he made a call. Louie winced as he detached the thing from his head. No answer from Pam or Vince. It was probably just as well; the glowing numerals on his watch warned him that it was past four.

What a night – the band had performed terribly and hardly anyone he knew had bothered to show up. On his way home he half-digested a pungent kebab prepared by a grease-spattered Camden Town vendor with filthy fingernails, and had almost reached his flat when some kind of *typhoon* set in. He smoked one very strong joint and drank a couple of cans of Red Stripe, but that did not explain why there was someone standing on the first floor scaffolding outside his bedroom, or why the lower half of the window was up, admitting the pelting rain.

His first thought – that Vince was playing some kind of trick on him – vaporised when he saw the size of the man. He was taller than Vince, hunched forward with his back turned, used to moving in a surreptitious manner. He reminded Louie of the skinny burglar in the cartoon version of *101 Dalmatians*. Clearly he had just exited the flat and was about to climb down to street level. The council were arranging for the front of the building to be repainted, and had warned him about security, but he had never considered the possibility of owning anything that someone else might want.

As the burglar turned and stepped back to the edge of the scaffolding platform, Louie lunged out through the window and grabbed his ankles. The effect was dramatic. The man above lost his balance and tottered back with a yelp of surprise, but as his feet were anchored he fell forward and turned upside down so that he was hanging by his boots. Louie released his hands and the burglar hit the street, landing on his head. The fall did not render him unconscious, but when Louie jumped down and sat astride his chest, he started blacking out. In the breast pocket of the intruder's jacket was a clear plastic envelope containing a computer disk. Since Vince had entrusted the manuscript to him, it had resided safely in the vegetable crisper of Louie's refrigerator. The disk was still ice-cold.

'Who put you up to this?' Louie asked, raising his victim's face from a puddle and breathing Red Stripe into it. No answer was forthcoming, so he dropped his new friend's head on the pavement a few times. The noise made him squeamish, so he slapped the pained face beneath him on the chops, then raised his skull by tightly holding onto his front teeth.

'Tell me where Vincent is. Have you done something to him?'

Although the burglar's arms were pinned he tried to beckon Louie closer by rolling his eyes, but when his captor leaned forward he nearly had his ear bitten off. Louie had no compunction then in sitting back hard until he heard one rib crack beneath his thighs, then another. When the burglar began to whimper in pain, Louie felt sure that he would find out anything he needed to know.

Vince wiped a string of icy mucus from his nose with the back of his hand and dug deep into the bin. The envelope was covered in chips and soaked in the remains of a can of cola someone had dropped in. He tore the sopping paper open and read:

The Challenge Of Nonconformity

Opened after Defoe's Year,
Blake and Bunyan make a show.
Paradise was founded here,
Seek the Elf King, go below.

Where was he supposed to go this time? For the sake of
Esther and Pam it would be necessary to unravel the latest
puzzle quickly, but where in London was it waiting for him?
He looked down at Trafalgar Square, where throngs of
clubbers were waiting for night buses, then up towards
Cambridge Circus at the thinning traffic. The first thing was
to get off the street and make a call to his lifeline, presuming
that Dr Masters and his Insomnia Squad were still living up
to their name.

He realised he must have been standing in the sweeping
rain for several minutes, trying to formulate a plan, when a
young woman, naked from the waist up and wrapped in a
vast sheet of clear plastic called out 'You all right, Vince?' as
she passed. Vince's ears and hands were numb. The girl
should have been frozen, but if she was she didn't show it.

'Hey, Meat Rack,' he shouted back, recognising her, 'what
are you doing dressed like that?'

A nightclub in Adelaide Street was emptying out its
customers, and pavements that had been deserted moments
before were filled with a laughing, chanting urban tribe. It
was as if a rainbow had splintered into human life and spilled
itself across the wet brown roadway. The girl stopped and
walked back. 'Christ, Vince, nobody calls me Meat Rack any
more, I'm just plain Caroline again. The old crowd's all split
up. Nobody stayed around. I'm surprised you're still here.

This city's gone to shit. It's all over.'

'You look like you're still having fun.'

She looked around at her friends. 'Us? We're just partying in the wreckage, baby. Picking over the ruins.' He looked at her in wonder. Hadn't someone else said the same thing tonight? She pointed out a skinny Asian man next to her. 'You remember Miserable Phil, don't you?'

'Sure, sure.' They shook hands almost as strangers, although they had once been united by music, parties, unemployment, the fun of being young and footloose. 'Frameboy and Travelling Matt are still with us, the last ones to leave, lazy sods. Remember them?'

'Of course I do.' He smiled, suddenly saddened. 'Which way you heading?'

'Who knows? We're foraging for food. You wanna come?'

'I'd like to. I can't.'

Meat Rack slipped her arm through his. She smelled of dry ice and peppermints. Her plastic sheet crackled. 'Not even for old times' sake?'

Vince looked about himself, disoriented, then up at the closed circuit cameras. If he was ever to slip away, now would be the time to do it. He joined the mafficking clubbers, hiding himself within their colourful nucleus, crossing the road by the London Coliseum to head towards Piccadilly Circus. At the first building he reached with a recessed, shadowed entrance, he squeezed Meat Rack's arm.

'Hey, look after yourself.'

'Don't worry about me. I'm going off into hibernation. Ain't gonna come out again until global warming's back. Stay fit. Have hope.'

He slipped away into the darkness. When he opened up the mobile phone, he found the battery completely depleted. He must have left the damned thing on. *Looks like I'm on my own this time*, he thought, as the rain dropped in freezing veils. He watched the clubbers disappear in the distance like a roving carnival of religious hysterics, invading the wet grey streets to search for converts.

Arthur Bryant accepted the mug of tea from Jane Masters and walked over to the window, drawing aside the curtain. Outside, the rain was starting to flood the streets of Battersea. 'How well did you know this fellow?' he asked.

'I spoke to him on the phone a couple of times, and met him face to face once,' explained Harold. 'Wells was friendly enough, aggressive and very confident. Smile on the face of the tiger and all that. Clearly used to having his own way. Dropped the smile and changed his voice to a sort of low bark the moment anyone disagreed with him, in that cornered manner the more rabid ministers adopt when they're being interviewed about a blunder.'

'What's his background?'

'As I told Vincent, there doesn't seem to be much written down about the League of Prometheus since the war. Sebastian and his members have been used to spin-doctoring any publicity that manages to leak out. When they can get away with it, of course. They don't like to be seen as obvious, so they put in a quiet word here and there. What it is to have friends in high places, eh? I collected a little material on him but never used any of it.'

'Why not?'

'I abandoned that avenue of enquiry after Wells put pressure on me.'

'Did you keep any documentation at all?'

'I saved some bits and pieces. I vaguely recall a couple of

articles about some personal tragedy he or his family suffered. The files should still be in the attic – if Jane hasn't thrown them out.'

'Now, Harold, you know I wouldn't dare touch any of your papers,' said Jane.

'Could you have a look for me?' asked Bryant. 'I'd be particularly interested in shedding some light on his personal life. We can't know what he's thinking at the moment, but it might help us if we fill in his background. Especially as we seem to be in a period of radio silence. It's a lucky chance this boy found you.'

'Lucky perhaps,' agreed Masters, 'but not much to do with chance. The moment you start investigating London's private clubs and societies you come up against the League of Prometheus in one form or another. It's just that most people don't get very much further.'

The sudden loud trill of the telephone startled everyone. When Maggie answered it she was surprised not to hear Vince's voice but that of an unknown man asking her questions.

'Slow down,' she snapped, 'I can't understand a word you're saying.'

'I'm sorry, I've just had a bit of a fight with someone and I think it's making me speedy. I'm trying to find Vincent Reynolds.'

'This isn't Directory Enquiries. Who are you?'

'No, I just – look, I got a message to call Vince, but there's no answer from his flat and he left your number on my machine, and everything's very – hyper, if you know what I mean –'

'Are you a friend or foe?' asked Maggie sharply.

'Friend! Friend! If there's something wrong, I want to help him.'

'Perhaps you should start by explaining yourself more clearly,' said Maggie, lighting a herbal cigarette.

'I think he might be in trouble. You won't believe me . . .'

She exhaled a plume of smoke. 'If this is about the League of Prometheus we're way ahead of you,' she offered.

'Let me talk to Doctor Masters.'

'It's for you.' Maggie handed him the phone, miffed. Masters spoke quietly, with an exactitude and attention to detail that had always defeated Maggie. She strained impatiently, trying to hear both ends of the conversation.

Louie had alighted from a night bus at the Trafalgar Square central stop. He did not realise that he was standing no more than a thousand yards from Vince when he made his call. Masters was able to verify that the man who had broken into his flat had not been feeding him false information, although he had simply said 'National Gallery' before passing out.

'So he should be right around here somewhere.'

'That's right,' said Masters. 'Our last contact point for him was at the side entrance of the National, just around the corner from your call box.'

Considering London was a home to seven million people and covered six hundred and one square miles, the coincidence of looking up and catching sight of the back of Vince's head should have startled him. It didn't, of course, because it was precisely the kind of thing that occurred in the capital every day. But locating Vince proved easier than catching up with him, for once Louie spotted his friend darting along the walls of the buildings in Charing Cross Road, he realised that dozens of home-going clubbers clogged the pavement between them. Something in the Camberwell Carrot he had smoked must have been impure because his stomach was turning over. He tried to concentrate as he kept the retreating figure in his sights, but as his quarry rounded the corner ahead, the gap between them grew frustratingly wider.

CHAPTER THIRTY-NINE

Captive Love

'IT'S NOT my fault,' said Pam, holding out her hands and rubbing the wrists. 'If you want me to stay tied up, it's your responsibility to make sure the knots work.'

'It's no use using pieces of film, they're not flexible enough.' Barwick threw the celluloid strips on the floor in disgust. He was tired of being everyone else's caretaker. If Pam escaped, he would doubtless be blamed and punished.

'He's the big mastermind, him upstairs, isn't he?' She pointed to the ceiling. 'He should take responsibility, not leave it all to you. The truth is obvious, he doesn't care what happens to anyone.' She spoke urgently, sure that someone would appear any minute to accuse her of having sent Xavier on a wild goose chase.

If Barwick had not been such a coward, he would have been able to admit how much he hated Sebastian, Caton-James and the rest. He had been thrust in their path for years, through school, through college, through family ties, and now through blood. He would never be free of them, any of them, ever.

'You don't understand,' he said miserably, 'nobody chooses to join the League, and nobody can ever leave it. Membership is by birth, and for life. That's what they tell you.'

Sometimes Barwick sat on the bench at the top of Primrose Hill and looked down across the sprawling city, and felt like a visitor from another planet. He had nothing in common with the people who walked the streets below, and wished he had. He was not quite good enough for the people of his own class. Caton-James and the rest thought him too slow, too lacking in style, too fat, too dull. But he would never be able to fit in anywhere else, no matter how hard he tried. Sometimes he thought of himself as a lift stuck between floors. He would always be an alien, awkwardly cemented into limiting social strata by his background. Pam wore her lower-middle class origins as proudly as a designer label, but in her case it fitted beautifully. She was beautiful.

'I don't want to escape and get you into trouble,' she was whispering to him, 'but let me make a phone call, just to a friend who can help Vince, that's all.' She threw him a pleading look. 'That's all.'

Her mobile phone was still in her handbag. If he took her to the alcove beneath the stairs, nobody would be able to hear her. Half of his colleagues were asleep in the big armchairs upstairs. Sebastian and the others had no reason to come down. 'All right,' he said finally, taking her hand. 'I'll be with you, but if you say one word about where you are, we're done for. Understand?'

She nodded thankfully.

'Follow me.'

Tucked safely in the shadows, Xavier Stevens watched and waited. Christ, what a night, he thought. The others were so panic-stricken about its events that they had lost all sense of its sport. Of course it was a serious matter, deadly serious, but Sebastian saw it simply as some kind of power-game to be played out, a way of scoring against his father. He saw right through Sebastian. Like all bullies, the man was a coward at heart. He always found someone else to do his dirty work.

Wells had done some dirty work tonight. He had not enjoyed killing the agent; it seemed unnecessary, but it was what Wells had wanted, and he was willing to pay. He smiled grimly. You could do anything in this city and get away with it, if you were familiar with the right routes.

Stevens moved forward and peered around the corner. Vince was still standing there by the shop window of Rymans, utterly immobilised. Why wasn't he phoning, asking his friends, taking action? Could it be that Wells had misjudged his stamina after all? He longed to step up to Vince and goad him into action, push him, shove him, stab at him, make him do something. Instead, he was forced to crouch and watch and wait while he arrived at his own independent conclusions. *Come on*, he urged him silently, *you can do it, work it out*. Stevens checked his watch. Not much time left now. Three more challenges and then the dawn. He wanted to be there when the fireworks began.

I can do this, Vince thought, I don't need anyone else's help. Time to show them what you're made of. He dried his hands as best as he could and reopened the page with numb fingers.

Opened after Defoe's Year. The capital letter on 'year' was a giveaway. Defoe had to be Daniel Defoe. One of his most famous works was *A Journal of the Plague Year*, so he was looking for something that opened the year after the Great Plague ended, presumably in 1666, the year of the Great Fire. Defoe was a famous Nonconformist, so that was the title of the challenge taken care of.

Blake and Bunyan make a show. He didn't know what to

make of this, beyond the fact that they were all writers.

Paradise was founded here conceivably referred to Milton and his *Paradise Lost*, which was contemporary to Defoe.

Seek the Elf King, go below was gibberish. Instinctively he felt drawn to the old inner City of London, but could find no logical justification for his choice. The hand that touched his shoulder while he was attempting to solve the conundrum shattered the page and nearly made him drop in his tracks.

While Masters was rooting about in the attic looking for his notes and clippings, the phone rang again downstairs. Maggie Armitage answered it on the second ring. She listened for a minute, then cupped her hand over the receiver and mouthed 'Who are all these people?' to Stanley Purbrick. This one was called Pam, and she also wanted to know where Vince was.

'I wish we knew, dear,' said Maggie, 'but he hasn't called us in over an hour, and we have no way of contacting him. Yes, I'll let him know you're safe if he rings again. Can he contact you? No, I see.'

Maggie replaced the receiver, puzzled. 'Sounded like she was calling from inside a cupboard,' she said.

The walls of the fuliginous cupboard were coated with coal dust, and once Pam started sneezing she could not stop. Barwick held the door open for her, his clumsy fantasies of seduction thwarted.

'Look here,' he began, starting towards her as she fished about in her bag for a handkerchief, 'suppose we just left, you and I, quickly and quietly by the servants' entrance? We could be far away from here before they find us gone.'

'Okay, but won't you get into trouble?' she said, trying to think through this new development as she blew coal from her nose.

'It'll be a lot worse than that,' said Barwick, grimacing. 'You can't leave the League, not once you know its secrets.'

'Tell me, Horace, why are they making Vince do this?' she asked. 'It's more than just a series of games, isn't it?'

'Oh, much more,' he agreed. 'You have no idea ...'

'If you don't agree with what the League is doing, you should tell me. Perhaps we can do something about it.'

'I agree in principal, what with the way the country is going and everything. But what he's planning is simply too dangerous to contemplate. The WBI is a government organisation. He can't do it without Vince, you see . . .'

'I don't understand,' she persisted as they headed for the stone staircase at the rear of the building. 'You have to tell me what he is going to do.'

'I can't do that. Too risky,' Barwick gasped, the effort of fast movement clearly having an adverse effect on him. 'He would have to kill me – and you. It's better that you don't know anything more.'

'And we just sit back and let this – thing – happen? Can't you go to the authorities? Someone with power?'

'How, when our families are the authorities?' he wheezed. The spiral staircase they had entered turned to the ground floor and a basement beyond. 'The people with power, we're all related one way or another.'

'You're telling me that this is about Sebastian getting back at his family?'

'Well, in part. I mean, his father, but everyone knows about that. Sebastian can never forgive him for what he did.'

The heavy oak doors to the courtyard stood no more than ten yards ahead. Pam prayed they weren't locked. 'Please, Horace, tell me where Vince is. It doesn't matter if I know now.'

'He should be on the seventh challenge. Xavier Stevens has gone back out there to keep an eye on him.'

'Where, Horace?' She forced her eyes to glisten. 'I must know where. Please.'

Finally he told her the location, proud to be the possessor of such privileged information. They had reached the bottom of the staircase. Freedom lay just a few short steps ahead.

'Listen Horace,' she said, drawing him close, 'you've been really nice to me. I want to thank you. You're not like the others.'

'I've been hoping you would feel that way,' he muttered sheepishly. 'They say hostages often fall in love with their captors, don't they? I've always wanted to meet someone who likes me for who I am, not what my family represents. Money always gets in the way.'

'Only if you've got it, sunshine,' she said, bringing her right knee sharply up into his unprotected groin. 'Don't get me wrong. I still think you're an arsehole.'

Barwick let out a howl and tipped backwards clutching his testicles. The shock set him off-balance and he fell hard on the steps, damaging his coccyx and barrelling down to the wall below. Pam ran for the exit.

The tradesman's door was unlocked. As she yanked it open and dashed out into the floodlit courtyard, something whistled in the air behind her. She looked back and saw St John Warner at the open stairwell window, reloading what appeared to be a crossbow. As she ran on across the gravelled yard, she cursed her decision to wear high-heeled shoes tonight.

Sebastian rested his forehead against the cold diamond pane. He had not foreseen that Vince would draft in others to help him, and at first had felt anger towards his opponent, but now he understood the rightness of it. He was a child of the street, after all; it was fitting that other such denizens should offer him advice, just as he used his own background. The League, its followers and friends were isolated from Vince's kind. They had underestimated the power of the nation's grass roots. This exercise would do them all good. There was a commotion in the courtyard below, and he looked out in time to see St John Warner firing his bloody crossbow at their hostage, for God's sake.

Praying that no one else was looking out of their windows while this farrago was unfolding, he rose from his chair and headed downstairs to instigate some disciplinary action. He wanted everyone else cleared from Vince's path now. If the girl or anyone else turned up again, he would have their bodies dumped in the river before dawn and low tide.

Old Bones

'WHAT'S THAT game show where they had to find things like the portrait of Elizabeth the First?' asked Stanley Purbrick. 'They had teams, and maps, and an annoying woman who kept barging about in a jump suit.'

'This is not a game show, Stanley,' said Masters, clearing a patch on the table and heaving a mildewed cardboard box onto it. 'There's a very good reason why our help is needed. If this boy is defeated and halted in his path, just as I was four years ago, the corruption will just continue to deepen, and soon the stain will be so ingrained that it will never be removed.' He began pulling damp cardboard files from the box and passing them to Arthur Bryant. 'It's not as if we have a constitution for our protection. Up until the Thatcher years we relied on a certain amount of common sense to guide us. Now the profit motive makes every action suspect.'

'Harold, dear, take your medication,' said Jane Masters. 'You know what happens when you get overexcited.'

'Well, it makes me angry,' he countered. 'I'm a so-called respected academic, I sit on a dozen advisory boards and yet I'm as powerless as a child dossing down in a shop doorway. What I don't understand is why we, as a country, aren't angrier about the erosion of our liberties. Look at the way we allow our Members of Parliament to retain positions in companies that show direct conflicts of interest. And good God, the opportunism! Shaw said that liberty means responsibility; that is why most men dread it.'

'He also said that an Englishman thinks he is moral when he is only uncomfortable,' interrupted Bryant. 'Who exactly are Sebastian Wells's parents?'

'His father is a former darling of the far right, bring back hanging, to hell with Europe, that sort of thing. He would have made the perfect conservative MP somewhere in the shires, a nominal position, a nice safe seat. Unfortunately it was his lot to be high-born. He's fascinated by the accumulation of corporations, and that's where it starts to get interesting.'

'Oh, why?'

'One senses there are all kinds of infringements. His wife is represented in a number of companies, either as a shareholder or on the board, and when you put their joint assets together – well,' he looked pointedly at Stanley Purbrick, 'a true conspiracy theorist would draw conclusions from their surprisingly fortuitous connections. For example, he has a company dealing in arms, she has machine exports, he has a shipping corporation, she has a security firm. They dovetail a little too neatly, and one could say that a pattern emerges. Old family connections aside, they seem to be part of a clique of business colleagues and friends that, if sat all together in a room, represent most of the more dubious financial fixers of the government's outer circle.'

'So we'd be stupid to mess with these people,' said Maggie airily, waving her wineglass at arm's length. 'This is nothing new. By the very nature of its existence, a modern government is always tainted. How can it not be? We can't live by Grecian ideals. This isn't a republic. Big business is not nice. We know that, and nobody can stop it without stopping the world.'

'We can stop Wells,' said Jane Masters. 'Can't we?'

Arthur Bryant looked up from the clipping he had been studying for the last few minutes. 'I don't know about that yet,' he said, 'but I rather think we have a way into the problem.'

Louie bought two doughy slices of pepperoni pizza from the Turkish vendor who was arguing in French with his Nigerian helper, and passed one to Vince. The traffic around Piccadilly Circus was pulsing slowly now, the city's breath shallow in the deepest part of the night, but most of the billboard neon was still ablaze, reflecting a sullen glow at the clouds racing low overhead.

'Thanks,' he said, barely comprehensible through his mouthful of food. 'I didn't realise how hungry I was. You shouldn't be seen around me, Louie. Everyone who comes close risks getting hurt.'

'Don't worry, mate, I've already given one bloke a punch up the bracket, trying to save your sodding book. I can look after myself. We'll see who gets hurt now.'

'Do you think Esther is really dead? I called her, but there was no answer.'

'I don't know. I guess you have to prepare yourself for the chance that she might be.'

'He mentioned Pam. There's no answer from her phone, either. Christ, if he's touched –'

'All right, calm down. You're not gonna help anyone by going crazy now. Tell you what, make this call while I get us some coffees.' Vince accepted the mobile phone from Louie. His fingers were still frozen, even though he had been holding the microwaved pizza slice. If only he hadn't bought that damned society magazine in the first place, no one would have been hurt. There was no way of turning back the clock, but there had to be some way of making amends. He called Harold Masters.

'I only cut it out because there was a picture of Sebastian Wells at the top,' said Masters. 'He cuts a terribly dashing figure, don't you think?'

The article was headed:

Mystery death at Howarth Lodge –
Open verdict forced by inquest.

The undergraduates who attended a post-exam house party at the country seat of Sir Nicholas Wells were expecting a weekend of fun and frivolity, but on Sunday the hi-jinks ended in tragedy when the body of an unconscious girl was pulled from the property's ornamental lake. For a few brief weeks Melanie Daniels was the pretty blonde girlfriend of Nicholas Wells' son, Sebastian. She had apparently fallen from the lake's jetty in a state of inebriation, and died on her way to hospital.

An inquest led by the Hon. Jasper Forthcairn, QC found no evidence of foul play, but suggested that the combination of barbiturates and alcohol found present in Daniels' bloodstream in large amounts was a major contributing factor to her death.

'Melanie was a happy girl with everything to live for,'

commented Anne Daniels, her mother. 'She had fallen in with the wrong crowd.'

Despite a recent public break-up with his son over issues raised by the controversial first annual conference of the Without Borders Initiative, Sir Horatio told the press: 'Sebastian is a clean living, decent young man. These girls are unable to resist the lure of an eligible, wealthy bachelor, and often succumb to addictive antisocial behaviour.'

Sebastian Wells had recently been suspended from college attendance after his controversial views on racism were made known at the WBI conference.

'There's something about the man I can't make out.' Bryant's eyes grew distant with thought, so that he looked more than ever like a ruminating tortoise. 'The family certainly seems to dominate, doesn't it? In nearly every one of these interviews the father has something strong to say about his son. Suggestive in itself.'

Maggie couldn't see how. She studied the photograph of Sebastian Wells on the front of a pamphlet entitled '*England and Her Foreign Population: Seduction of the Innocents*' and noted his colour combinations, unusual for an Aries. The telephone, which had now been placed in the centre of the table like an altar-piece, rang suddenly and she swept it up in a jewelled paw.

'Vincent! Where are you? We've been so worried!' She listened, then threw her hand over the mouthpiece. 'He's eating pizza in Piccadilly Circus, apparently,' she told everyone. 'Do you have *any idea* how bad that is for you? Do you have the next challenge? Then give it to us.' She waggled her fingers in front of her. 'Pen, pen, pen.'

As she wrote, the others returned to the table and gathered around her. 'Yes, go on. Nonconformity, yes, okay – let me see if I have it right – *Opened after Defoe's Year, Blake and Bunyan make a show. Paradise was founded here, Seek the Elf King, go below.* Plague year, yes, I imagine that's correct. Hang on.' She turned to the assembled group, held up the sheet of paper on which she had scribbled the verse, gave them ten seconds to read it and asked 'Any ideas?'

'They were all nonconformists, religiously speaking,' said Purbrick. 'Blake and Bunyan, what's the connection there?'

'Well, they were contemporaries,' said Jane.

'That's right,' agreed Masters. 'I wonder why it's written in rhyme. The other challenges are all prose.'

'Because of Milton?'

'I went to visit Blake's grave once,' said Maggie. 'He was buried with Catherine, his wife. His headstone was a great disappointment, a miserable little piece of discoloured –'

'Isn't Bunyan buried in the same place?' asked Bryant. 'Yes, I'm sure he is. And Defoe as well. Damn, what is it called –'

Jane Masters was already searching the shelves, and pulled down a slim volume entitled *The Cemeteries Of London*. 'Here you are,' she said. 'Bunhill Fields, a graveyard allocated to nonconformists, who were banned from burial in Church of England cemeteries for their refusal to use C of E prayer-books in their services. John Bunyan, William Blake and Daniel Defoe are all buried near each other, Milton wrote *Paradise Lost* on a site in Bunhill Row, overlooking the graves. Nothing about imps or elves, though.'

'Any fairy-tale authors?' asked Bryant hopefully. 'Tolkien isn't planted there by any chance?'

'It doesn't say. Bunhill presumably comes from

"Bone-hill", as they transferred the bones from St Paul's charnel house there for burial. He has to get to the City Road, near Old Street station.'

Maggie relayed the information, then covered the receiver once more. 'He's not thrilled about being sent to a graveyard in a storm in the middle of the night. He wants to know what he's supposed to be looking for.'

'Tell him he'll have to look around when he gets there. Ask him if he needs anything.'

'He says he's cold and wet, but okay. He's found that friend of his, the weird one who rang earlier.'

'The one who sounded really stoned?' complained Purbrick, sitting back and folding his arms. 'Wonderful. That's all we needed.'

CHAPTER FORTY-ONE

The Elf King

RAIN BATTERED the tops of the great plane trees looming over Bunhill Row and bounced over the gutters as Vince and Louie left their taxi outside The Artillery Arms to approach the locked gate of the cemetery. Here, as in so many parts of the city, the landscape was divided into buildings that had survived the Blitz and those that had been utterly devastated. Renovated Peabody Estate homes shared space with the blank brick walls of post-war brutalist office blocks. Beyond them was the heavy dark foliage of the cemetery, a constant green space in a changing world. Most of the tombstones within had been worn smooth with age, their epitaphs crumbling to dust in the wind and rain. Only those few carved on slate or granite remained decipherable.

'I used to come here to eat my lunch when I was a motor-cycle courier,' said Louie as he clambered over the low railings. 'Didn't know there was anyone famous buried here, though. You don't look around when it's your turf, you know? Not like when you're a visitor.' He shook water from his jacket. 'I once got breathalysed by the lads in Bishopsgate nick, just up the road from here. They were a nice bunch. Gave me tea, biscuits and everything. Bourbons.'

'Yeah, and they took your licence away for a year.'

'What are we looking for, exactly?'

'I wish I knew,' said Vince. 'Give us a hand over.' He hopped across onto the neatly mown grass.

While they sheltered under a tree, considering how best to tackle their search of the cemetery, the familiar thrumming of a taxi engine grew behind them, and Vince was surprised to see his old schoolfriend paying the driver and asking for a receipt.

'Pam?' He stepped up to the railing. 'Are you okay? How did you find us?'

'Sebastian had me tied to a post but I got away,' she said breathlessly. 'It was like something out of a Bruce Willis film. Nothing like that has ever happened to me before. These people are really peculiar, Vince, they fired arrows at me for heaven's sake, and they're planning something –'

'What are you talking about? Where have you been?'

'There was someone watching you at Red Lion Square. I followed him back to this gothic sort of *abbey* near Chelsea embankment and they tried to get me to tell them where you kept your manuscripts. I didn't tell them the truth. They've destroyed your disks, though. They smashed up your flat.'

'Christ, Pam, you could have been killed.'

'This book had better be worth it,' said Louie, pulling the computer disk from his jacket.

'What on earth are you doing walking around with that on you?' asked Vince.

'I thought it would be safer if I kept it with me. Fucking hell, don't shout, I've had a hard night. I had to take this off some geezer who'd nicked it from my flat.'

'Louie, what are you doing here?' asked Pam. 'Is he all right?'

'He's a bit distraught.' Vince looked from one to the other. 'Are we expecting anyone else? Perhaps you've invited my mother along too?'

'No, there's just us. I thought you'd be pleased.'

Vince shook his head in defeat. 'Well, now that everyone's here, I guess you might as well help. But when they find out, believe me, there's going to be trouble about this.'

Caton-James lifted his legs from the desk and tipped his chair away from the monitors. 'That's it,' he said, 'that's enough.' He punched out Sebastian's number and waited for him to answer. 'He's having a fucking school reunion party outside the cemetery,' he complained, 'standing there talking to his friends in the pissing rain like it's all some big joke. Either you stop this farce now or –'

'Or what?' asked Sebastian.

'We've got enough. This is the seventh, and seven should do it. We've won. We can get rid of the others.'

'No. I want them all.'

'Why do you need the other three, for God's sake?'

'It's foolproof then. Ten out of ten, don't you see? No other explanation needed.'

'All right, but we have to get rid of his friends, and do it right now.'

'I'll have to agree with that. What do you suggest?'

'Where's Xavier?'

'He should be somewhere near the cemetery by now. He's supposed to be keeping Reynolds in his sights. You'd better give him a call.' The line fell silent for a moment. 'God knows how he's supposed to get the bodies from there to the river without arousing suspicion. He'll need a larger vehicle than his bike, that's for sure. Have we got any cars in the area?'

'The Rover's nearby, but it'll need a driver, someone who can keep his mouth shut.'

'Wake up Protheroe. He's monitoring CCTVs for us at Liverpool Street station. Get him out on the street. The fresh air will do him good.'

'I'll stay on this side and keep a lookout,' whispered Pam, even though the street was deserted. 'I'm not fond of cemeteries.' Rain dropped straight and hard on her head and shoulders. The noise of the downpour drowned out any other sound. The colour of her soaked navy-blue suit had run, staining her blouse and her tights. It looked like someone had thrown several pots of ink at her. She would make sure that Vince bought her a new outfit if they survived the night.

The cemetery was sectioned off to protect its more fragile homes. The headstones were tall and thin, often the size of a man, and most had been blown flat by bombs during the Second World War, although their owners were among the few residents in the area who had not lain awake all night waiting for the engines of the V1s to cut out overhead. Louie and Vince found nothing remotely elfish on or around any of the graves. The more famous, and therefore more visited, tombstones had all been repositioned in the centre of the cemetery, on or around its gravel path. The place had lost the chaotic untidiness it had possessed between the wars, and looked the worse for it.

'It would help if we knew what we were looking for,' Louie complained. 'I've never heard of any bloody Elf King.'

It was eerie here even in broad daylight, but worse now with the rain spattering from the claw-like branches of the plane trees, and the streetlamps strobing jaundiced shadows. Beyond the cemetery railing, Pam wrapped her arms around her dripping jacket and tried to stamp some life back into her frozen feet. In doing so, she broke the heel of her shoe. She was staring down at the fracture, trying to think of a way to mend it when she saw the embossed lettering.

'Oh my God. Vince! Louie!' She threw a discreet distress call over the cemetery wall and waited for a response, but none was forthcoming. 'Vince?'

She looked back at the raised metal letters of the manhole cover. It read METROPOLITAN WATER BOARD SV SELF LOCKING PLATE, but the lettering on either side of the cover had worn down to leave the central raised section – ELF KING.

What did the instructions say?

Go below.

Carefully hitching up her soaked skirt, she pulled at the sides of the iron disc and found that it had already been loosened. It shifted easily, so that she was able to roll it aside and stare down into distant rushing darkness.

CHAPTER FORTY-TWO

Aqua Mortis

THE IRON-RUNGED ladder was so cold she was afraid for a moment that her hands might stick to it. She fixed the pen-light torch Vince had left her in the belt-loop of her skirt, and its narrow pool of light instantly revealed the stark white oblong of the letter, weighted down with a piece of brick on a dry stone ledge ten feet underneath her. The rushing water below must surely contain sewage; she imagined that the SV on the manhole cover stood for 'Sewage Valve', but in this cold temperature it thankfully had little odour. Climbing into a sewer during a thunderstorm in high-heels was not some-thing she had ever intended to do in her lifetime. She knew she should have waited for Vince and Louie to come back, but it was a chance to prove herself and do something proactive. It was time women took more of an initiative, she told herself.

It was an easy climb, despite the fact that the drain was narrow and one of her heels was broken. She collected the letter from the ledge, tossing the brick that pinned it into the black waters, then folded the paper and slipped it into her handbag.

She started up the ladder again. At the top, she lobbed her

bag back onto the pavement and was about to climb out when the manhole cover abruptly slid back in place with a clang, catching her on the side of the head, and she dropped from the ladder, down into the roaring black spray.

'She drowned,' said Harold Masters. 'It was an accident. The hour was late, the girl was high, on drugs, on drink. It was his son's party, and the boy was blamed. Twenty-one years of age. His nascent career never recovered after that. Surely that's enough to make anyone bitter.'

Bryant pushed a sheaf of clippings in his colleague's direction. 'Come on, Harold,' he said, 'just look at Wells's background. He comes from a long line of empire builders, the so-called backbone of the nation. Sebastian's future had been decided for him before he was even born. His father was a supporter of Mosley, a hardline member of the League of Prometheus, its president for a number of years at a time when their membership was swollen with patriots, and his son took up the life almost at once. Look at his extra-curricular track record at Oxford. He was set on becoming a leader of men. And yet he ruins his chances with this one slip-up.'

'It's a human life we're talking about,' said Maggie, 'not just a "slip-up". Besides, a lot of bright young men and women lost their way during their college years.'

'I know, but this doesn't ring true,' complained Bryant, rubbing a weary hand across his face. 'There's something else.'

'Well, I don't know what you expect to find,' said Purbrick. 'The son simply went to the bad.'

'Try reading the clippings chronologically,' Bryant suggested.

'Really, I don't see how this will help.'

'Something happened between Wells *pere et fils*. Look at this, in 1988 they shared a platform at a local rally, completely in agreement. The following year, the same thing, joint appearances and then – 1990, the son appears alone, and the father has suddenly retired from public speaking. The son even speaks out in public against his own father, who by this time has changed his political affiliations. And this girl drowned in the summer of 1989. Now what does that suggest to you?'

'They fell out over the girl's death,' said Jane. 'It would be more surprising if they hadn't. Where was the mother while all this was going on?'

'She dropped out of the picture some years earlier. Lives in France.'

'Later the father took to the lecture circuit without his son,' Masters pointed out. 'He remained a Conservative, but his position was shifting. Getting soft in his dotage, the son told the papers. Sebastian kept a hard line on immigration, while his father founded that initiative, the Without Borders thing. Supposed to bring down trade barriers. Although I imagine the old man set it up so that his business interests would benefit from changes in the migration laws, bring more wage slaves into Britain, that sort of malarkey. Their flags are out all along the Mall this week. There must be something going on.'

'It's as if father and son were competing with one another,' muttered Bryant.

'That's right. Sebastian is fresher, younger, the stronger of the two. He had an advantage over the old man, he was heading for the top. Then the scandal of Melanie Daniels's death hit him, and he never recovered his credibility. In the battle of ideologies, the father somehow won. This is very curious.'

'I really don't see what's so odd,' said Maggie impatiently, 'or how it helps anyone. We should be helping Vince find this Elf King.'

'He's looking for it now,' said Masters. 'I'm sure he'll call us as soon as he has news. I'm going upstairs to check on something. Bryant, will you come with me?'

'Certainly, old man. You know, I have an idea ...'

'We should never let those two get together,' said Jane, wearily pouring herself a scotch. 'Heaven knows what they'll hatch up.' It was safe to assume that she would be preparing a cooked breakfast for five this morning, shortly after the arrival of dawn. The Insomnia Squad had passed long nights before, but never anything like this.

'She wouldn't have just left it here,' said Vince, picking up the sodden bag and turning it by its strap. 'She must be around somewhere.' Louie walked to the corner and returned. 'Nope, no sign of anybody.'

'Didn't you hear anything?'

Louie narrowed his eyes, the rain spattering across his forehead. Above him, thunder grumbled. 'In this?'

'She wouldn't have left without me.' Vince opened the bag and peered in. He instantly recognised the envelope. 'Looks like she found it.' He pulled it out, noting that it had not been opened.

'Where, though? Where was she standing just before I climbed over the railings after you?' They looked around, but it was still a few minutes before they saw the manhole lid.

Whoever had put it back had stamped it into place, knocking off pieces of the paving stone's cement edging. The cover was now firmly jammed. Louie searched around for some kind of lever, and picked up a broken section of branch. He tried to wedge it under one end of the lid, but the wood was wet, and split. Vince found a discarded hubcap in the gutter and after chipping away at the cement edging they jammed it beneath the edge of the lid, but it took another five minutes to prise the iron disc from its setting.

'Aqua Mortis,' said Louie, kneeling and peering into the blackness. 'That's what they used to call the Thames. Water of death. So much sewage flowed into it. The stench alone was enough to kill you. You don't think she's down there, do you?'

'With the Elf King? Somebody pulled the thing up. Pamela!' yelled Vince, but the cry was lost in the noise of churning water. The pipes were thumping and gurgling with the deluge of torrential rain. It was a pity he had given his torch to Pam. He could see no more than three or four feet into the top of the shaft.

'I don't think I can go down there,' said Louie. 'I get claustrophobia.'

'Suppose she reached up to throw the bag out and the lid fell back on her, knocking her down the steps to the bottom? She might be just out of reach, unconscious.'

'And she might be dead. Suppose there's someone else here? You yourself said they don't want you talking to anyone.'

Vince stared at Louie. 'You know we have to go and look.'

'Shit.'

The next sound to pass between them was that of an arrow cleaving the air. Louie looked back at Vince's wide eyes and dropping jaw, then down at the side of his own thigh, from which protruded six inches of slim aluminium shaft. 'Man, I don't *believe* it,' was all he managed to say before Xavier Stevens kicked him over the manhole-mouth. Vince scrambled to his feet and heard the crossbow reload in his direction. Louie tried to maintain his balance but fell back into the sewage shaft.

The water level had risen since Pam climbed down to retrieve the letter. There was a scrape of brickwork and an echoing splash when Louie hit the bottom.

Stevens kicked the heavy lid back into place again, stamped it hard into the surround with a steel-capped boot and hesitated in front of Vince, staring him down, daring him to move. He was tempted to finish the job and face the consequences later. He wasn't afraid of anything Sebastian might threaten him with. But then his bloodlust subsided, and he began thinking practically. He'd done the League a favour. Caton-James had called him to say that Protheroe was bringing something to put the bodies in, but he would not be needed now. Stevens returned to his motorbike and kicked it into life. This night was going to cost Sebastian dearly. They were going to discover that his silence had a painfully high price.

Vince helplessly tried to tear the lid from the drain, but it was too firmly wedged in place now to shift without tools. He darted across the road and hammered on the door of the saloon bar, but no lights came on, no heads appeared at the windows above. Running around the corner, he rang the bell of the first flat he chanced upon. No answer again. Given the late hour and the inclemency of the weather, it was hardly surprising that no one was prepared to open their door to a stranger in the street.

Returning to collect Pam's fallen bag, he removed her mobile phone, walked back to the comparative shelter of the pub doorway and punched out Masters's number. The doctor answered on the second ring, listened to what had happened and promised to call the police immediately.

'I can't get the lid up by myself,' Vince shouted above the drumming rain, 'it's stuck in place.'

'You mustn't panic,' said Masters. 'Let's think this through. In normal weather he'd probably be able to go along to the next valve shaft and surface there, but in this downpour the tunnel may well be flooded all the way to the roof. Jane's calling the police on our other line, Vince. You'd better get away from there fast.'

'I can't just leave them like this. Jesus, they might both be –'

'There's nothing more you can do, is there?'

'Not without equipment, people to help me –'

'Exactly. If you stop now, they'll have suffered for no purpose. You *have* to keep going.'

'I can't –'

'You can. You say you have the new envelope. Have you opened it yet?'

'No,' he said, 'Jesus Christ –'

'If you don't do it and stay calm, Vince, everything is lost.'

'Okay. Hold on.' He pulled the sopping letter from his pocket, tore off the end and attempted to read the paper inside.

<u>The Challenge Of The Hours</u>

The night of September 3rd and the passing of Proserpine.

A Sunday evening near Sadler's Wells with Diana and her cuckold Actaeon.

Noon at L'Eglise des Grecs in Hog Lane, where a good woman is silent.

Aurora arrives at St Paul's at five to eight, less pious than she appears.

The words had been transcribed with a fountain pen as usual, and were once again in a different hand. It was a wonder the rain had not ruined them. He wondered what effect water would have on the chemical treatment of the paper. Vince read the letter aloud, pausing to allow the doctor time to jot each sentence down.

'I can hardly hear you, the rain's coming down so hard,' he shouted.

'I said I think we have a double bluff here,' Masters told him. 'At first appearance it's quite simple, but no, the more I think about it the more confusing it becomes.'

'Simple?' He could not share the doctor's excitement for the game. It was fine for him; he was warm and dry and safe. Vince just wanted to solve the damned thing and find out what had happened to his friends. His boots were full of water and rain was dripping inside his collar, down his spine.

'This is to do with a set of paintings,' said Masters. 'Hogarth's four famous *Times of the Day* paintings to be exact, *Morning, Noon, Evening* and *Night*. They're right here in London. The problem is, they're absolutely stuffed with allegorical allusions that point in all sorts of different directions. We have too many clues to follow.'

'Couldn't it be simpler than that?' asked Vince, forcing himself to think clearly. 'Surely Sebastian wasn't expecting me to work out the symbolism in paintings at five o'clock in the morning.'

'I think that's precisely what he wants you to do,' replied Masters. 'Don't you see, he's thrusting his preferred kind of education on you, British, classical, old school. And these paintings are games, filled with little puzzles, just the sort of thing he likes.'

'I've seen the Hogarth pictures at the Tate Gallery. Couldn't I be intended to go there?'

'What would be the point of specifying the Hogarth pictures so exactly when any artist exhibited at the Tate would do? And why go into such detail about them? No, the answer has to be in the paintings themselves.'

'Do you have any reproductions of them to hand?'

'I probably have quite a few. They're featured in a great many art volumes. Are you sheltering somewhere out of the wet?'

'No.'

'Listen, you'd better make yourself scarce from there if the police are on their way. It's going to take us a few minutes to locate reproductions of the paintings and examine them. We'll call you back.'

He gave Masters his new number and rang off. With a hiss of exasperation, he stepped back into the drenching downpour.

Louie could feel something cold and wet pressing against him in the icy rushing torrent, something with the heaviness of flesh and bone. It thumped against his burning thigh as the water pounded around him, dragging at his limbs. He reached down into the freezing stream and grabbed a human arm, pulling it nearer. Pam was the worse for wear but still very much alive, and began coughing violently as soon as he raised her head. There seemed to be a stone slab set halfway across the shaft, about two feet down in the water. They were safe so long as they managed to stay on it, as she had; to step off would mean being swept away along the tunnel to who knew where. Forcing one arm around Pam's waist, he used the other to cling to the iron rungs, but had no strength to pull the pair of them free from the churning river.

'Hit my head,' yelled Pam miserably. Louie was so surprised he nearly dropped her. 'Someone let the lid fall on my head. Can't we get out?'

'No, the cover's been put back in place,' he explained. 'Are you strong enough to hold onto something?'

'I think so.'

He gently pushed her through the water to the side wall and wrapped her fingers around the rungs. 'Now hold tight. I'll see if I can get the lid off. Don't let go, whatever you do.'

Slowly, painfully, he climbed the rungs one at a time until his head was level with the top of the shaft. With his free hand he attempted to push the lid free, but there was not even a quarter-inch of movement. His right thigh, where the cross-bow dart had entered, felt as though it was on fire. God only knew how many inoculations he would need if they ever got out of here alive.

He stepped down a rung to try and get a better grip, and the aluminium shaft of the dart caught inside one of the ladder struts, causing him to yell out in pain. His fingers closed on air as the rung eluded his grasp, and he fell back. For a moment he lay across the shaft breathing hard, his shoulder against the slime-covered wall opposite. Then as Pam screamed his name he slipped again and fell feet first, bypassing the ledge, into the storm-driven cloacal rage below.

CHAPTER FORTY-THREE

Night And Day

'BUT ARTHUR, we need your knowledge down here,' pleaded Maggie Armitage. 'You still remember all the old, esoteric stuff even I've forgotten.'

'I'm not sure I take that as a compliment,' replied the elderly detective. 'Anyway, there are too many cooks in this room. You need to go over those paintings inch by inch, preferably with a magnifying glass. Someone should be working out what the League of Prometheus is up to.'

'Surely we know that already.'

'No,' said Bryant emphatically, 'that is precisely what we don't know, beyond the fact that Vincent Reynolds is being used. Could their meeting have been prearranged right from the outset, d'you suppose?'

'I don't see how,' answered Masters. 'Vincent says he found Sebastian's name in a magazine.'

'Hmm. Harold, may I borrow your wife?' He extended his hand. 'Jane, you have a lively mind. I know it's late, but you wouldn't mind helping me for a few minutes, would you?'

'Not at all,' replied Jane, flattered. 'What do you want me to do?'

'I'm not a fan of the Internet, as you know. It seems to me

rather like the stack of magazines one always finds in dentists' waiting rooms. They cover all the subjects you have no interest in reading about, and the only pages you'd like to read are partially missing. Still, it could be useful in this situation. Harold was telling me that you use it at the museum, and that you have a connection set up here. Can you show me how to locate those page-things?'

'Web-sites, yes, of course. I'll show you where the terminal is.' She led the way upstairs. Unlike his partner John May, who was in the thrall of all things cybernetic, Bryant had no love or understanding of technology. Its usefulness in locating information, however, could not be denied. He needed to probe deeper into the newspaper files for reports of the drowning of Melanie Daniels, and knew that he could probably access all the archival material he needed through the Internet. At the back of his mind was the suspicion that Sebastian had somehow been responsible for the girl's death. Either it was an accident that he had unwittingly caused, or he had actually murdered her in a fit of anger. Suppose Sir Nicholas had discovered the truth, and had refused to help his boy out of the situation? Surely that was reason enough for father and son to become estranged?

And yet this alone was not enough to explain the League's mobilisation in the last few hours. It seemed unlikely that an accident occurring over seven years ago had any bearing on the drama now being played out, but what else did they have to go on? As he seated himself before the console and Jane switched on the modem for him, he realised how little time there was left before the dawn would start shedding its unwelcome light on the events of the night.

'Let's have a good look at these pictures,' said Masters. He adjusted his bifocals and scanned the page. 'We'll take the clues in the order that they were written down. *The night of September 3rd and the passing of Proserpine.*' He opened a heavy, battered copy of *The Works of William Hogarth*, bound in brown leather, and located the *Times of the Day* engravings. The sequence of four ended with *Night*. 'Well, Proserpine is Persephone, the wife of Hades, the goddess of the underworld ...'

'I know a fair amount about these pictures,' said Maggie keenly. 'Hogarth is often cited by our coven members because of his reliance on symbolism and myth. The members like that sort of thing. Look, here, at the *Night* picture.' She tapped it with a crimson nail. 'It's apparently set in Hartshorn Lane, Charing Cross. The road is long gone, of course. The oak boughs on the sign and the oak leaves in the freemason's hat suggest the date – May 29th, the anniversary of Charles the Second's restoration. There's a crashed coach in the bottom right-hand corner. I think it's meant as a sort of nasty parody of Persephone bringing on the night. Most of Hogarth's jests have a sadistic edge created by his love of paradox. There's another joke in the surrounding scene – rather than preparing for bed, everyone is getting ready to go out.'

'That's what Vince has done, isn't it?' said Purbrick. 'He's been forced to swap night for day, going out when everyone else has gone to bed.'

Maggie turned the page back and pointed to a reproduction of *Evening*. '*Diana and her cuckold Actaeon*. We know this is who the painting is meant to represent because the characters are painted on the fan held by the central character. The spirit of Diana hangs over the picture, but in a sort of perverse parody. Actaeon was changed into a stag for looking upon Artemis while she was bathing, but here he's been turned into a cuckold. He's standing in front of a bull.'

'What does that mean?' asked Purbrick.

'It looks like he has horns. Putting horns on a man is the traditional manner of showing that his wife is unfaithful, Stanley, surely you know that.'

'I don't see how it helps us,' Purbrick complained.

'According to these notes it's supposed to be five in the afternoon because there's a milkmaid milking a cow in the background, and we're at Sadler's Wells. Those are the hills of Highgate in the distance.'

'Not much help. Turn to the next one.'

'*Noon*,' said Maggie, holding up the third reproduction. 'Ruled by Apollo, associated with the sun, and Venus, whose love is inverted here to be symbolised by a vulgar marriage and various earthy lusts, lots of sloppy feasting and debauchery.'

'I like this one,' said Purbrick. 'It's a bit saucy. *Where the good woman is silent*. Who is the good woman, then?'

'She's on the sign outside the inn.'

'But she's got no head.'

'That's what makes her good; she can't nag.'

'Hmm. What about the last picture?'

'*Morning*. The church dial says five to eight. An old maid crossing Covent Garden Square. She's dressed in yellow, the colour of the dawn sun, like the goddess Aurora –'

'Like the fire that Prometheus himself carries,' added Purbrick.

'That's right. She's on her way to church, but this is another inversion, another cruel paradox. She's peppered with black spots, venereal marks, and dressed less for religious service than personal vanity, hence *less pious than she appears*. She looks more like she's been out all night and is going to church to repent her carnal sins.'

'Well, the symbolism of the paintings is obvious, then, isn't it?' said Purbrick. 'He's commenting on Vincent.'

'How do you mean?' asked Maggie.

'The four goddesses, they all represent some aspect of what Sebastian perceives to be Vincent's world tonight. Persephone runs into the night and into the underworld, Diana the huntress takes on a challenge, Venus the lover turns the love into sin, and Aurora is the dawn-bringer, carrier of fire. Vincent befriended Sebastian, but the friendship soured under false pretences, that's Venus –'

'It's a bit different to love, though, isn't it?'

'Not in the classical sense, not at all. Friendship between males is seen in terms quite as strong as love, and governed by exactly the same rules of loyalty and duty. Next, Vincent ran into the night at Sebastian's instruction, he accepted the challenge and hunted through the fields for him –'

'*Fields*, Stanley?' Maggie raised an eyebrow.

'Indeed, for what will you find beneath the concrete of the city? *Fields,* Margaret, fields and the bones of Londoners. But according to these pictures, there's one thing Vincent hasn't done yet.'

'He hasn't brought in the dawn.'

'Right. That's where he has to go, where the character in the fourth painting is going, to Covent Garden, to the portico of St Paul's Church, featured in the picture. At least, that's what we're meant to think. But it's another trick, you see.'

'You mean because the painting is actually back to front. Hogarth always drew in a mirror.'

'No, no, it's to do with the church. I used to attend there

when I was younger, so I know this is true,' said Purbrick proudly. 'Inigo Jones outraged the clerics when he completed St Paul's in 1633, because he placed the altar at the west instead of the east end. It was something quite unheard of. He wanted his grand portico to face east into the new piazza, but in the face of so much ecclesiastical protest he resited the altar without changing the church's overall design. By doing so, he turned the church back-to-front, transforming the grand portico into a fake doorway, reducing it to a mere stage, where street entertainers now perform to the crowds.'

'Good heavens.'

'He created a paradox, a backward church that almost mocks itself with jugglers and fire-eaters instead of holy men.'

'Stanley, there's life left in you yet,' muttered Maggie, amazed.

If he reached up he could feel the curved brick ceiling at his fingertips, but there was no break in the water above him. The tunnel was completely filled. Another jutting stone ledge scraped past Louie, and he twisted his body, mindful of the metal rod still protruding from his thigh. He was running out of breath. The trick was not to panic. He allowed his body to go limp and be carried by the buffeting current.

The tunnel swept sharply to the right and up slightly, so that he could feel the slime-covered base of the sewer rapidly passing beneath his boots. Moments later he burst from the freezing water into air, propelled to a hard landing on the far side of a large iron grid, down through which the overflow from the tunnel was rushing. A faint grey light showed from above, allowing him to make out the hexagonal shape of the broad Victorian air-shaft. He reached down to his thigh and found the steel shaft of the arrow gone, wrenched free in the vortex.

Things got better after that. Pam had been pulled loose in his fall and now appeared behind him, although he was too late to break her fall as she burst from the tunnel and landed on the drainage grid. It took all his strength to drag her free of the torrent before she could swallow any more effluent. Water also spattered his face from above. Rain was falling through the large iron pores of a rectangular drain lid. Pam was not conscious, but was at least breathing hard. He rested his head against the green-slimed wall and allowed the falling raindrops to wash the filth from his face. Then he pulled Pam against the wall at his back and began looking for the ladder that he knew would take them to the surface and safety.

It was only when he opened his jacket to squeeze some of the water out that he realised what had happened. The disk he had fought to save, Vince's final copy of the manuscript, had been sucked from his clothes and washed away, the fragile magnetic square lost in the surf of detritus thundering through its channel beneath the city.

'Interesting,' said Bryant, 'this bit here about the inquest.' They had tapped into the only report that had so far made it onto the Internet, a web-site dedicated to celebrity criminal cases. He tapped the scrolling screen with the end of his biro. Jane shifted closer on the piano stool they were awkwardly sharing. 'The coroner's report on Melanie Daniels suggested that there was no sign of panic in the victim. Drowners usually start to hyperventilate when they inhale water into their lungs. No cadaveric spasms, few diatoms. It's not symptomatic of drowning. I'm surprised the verdict was misadventure.'

'I'm not sure what you're looking for,' said Jane.

'I'm not sure myself, but this is all very suggestive. Daniels was relaxed when she went into the water, if not unconscious. How could that be?'

'She must have been pretty out of it.'

'Oh come on, the party was late in the year, the lake would have been freezing cold. If she was so drunk and stoned that she couldn't even feel the icy water pouring into her mouth, how did she even manage to get as far as the end of a narrow jetty in semi-darkness?'

'You think someone took her down to the lake and made it look like an accident?'

'It's a possibility, yes.'

'But wouldn't the coroner have discovered that?'

'He should have done. Tell me, is there a Debrett's *Who's Who* on database?'

'I should think so. Who do you want to look up?'

'Jasper Forthcairn, QC, the coroner in charge of the case.'

So. It was Covent Garden for the ninth stop.

Vince closed up the mobile phone and wearily swung his bag onto his shoulder. He stepped out of the sheltering doorway into the deadening downpour. His wet jeans were chafing the tops of his legs, but he barely registered the discomfort. He felt helpless about the fate of Louie and Pam. He was angry with himself and Sebastian, for allowing things to go this far, for involving and injuring others. When he thought of that smug, smiling face he longed to swing one good punch at it and knock a few teeth loose. Limping back to Liverpool Street, shuffling along like a sodden scarecrow, he finally managed to hail a cab and climbed in, squelching down onto the seat and turning the heater on full to try to dry himself a little.

'Forgive me for saying so, mate,' said the driver, 'but you look like something the bleedin' cat dragged in, an' you're makin' my seat wet. Here.' He passed Vince a dry towel.

'Thank you, that's very kind.' He buried his face in the warm scented nap of the cloth, then ruffled his hair dry. For the next ten minutes he felt safe and protected inside the latter-day hackney carriage, as it purred through the rainy streets. The major routes were growing busier now as the first commuters started coming into the city. He must have fallen asleep, because it seemed only moments later that the taxi had stopped and the driver was calling to him through the window.

'Here you are, tosh, this where you wanna be? You won't find anything open around here until about nine.'

'This is fine, thanks.' Vince paid him and alighted back into the rain. There was no sign of light in the sky yet. Dawn was still some way off. The market was empty, the shops in darkness, the cobbled square devoid of human life. A small funfair stood on the north side, its red and yellow round-abouts and sideshows boarded up against the weather and the night.

He headed for what he took to be the front entrance of St Paul's Church, then remembered Dr Masters' advice, that the portico in the painting was a false front, existing separately at the rear of the building. Wiping the water from his eyes, he slowly made his way across the cobbled square.

CHAPTER FORTY-FOUR

The Trickster

THE POLICE constable looked around for something to wedge under the lid of the manhole cover, but it was hard to see in the rain that thundered down around them outside the little park.

'I'll tell you why,' he told his partner. 'Because it's a funny time to make a crank call and the caller didn't sound pissed or nuts, he was very well spoken in fact, so the desk sergeant thought it was worth checking out.'

'If somebody fell down there, how come the lid's back in place?' asked his partner, picking up the same length of branch Louie had used to try to open the drain. 'How about this?' When employed as a lever, the wood cracked further along its length. He tossed it aside and looked around for something else.

'Get a tyre iron from the car.'

He returned with the iron and jammed it into the rim of the drain. After a few moments of hard pressure it burst up, and the constable was able to carefully roll the lid aside. He shone his torch down into blackness. The rushing water was now only two feet below the opening.

'The sewer level must have risen in the rainstorm,' he

pointed out to his colleague. 'Sudden rainstorms have been known to blow these manhole covers clean off. If anyone really had fallen in half an hour ago, they'd be long drowned by now.'

Louie pushed against the grid. Although it was nearly three feet square he found it was lighter than he had expected, and moved aside easily. He gingerly raised his head and looked out. The shaft was situated in the middle of the road in a quiet backstreet to the rear of the Peabody Trust buildings. He shoved the lid aside and went back for Pam. She was conscious now, but shaking violently with cold and barely coherent. Slipping his arm around her shoulder, he helped her to climb the eight rungs to the top of the shaft, then lifted her beneath the armpits until she was capable of dragging herself out into the roadway.

'Better get you some dry clothes before you catch pneumonia,' said Louie, pulling Pam to her feet and rubbing life into her shoulders. 'Vince will have to manage without us now.' The wound on his leg was throbbing badly, the skin around the opening starting to harden and swell. Before either of them could rest tonight, they would have to check themselves into a casualty ward somewhere. He hoped that Vincent, wherever he was, was having better luck.

'I am, by nature, a suspicious man,' said Bryant, turning his gimlet eyes from the screen and running a hand across his bald pate. 'There has to be something other than this. It isn't just a matter of principal or class. Sebastian Wells is denied a parliamentary position because he's an Honourable. He has to make his presence felt in another way. Even if it's under-hand. Even if he never fully receives public credit for it. He's not bothered about publicity, more than likely shies away from it. Prefers to work behind the scenes, be the hidden puppetmaster. But what does he want?' He gave Jane's arm an anxious prod.

'I don't know,' she answered, 'power? Isn't that what they normally want?'

'I suppose he wants his hand on the tiller of the country. That's why he revived the League of Prometheus. It would have faded away without his intervention. His father had lost faith in it. Under his waning tutelage the membership had dwindled away to almost nothing. Sebastian built it back up, made it strong again. Of course, it must have been quite convenient to have the glorious capitalistic eighties arrive in the nick of time. No doubt the Thatcher years provided all kinds of reciprocal benefits. But where does Vince fit into all this?'

'Perhaps Wells was lonely. Intrigued. Perhaps he fell in love with him.' Jane shrugged. 'Who knows with these public-school types?'

'One thing's for sure, though. He thought he'd found someone who could play his games, but Vince not only rejected his friendship, he threatened to make him a laughing stock.'

'Then isn't that cause enough for revenge?'

Bryant thought for a moment. 'No,' he said finally. 'Wells would never normally choose a working-class man as a confidant, especially one like Vince. It goes against his grain, against everything he stands for. Look through Harold's articles and you can see how obsessed with his image Wells is. Why would he bother to cultivate himself so carefully and then take frivolous risks?' Bryant worried a fingernail in his dentures. 'Their first meeting might have been an accident, but it was a fortuitous one. I think Wells agreed to be befriended by Vince for a very specific reason. What have you got there?'

'I just ran a search on topics related to the League and this came up. Looks like it's downloading from somewhere on the eastern seaboard of the USA.'

'The Eulenspiegel Society?'

They watched as the web-site slowly built itself in layers of colour that revealed an engraving of a long-haired man in a red hat and a cloak.

'My god, it's a special interest sex group – masochists. I don't see the connection . . .'

'Wait, look. There's a link to their house magazine. Ready for this? It's called the "Prometheus Periodical".'

'It figures. Prometheus was the wisest of his race. He persuaded Zeus not to destroy the world and brought fire to mankind, for which he was punished by living a life of eternal torment, chained to a rock and having his liver torn out by an eagle each day. I guess that would appeal to masochists. We know the name Prometheus means "forethought", and its symbol is the swastika. But who is Eulenspiegel?'

'Hold on.' With the file fully loaded, Jane scrolled down through the pages, stopping and reading. ' "*Till Eulenspiegel*. Fourteenth-century German trickster, representative of the individual taking revenge upon society. Cunning, brutal and obscene by nature, fond of jests, puns and practical jokes, he always outwits those in authority. The subject of all kinds of musical and literary works, translated into many languages including Dutch, French and Latin. Richard Strauss wrote a symphonic poem about him." '

'Sounds like Sebastian found himself the ideal role model. It throws a little light on the nature of the League of

Prometheus, but it doesn't offer us any immediate help. The trickster. The revenger. But against whom, and how? This is going around in circles. I have to speak to Vince again. Can you get him on the phone?'

Vince had just reached the great false-fronted portico of St Paul's Church, and was searching the rainsoaked walls for his next envelope when the mobile began buzzing in his jacket.

'Vince, this is Mr Bryant,' said Bryant, shouting unnecessarily. 'Where are you?'

'I'm in Covent Garden. Tell Doctor Masters I haven't found the envelope yet. The churchyard's locked up. I'm going to have to scale the gate, and there are security cameras mounted at either end.'

'Before you do that I need you to think carefully for me. What do you think Sebastian will do if you beat him in the next couple of hours?'

'I don't know. I hope he'll keep his end of the bargain. I think he will. He's kind of rule-bound. Honour and duty. Prides himself on behaving like a gentleman.'

'That doesn't mean much any more. There must be something . . .'

'He loves games and tricks, but you know that.'

'Vince, what are his friends like?'

'Snooty. I didn't get introduced to many of them.'

'What about his parents?'

'Divorced. Didn't meet them. He hates his father with a vengeance.'

'Oh, really? Why do you think that is?'

'I'm not sure, but there's definitely bad blood between them.'

'Did he ever tell you what his father actually does?'

'He used to head the League, but now he's some kind of

business consultant at the DTI, heading up boring Euro-committees.'

'You see, Vince, I'm trying to think how best to explain my thinking; could all of this be providing him with a way of getting at his father?'

'You mean it's a personal matter? I wouldn't be surprised. He's angry with me, angry with his old man, probably capable of being angry with the whole world. But I don't see how he could do anything about it like this.'

'Neither do I. I'm afraid I can't help you in your physical search. That's Doctor Masters's department. All I can do is dig further into Wells's background history and hope something turns up in time.' He rang off as Jane Masters downloaded a fresh set of files on her PC.

'I'm absolutely convinced that the solution to this conundrum is right here in front of us, Jane,' said Bryant. 'It's not out there, it's somewhere in the past. This is my area of speciality, you know.'

'I'm sorry we're making you work on your sabbatical,' Jane apologised, although she knew that Bryant welcomed any opportunity to break with routine while he waited for May to return from abroad.

'If we assume Sebastian has a hidden agenda, what's his method for implementing it? Suppose he and his father fell out after the Melanie Daniels inquest. I find myself wondering whether the old man fixed the coroner in order to save his son from a murder charge, but if that was the case, Sebastian would owe his father a huge debt of gratitude, not be angry with him. Let's suppose for the sake of argument that he has a powerful reason for hating his old man. And by doing something tonight he can take revenge, for the League and for himself.'

'But how?'

'What would hurt his father most? Making the League strong again? He's certainly been trying to do that these last few years. Call up Sir Nicholas's file once more.'

Jane returned to the Internet address and waited while further information downloaded onto her screen. 'Here we are, full biographical details, current positions held, boards on which he sits – or publicly admits to sitting on, no current social background.'

'Can we pull information on each of these groups in turn and get work agendas and calendars from them?'

'I suppose so. Of course, it will be limited to knowledge they're prepared to make available to press and public.'

'How long will it take?'

'I'm not sure. It depends on who holds the information and how much of it they release. How soon do you need it?'

'Let's put it this way; Vince finishes his challenges at dawn, which I suppose will be around 7:45 a.m. this morning. Something will have to happen then; either Sebastian will keep his promise and let him go, and he'll be free to publish his book, or he'll break his word and stop Vince for good. Or he'll implement some kind of action that fulfils his plans. Whichever route he takes, we'll know soon enough. I don't like surprises, Jane, they make me nervous.'

He glanced back at the screen and saw that the screen had filled with dense blue type. At the top was the yellow circular star logo of the EC.

'The EC's Without Borders Initiative,' said Jane. 'Sebastian's father is founder and present chairman. There's an access address for their manifesto if you can be bothered – member countries, outline of objectives, information pack, stuff like that.'

'Part of the answer is right here,' said Bryant suddenly. 'We know Sir Nick had a change of heart, from old Tory to new Liberal. Imagine: he sets up this initiative, ready to exploit the pants off the labour market, then has a pang of conscience and drops the hidden agenda in favour of doing genuine good.'

'It would explain the rift between father and son.'

'Sebastian is betrayed, and the initiative from which he'd hoped to profit becomes the new enemy. What about a listing of their meetings, their monthly schedule?' asked Bryant. He had remembered seeing European flags lining The Mall only yesterday. 'Confound this thing. How do I move to the next page?' Bryant sat before the computer helplessly.

'Click here, Arthur. It makes the copy scroll. Look.'

WITHOUT BORDERS is an EC initiative aimed at reducing and ultimately eliminating immigration restrictions between member communities.

'Little Englanders won't like that at all. Member countries presently in London for annual conference. Odd coincidence.'

'What is?'

'It starts today. Even better. Officially opens this morning. What does it say next to the address?' Bryant's nose was almost touching the screen. 'Why do they make the print so small?'

Jane read for him. 'This important conference is attended by all key member delegates.'

'Highlight those nationalities, would you?'

'I'll have a go.' Jane was beginning to wonder if they were wasting their time, so close to Vince's deadline. She flicked the cursor to the sections of the schedule that were marked in a deeper shade of blue. A series of names and titles began to scroll down.

'Ten of them.'

'Ten men. Ten challenges.'

'What?'

'Oh, nothing. How about a list of their registered offices? Not in their resident countries. London addresses someone might use if they wanted to help, or needed press information.'

'Hang on.' Jane backed up to *Information Packs: UK Contact Addresses For Member Countries* and clicked on the blue title.

'There's your answer.' Bryant sat back, as smug as a cat.

'I don't see –' Jane began, stopping as she studied the office locations. The screen shone rectangles of cobalt on her eyes. 'Good God.'

'Victoria. The Strand. Muswell Hill Broadway. Puddle Dock. Red Lion Square. Vauxhall Bridge Road. St Martin's Lane. City Road. Bedford Street. Covent Garden.'

'It's a list of all the places Vince has visited in the night.'

'Do you see? Sebastian had to make Vincent carry out all the challenges alone. He needed him to unravel each of the clues in turn. I thought it odd that he should get rid of everyone who's been at the boy's side, and yet allow us to continue helping him.'

'I don't see how he could have stopped us –'

'With the resources at his command he could have done so very easily, but he didn't dare. We were making sure Vince reached each of his destinations. Besides, he didn't need to stop us.'

'Why not?'

'Because we couldn't be seen. Don't you understand? He only had to stop the ones who could physically be seen.' Bryant stabbed a bony forefinger at the air. 'Up there. All very clever.'

The revelation, such as it was, escaped her. 'I'm not sure I follow, Arthur.'

'The surveillance cameras. All those closed circuit television networks. All those security monitors busily cutting crime statistics in the capital. In the course of one night, Vincent Reynolds has been photographed at every single one of the official addresses of the members attending the conference. So if anything bad happens when it opens, guess who's the perfect scapegoat? And short of smearing his hands with blood, we've unwittingly helped to pin the blame on him.'

'But surely if something did occur, Vince could explain what's really been happening . . .'

'How? By relating some half-baked story about being persecuted through the night, with no one to back it up, not even us. After all, we haven't seen any of these supposed self-destructing 'notes' he's been finding, have we? No one will believe him, Jane. There's no evidence. The League is adept at covering its tracks. Even if he's kept the remains of the letters, they mean nothing by themselves. No wonder Sebastian was so careful in his selection of a dupe. A working-class man with a dodgy background! In his eyes, Vince is just the sort of person who would resent an organisation dedicated to ending immigration restrictions. How better to show that it's the will of the common people to remain an island? How better back up his inflammatory speeches with an "I told you so", to prove that the working classes are dangerous and must be controlled?'

'Vince is still out there collecting the details of the final destination. Won't Sebastian want to place him at the site?'

'Crikey, that's a thought. Does it specify the location on the EC schedule?'

Jane checked the screen. 'No. I don't suppose they would post the conference location in public view for security reasons.'

'Then we'll have to figure it out from the clue. Call Vince again.'

'Are you going to tell him about Sebastian's plans?'

'I have to. God, we owe him that.'

'Suppose he doesn't want to go on once he knows?'

'I don't think it will make any difference to him,' said Bryant. 'I mean. Would you stop now?'

He picked up the telephone receiver and dialled.

CHAPTER FORTY-FIVE

Monkey Business

I CANNOT by the progress of the stars give guess how near to day, he thought, feeling like Brutus in his long night of torment before the death of Caesar. The rain pattered against the windows in ripples, a drenching cloak for an inhospitable world.

Sebastian felt that the false-fronted church, featured with such neat hypocrisy in Hogarth's painting, provided an appropriate setting for this latest envelope. Its discovery would wind Vincent up and send him off again like a little clockwork toy along a track. The poor lad had never supposed that there might be more than one level to the game. A pity really, for it reduced his status as a player.

Sebastian could afford to sit back and watch the fireworks. Rather more than fireworks, perhaps. The Semtex-derivative that Xavier's boys had planted was quite untraceable, thanks to the fact that it had been passed on a false (and very expensive) route through several different countries. An explosive device, the traditional choice of traitors from Guy Fawkes onward, classic and simple, a truly *London* weapon. It had been a stroke of genius to coat the envelopes in traces of the stuff so that by now it completely covered Vincent's hands and clothes.

A warm dark feeling grew within his chest. Prometheus was placing a spark to his kindling, about to bring fire to mankind once more . . .

Thanks to his careful planning, the coming day's events were now a foregone conclusion. Following the tip-off Caton-James was preparing to make, Vincent would be picked up and interrogated. The police would realise that the boy had no alibi for the night. They would discover that he could be placed at every single member's London address, with the proof neatly provided on ten separate videotaping systems.

Vincent could tell them of his challenge, but would be able to offer no proof beyond some indecipherable shards of paper (if he had managed to keep any of them) which only made him look more of a fruitcake. That had been another smart move, to use paper stolen from his apartment. He would take them to the Holborn chamber, and they would find nothing. He might even be able to lead them to their Chelsea headquarters, but the police would still find nothing.

No doubt at one stage Vince would cite the death of his agent as proof of unseen forces at work, but here Sebastian had boxed clever. With admirable restraint he had avoided the obvious route of planting evidence that would incriminate Vincent in the murder – for how could the boy have been in two places at once? The videotapes that had filmed him through the night were time-coded. Instead, Xavier had been instructed to make his violence appear to be the result of a bungled burglary.

Then there was Harold Masters. The doctor might attempt to lodge some kind of complaint, but he had a history of attacking the League. Better still, he had a history of mental instability, having suffered a nervous breakdown in 1987. The only loose cannon was the girl, Pam, but she was presumably lost at sea along with the other one, Louie, and anyway her word meant nothing to anyone. Nobody really listened to people like that. No proof, no power, any of them. It was perfect.

Sebastian tipped back his chair and rooted around in his jacket for the Cuban cigar he had been saving. In a little over an hour the power of Prometheus would be fully restored. A gesture would have been made, and its effects felt. In time, there would be other gestures, just as successful as this. He exhaled a plume of blue smoke and permitted himself a small grim smile of satisfaction.

'I've got the ninth envelope,' said Vince, 'it was sellotaped behind a pillar at the other end of the church, the real front. Can you hear me? I'm having to shout because the rain's coming down so hard.'

'What does it say?'

'Hang on a minute.' He had trouble tearing open the plastic bag inside which the envelope had been sealed, and then managed to rip the foolscap sheet in his haste.

'Oh, great.'

'Well?'

'Listen to this little lot. You're going to need a pencil.' He looked back at the page.

The Challenge Of Decimus Burton

To keep this baby free from hurt,
He's dressed in a cap and Guernsey shirt;
They've got him a nurse and he sits on her knee,

And she calls him her Tommy

Bevy
Descent
Muster
Murder
Obstinacy
Pod
Serge
Smack

He waited while Masters relayed the list to the others.

'The poem feels like it's a word short in the last line.' Maggie rechecked the words she had copied into her notebook. 'It doesn't scan properly.'

'For God's sake, that's hardly important, is it?' complained Purbrick.

'Perhaps you're meant to supply the missing word,' she replied indignantly. 'Perhaps that's the whole point.'

'What does it need in order to scan? I mean, how many syllables?'

Maggie bounced her fingers over the page. 'Dum-dah-dah. Three.'

'Chimpanzee,' said Harold Masters, rising and going to the bookcase behind his chair. 'Chim-Pan-Zee. Decimus Burton. I mean, I'm guessing but it seems the most likely answer.'

'Forgive us, Harold,' said Maggie, with more than a trace of sarcasm, 'we're not all as well-read as you. Explain please.'

'Decimus Burton planned out the Zoological Society of London, as it was then known in 1826. London Zoo, as it's now called. There's a book here somewhere.'

'*Conservation In Action?*'

'That's the one.'

'To your left, up one shelf.'

Masters pulled down the photographic volume and opened it at the first chapter.

'Tommy the chimpanzee arrived in 1835,' he explained. 'A wonderful novelty in those days. Someone called Theodore Hook was moved to write a poem about him.'

'Vincent's poem?'

'I can't imagine there are any others. During the war the keepers packed off most of the animals to stop them from getting shell-shocked, but they ate the contents of the aquarium. This is interesting; someone cut a foot off Alice the elephant's trunk one bank holiday in 1870. Why would anyone do that?'

'More to the point, why would Sebastian send Vince to London Zoo?' asked Maggie. 'Nobody lives there. He doesn't need to have him appear before surveillance cameras at the monkey house, surely.'

'You're forgetting one thing. The only way to get to the zoo is by passing some of the most politically sensitive homes in the whole of London, the grace and favour properties of Regent's Park.'

They called Vince. Within another three minutes he was on his way north, precisely on time and exactly as Sebastian had planned from the start.

CHAPTER FORTY-SIX

Spine

VINCE CRUNCHED two more uppers between his teeth and sat back in the cab, listening to the rain beating on the roof. He tried to force the puzzle through his tired brain. If what Masters had just told him about Sebastian and the creation of evidence from the surveillance cameras was true, what was the point of traipsing onwards to the zoo at all? His role in the game was almost finished. It only remained to be photographed in the last position and captured by the police, so that he could be blamed for whatever atrocity Sebastian had planned for his father's convention.

So why bother fitting in with Sebastian's plans? Wasn't he safer heading home right now? Except, of course, the League would have considered such an eventuality. It would not be safe to return to his flat. He had no doubt that if the police didn't get him, Sebastian's more violent acquaintances would be standing by to finish the job.

The cab sloshed across the pitted tarmac at Euston Tower and ploughed on through the storm up to Camden Town. It reached the park and entered the first of the gates into Outer Circle. Here the government departments were hidden behind trompe l'oeil mock-Grecian temples, painted a glaring white and set back from the road. Bedecked with posturing statues, they reminded Vince of over-iced wedding cakes, the apotheosis of good taste to some, the ultimate in kitsch to others.

Smearing a path through the steamed-over window with the back of his hand, he could make out the parade of security cameras mounted on grey steel poles. The curving park road bristled with them. Masters's theory had to be wrong; how could they record him speeding past through the condensation of a cabbie's window? Perhaps Sebastian had not allowed for the vagaries of the climate.

No. He would have thought of everything. Technology had ways of enhancing recorded images. He thought back over the night's challenges, trying to understand.

It was then that he remembered that this was the *ninth* challenge, and the final one was to follow. He ran through each of the journeys he had made and came to the same result. The League's letter had specifically stated that the challenge started at Victoria, which made the Savoy the first.

All of which meant that Vince was being sent north on a wild goose chase. He tried to remember how Sebastian's mind worked. He checked his watch: 6:13 a.m. He felt sure now that this was a ploy to keep him out of the way until the appointed hour, so that he would arrive in the final destination at exactly the right time. Sebastian would want him placed at the scene of the crime, just to make sure. It was the most incriminating piece of evidence he could manufacture, short of putting a smoking gun in his hand. And it was a way of maintaining the balance of the game, to fairly provide each member of the League with a chance to test him.

Ten members, ten challenges.

One envelope still to find.

But where was he supposed to start looking? Inside the monkey house of London Zoo?

Xavier Stevens stood in the rain outside Sebastian's Chelsea headquarters, looking up at the dimly-lit first-floor windows. He was in a deepening black rage. Not only had he been forced to perform all the dirty work as usual, but Sebastian had refused to authorise additional payment for the extra risks he had taken. He actually had the nerve to complain about the way the last task was handled. Why had the bodies not been taken to the river as he had requested? Where were they, in fact? Did he even think to bring back proof that they had been disposed of? Sebastian conveniently glossed over the fact that he had given Stevens carte blanche to remove any obstacles in his path, and that this had resulted in as many as six probable deaths.

It was obvious that the leader of the League of Prometheus resented his ability to achieve results, and that the others had only agreed to allow Stevens's induction into the group because he was prepared to carry out the kind of actions they were too cowardly to handle themselves. That was fine; he had not expected to be liked. He was quite prepared to settle for fear and respect. But Sebastian repeatedly made him appear a fool, and was happy to humiliate him in front of others over what, for him, was a relatively trifling sum of money. He had been sent packing without full payment, and was now determined to have the final say.

Stevens had overheard enough to understand what they were planning, and realised that the best way to hurt Sebastian was to upset the outcome of his scheme. He knew that the events of the night hinged on the League's scapegoat being set in place, because Sebastian had reluctantly told him

Disturbia

why he needed Vincent photographed alone.

If the scapegoat was permanently removed from the game, the police would have to search out a new suspect. Stevens had an apposite suspect in mind. He checked his watch. If he was still hitting the schedule, Reynolds would be on his way to London Zoo by now. Let them find his body there with Sebastian's name attached to it, he thought bitterly. Let's see just how brave and powerful the League could be then.

Stevens hoisted a black leather pack on his shoulders, climbed back on his motorcycle and headed north.

'They have to be something to do with animals,' said Stanley Purbrick, pulling at a loose thread in his cardigan. 'Although I've never heard of anything called a *Murder* or a *Bevy*. There are animals in Lombard Street, hanging from the signs, gold locusts and frogs and things.'

Maggie was nearly asleep. Her face was sliding down her arm. Jane set another mug of coffee before her on the table. She took a sip and forced herself to perk up. She stared blearily at the list. 'They're collective nouns,' she exclaimed, surprising even herself. 'You know, like an "unkindness of ravens". Where's the thesaurus?'

They eventually found the collective nouns catalogued not under 'Animals' but 'Assembly', an entry which in itself required a certain amount of lateral thinking to locate. In another minute or two, however, Maggie had translated the list back into the animal kingdom:

Larks, pheasants
Woodpeckers
Penguins
Crows

Buffalo
Seals
Herons
Jellyfish

They called Vince and got through just as he was alighting from the taxi a hundred yards or so from the deserted main gate of the zoo.

'You're going to have to climb over the railings and avoid the night watchmen for this one,' said Masters. 'I don't think you're meant to head for the monkey house. The chimpanzee poem was just to get you to the zoo. The list contains the pointers. Try the buffaloes. We think they're on the far side of the gardens.'

'Wait a minute, hold on here.' Purbrick raised his palm. 'Why send him after the buffalo? How do you know it's not, say, the jellyfish?'

'The buffalo is the only four-legged creature on the list,' said Maggie, rolling her eyes in exaggerated impatience. 'Have you ever seen a jellyfish with legs? Honestly, Stanley, get a grip.'

'The jellyfish is the only one without a spine,' sulked Purbrick.

'Trust you to champion the one creature that has no backbone.' She patted his hand.

'The jellyfish is an oriental delicacy.' He puffed defensively. 'You cook it until it has a consistency you can squish through your teeth.'

'That's a tad more than I need to know,' said Maggie. 'Drink your tea and take a nap, dear.'

The railings were not high, but they were sharpened to an

array of severe points. In addition, several cameras were visible through the undergrowth, and what appeared to be a guard post stood inside the low white-framed entrance. Vince decided that it would be best to get nearer to the buffalo enclosure from the outside of the park, rather than risk running through the centre of the gardens accompanied by the hooting of disturbed orang-utans. Luckily, a series of useful maps mounted inside the railings pointed him in the right direction. At the nearest possible point to the bison and buffalo enclosure, he painfully shunted himself over the black iron fence.

He held fond memories of visiting the animals as a child, but a return visit last year had proven a depressing experience. Many of the display cages in the almost-bankrupt zoo had been boarded up, their animals dispersed. Paint peeled from the parrot house, where dejected birds now concealed their once-radiant plumage as if ashamed of their diminished circumstances, and there had been a man selling encyclopedias in the gloomy calm of the aquarium. Indeed, the place seemed torn between a desire to present itself as an ecology centre and the need to make money. In the distance Vince could see a carnival-yellow bouncy castle and fast-food kiosks lining the once-grand central square. The schizophrenic nature of the place had been summed up by the fact that the tiger pelts and alligator handbags confiscated from smugglers and displayed beside cages as examples of callous commercialism had been forced to carry 'Not For Sale' tags.

If there were any buffalo outside tonight, sleeping beneath the dripping trees, he certainly could not see them. The pathways stretching off between the enclosures were rainswept and deserted. He clambered over the low iron fence and walked through the wet straw-strewn pasture. Presumably the animals were kept in on a night like tonight, when the overhead storm might panic them. He reached the holding pens, but there were padlocks fastened on the doors.

He folded open the mobile phone and punched out Masters's number, confident that his voice would be concealed by the noise of the rain in the trees. 'I can't see anything here for me,' he told the doctor. 'There's nothing in the exterior section of the enclosure, and the rest of the place is locked up tight. Are you sure I'm meant to be heading for the buffaloes?'

'Well, no,' Masters admitted. 'But nothing else really strikes us as the odd man out.'

'What about the penguins?' he offered. 'They're the only creatures on the list that are unable to fulfil one of the main functions of their species.'

'Oh, I see what you mean – they can't fly, can they? But why would that single them out for attention?'

Vince thought for a moment. He tried to recall his half-drunk conversations with Sebastian in the elegant restaurants they had frequented as friends. All those class-comparison lists they had made together; songs, schools, painters, architects, writers, pastimes – no animals had been mentioned, though he remembered Sebastian's sharp little denigrations of his heroes (Albert Camus 'too lefty-liberal'), and the admiration he had expressed for his own idols (Albert Speer 'a misguided visionary'). But why would he have mentioned Decimus Burton in the clue? Why name an architect? As the answer descended upon him, he could not help but chuckle at the crafty little paradox Sebastian had presented.

'Vince, are you still there?' asked Masters, alarmed.

'Yes,' he replied. 'I think I detect the hand of the author in this challenge. It's one of Sebastian's own. And it's not about the animals at all. It's about the zoo.' He stepped out from the eave of the barn and headed back towards the edge of the enclosure.

'What do you mean?'

'Sebastian and I have very different heroes. I expressed an admiration for Berthold Lubetkin, the great social architect who once said "Nothing is too good for ordinary people". Sebastian violently disagreed with me.'

'I'm sorry, I don't see the connection.'

'Lubetkin designed a masterpiece for the London Zoo. Hang on a second.' He climbed across the fence and dropped onto the concrete walkway ahead. 'During the last century this was one of the few private properties open to the public that truly cut across class distinctions. It was where the proletariat came to promenade. Its very name came from a popular music hall song. And in 1936, Lubetkin built a penguin pool for the zoo. Don't you see? It's Sebastian's comment on his perceived failure of such high ideals. A brilliant social designer and humanitarian is now solely remembered for a building that houses flightless birds.'

The white oval of the sunken pool, dazzling even in rain and darkness, was in sight. He rang off and sprinted along the edges of the path until he was forced out into an open concourse. The pounding rainstorm had at least driven any patrolling security guards back into their offices. Vince ran up to the edge and peered in. A handful of bedraggled penguins stood around the lip of the cobalt pool, sheltering from the downpour. Across the centre, two sweeping white ramps curled around each other in an elegant descent to water level. On the top one stood a figure dressed in black and white motorcycle leathers, holding a pale envelope.

He held the envelope high. 'If you want to capture the last

challenge, Mister Reynolds, you'll have to take it from me.'

Vince was exhausted. The thought of climbing into the penguin pool and having a fist-fight with a complete stranger was not one which appealed, but he seemed to have no choice in the matter. Setting his duffel bag against the wall, he searched for a way down. He would have to climb onto the same ramp occupied by his challenger, and it looked too fragile to support one man, let alone two.

As he lowered himself over the wall and his boots connected with the ramp, Stevens came at him.

Vince saw the knife in his right hand, but there was no way of avoiding it without losing his balance on the narrow walkway. The tip of the blade caught in the wet mesh of his jacket sleeve as Stevens's body came into contact with his. He could feel the edge of the knife twisting and pushing harder into his arm. But he was above Stevens on the ramp, still standing on a dry section of the white-painted concrete, and was able to gain more leverage.

Shoving down with all his might, he shifted his attacker back, and in doing so freed Stevens's arm to slash at him again. This time the blade cut wide above his face, missing by several inches. Seizing the time created by the continuing momentum of the action, he brought his knee up to Stevens's groin, only to find the move blocked by the other man's leg. But the assault was enough to shift their balance. He could feel the ramp bouncing dangerously beneath them as they fell, rolling and sliding over each other around the sharp curve. Below, a number of penguins scattered madly into the water.

In the brief moment that Vince lost sight of the knife it came at him again, this time from above, arcing down and sticking into his left bicep. The jacket prevented it from penetrating deeply, but the sensation snatched his breath away and sent shockwaves through the nerves in his limbs. He rolled over the edge of the ramp and fell, narrowly missing another walkway. He landed in the shallow pool on his back, and the shock of the fish-reeking icy water threw him up on his knees just as Stevens dropped from above.

Vince brought his head down to protect himself. Stevens crashed across him and kicked down hard, catching him in the solar plexus with his boot. Winded, he slapped back into the water as Stevens rose and waded towards him, the knife gleaming dully in his gloved hand.

What made Vince grab the passing seabird by its feet and brandish it at his attacker he would never know, but the struggling penguin was understandably miffed at finding itself faced with what appeared to be a giant rival penguin, and started viciously slashing at Stevens with the sides of its razor-sharp beak. Within seconds it had sawn through the black leather collar of Stevens' tunic and was biting his neck. The assassin screamed, dropping the knife and falling back, but the penguin kept coming at him, nipping, snapping and chattering as it forced him under the ramp, where Vince was able to boot him hard enough in the side of the head to render him unconscious.

As he slipped and slid back up the incline, grabbing at the sides of the ramp to stop himself from falling, Vince snatched up the dripping envelope that had fallen to its centre. He looked back in time to see the penguin, satisfied that it had exacted vengeance on an interloper, hopping from Stevens's inert black and white body and swimming away with a satisfied wiggle in its tail. Without flight, thought Vince, but not without fight.

CHAPTER FORTY-SEVEN

Departures

'OKAY, THERE'S a badge of some kind, red and blue enamel, with lettering on it. WBI.'

'The "Without Borders Initiative". What else?'

'Today's date, and some kind of serial number.'

'That's your pass,' said Masters. 'My guess is that he wants you inside the perimeter of the WBI's meeting-place. You have less chance of being arrested under suspicion if you're outside the immediate crime area. What else is there?'

'The final letter. I'll read it to you.'

The Challenge Of The Warrior Queen

'Fear not, isle of blowing woodland, isle of silvery parapets!
Tho' the Roman eagle shadow thee, tho' the gathering enemy narrow thee,
Thou shalt wax and he shall dwindle, thou shalt be the mighty one yet!
Thine the liberty, thine the glory, thine the deeds to be celebrated.'

Farewell, Queen Of The Iceni.
Your fate decided by a hare,
Loftily charioted, keeping victory in defeat,
Where you were slain, your subjects now depart.

'This looks like it might be easier than I expected,' said Vince, cradling the phone beneath his chin. 'I thought the last one would be a bastard. I've got one hour to solve it, which would bring us to eight o'clock.' He checked his watch, but it had been damaged in the fight. His arm throbbed dully, the bloody wound sticking to his shirt. 'It's Boadicea, isn't it? She fought in the shadow of the Roman eagle. She was the queen of the Iceni in Norfolk. Wasn't there something about a running hare?'

'That's right,' replied Masters, relaying information from Arthur Bryant. 'The Romans plundered her possessions, flogged her and raped her daughters, so she led an uprising against them. She needed to convince her troops by showing them an omen, so she released a hare which ran in an auspicious direction, one that revealed the favour of the goddess Adraste, the bestower of victory.'

'Hence *keeping victory in defeat*?'

'No, that probably refers to her name, which means "victory". It was the only thing she kept. The battle was lost and she was killed, but her fame lives on because, paradoxically, she came to represent the kind of patriotic fantasy figure that children were raised on, this image of the heroic champion who freed the Britons. I'm sure she figured heavily in Sebastian's upbringing.'

'The lines are from Tennyson,' Maggie called out, 'as is the reference to her being *Loftily charioted*. He helped to raise her profile immensely, and a statue was built to her.'

'Where?'

'It's on the Embankment right near Big Ben, absolutely enormous, you can't miss it. I guess that must be your final destination.'

'No,' said Vince, staring out into the rain. '*Where you were slain, your subjects now depart.* He's playing another trick on me.'

'What do you mean?'

'Oh, come on. It's one of those stupid schoolkid things you remember from history class. He doesn't mean me to go to her statue on the Embankment at all. He wants me to go to King's Cross station. Boadicea is supposed to have fallen in battle there. Platform Ten, to be exact.'

'God, I'd forgotten all about that. The station's meant to be built on the ancient battle-site, isn't it?'

'The thing about her being buried under the platform is just a piece of nonsense,' he heard Bryant say, 'one of those things teachers always used to tell children to spark their interest.'

'But you're right, it fits,' Masters agreed. 'They can't be holding an international conference on a train, can they?'

'I imagine they're boarding a train for somewhere in the countryside,' Vince replied. 'If it's due to set off at 8:00 a.m., they'll be gathered in the station concourse beforehand. They might even be there already, which means that Sebastian can strike at any time.'

'Don't you see how dangerous it is, sending him there alone?' said Maggie. 'It's what Sebastian is expecting. At least let Arthur call someone. Suppose Vince gets inside the security area and a bomb goes off, or a sniper opens fire? Suppose he's injured? Or arrested, just as the League has planned? Vince has played into their hands every step of the way – and we're still helping him because that's the only thing we can do. But if we don't do something different and disturb their expectations, they'll have won. It may already be too late.'

The open line on the speaker-phone crackled between them. They were assembled around the dining-room table once more, but were unable to agree on a course of action. When Maggie complained about this, Masters snapped. 'Well, what do you expect?' he shouted, 'we're academics. We've never had to put anything into practice.'

'Somebody has to this time,' Maggie replied. 'Unless you're prepared to see innocent people die. Why don't we just tell Vince to contact the first policeman he sees, and to stay out of the security area?'

Vince's voice cut through the static so loudly that they all jumped. 'I'm not going to the station,' he announced.

'What do you mean?'

'I'm turning the cab around. The road here is all dug up. I don't know how long it's going to take to get to King's Cross. It's a main-line terminus, and at this time of the morning it'll be packed. I'll never be able to convince anyone in authority to clear the area in time. Besides, for all I know, they're waiting for me to be sighted entering the station. It could be their signal to attack. I've a better idea.'

'Thank God,' said Maggie. 'I thought you would reach the station, find the train pulling out and leap on a motorcycle to head it off at a level crossing.'

'You ought to read less and get out more,' said Purbrick. 'Vince, what's your idea?'

'You have to call the police from there and get them to evacuate the train and the station.'

'If you can't do it, what chance do we have? They'll think it's a crank call.'

'Surely not if you have Mr Bryant call, and make him quote the security number on the badge,' Vince explained, reading it back. Sebastian would live to regret the inclusion of the little enamel pin in his final package. It was the one tangible piece of evidence that could be used against him, and Vince had every intention of doing so.

'Where are you going now?' asked Masters.

'I don't want to tell you, in case they've got someone monitoring the line. I'll be fine, don't worry. It's just some unfinished business.'

There was a crackle of disconnection, and the line went dead.

CHAPTER FORTY-EIGHT

The Final Paradox

SEBASTIAN LOOKED around the room, at the mangled leg of beef dripping bloody gravy on the sideboard, the congealed plates from last night's dinner, the ashtrays overflowing with joints and the discarded winebottles, and despaired of ever instilling his colleagues with the discipline of their forefathers, men who had at least been given the chance to run an empire, if not to build one.

Things were falling apart. Prisoners escaping. Stevens demanding money. St John Warner running amok with a *crossbow*, for God's sake. Worse, he knew that something had gone wrong with the game. The members of the League who were still awake and sober were downstairs watching breakfast TV and listening to the radio, waiting for first reports of the bomb, but he could hear no sound from them. They were staying away from him, shamefaced and embarrassed, weasels slinking from the fox.

Xavier Stevens had failed to return after their argument over the price of lives. The monitors showed no sign of Vincent Reynolds anywhere near the station. By now the meeting place of the European tribunal should have been damaged by a devastating explosion, the fabric of the building rent asunder, commuters sitting up in dazed and bloody confusion, TV stations preparing bulletins for traffic disruption caused by yet another city bomb as plucky Londoners took it on the nose again.

He checked his watch once more. 7:33 a.m. The WBI members had been asked to convene in front of their platform at 7:30 a.m., and the bomb's timer-mechanism had also been set at half-past the hour. It could only mean one thing. The police had somehow located the device, and had managed to either defuse or remove it. It was possible, he supposed, that the device itself was faulty, but unlikely considering the number of tests he had specified before taking delivery –

'Hello, Sebastian.'

A figure was standing in the doorway watching him. Vincent looked terrible. Soaked and grey and sick. There was blood dribbling from his right arm onto the carpet. He smelled of fish.

'Well well, I suppose you'd better come in. I'm glad you found your way to the inner sanctum,' said Sebastian casually. He turned from Vince to the lawns below the window, now revealing themselves beneath the thinning veils of night. 'I rather wondered if you might find me. The girl, I suppose.'

'That's right,' said Vince. 'You shouldn't have dismissed the girl. The upper echelon have always undervalued their women.'

'For God's sake don't start. Sit down before you fall down. We have something to discuss, you and I.' He looked around for the decanter and located it under his chair, almost empty. He noticed that his hands were shaking. 'You came very close to winning the challenge for a while.'

'What are you talking about?' said Vince. 'I beat you. I

solved all of the tests you set for me. By now the bomb squad should have cordoned off your device and defused it. I hope you're going to show grace in defeat.'

'I can't acknowledge defeat, Vincent, you must see that. After all, you can't publish. We destroyed your disks, your notes, your manuscripts, your commissioning editor, your agent. And we can do it again whenever we like. You have no evidence beyond your own admittedly faulty memory. Who are they going to believe, the toff or the tout?' He permitted himself a victorious smile. 'You broke the rules I laid down. I warned you about tampering with the code of honour.'

'What honour? You call attacking people and trying to kill them honourable?'

'It depends on what you're protecting. I'd ask you to consider joining the League if you weren't so much against it. We're dying. Look around you. We don't have the common touch, you see, and so much of the world does now. We need fresh blood to help take us into the next milennium.' Sebastian stared at him as though examining a creature from another planet. 'All my hard work has been in vain. You still have no concept of the people who run the city.'

'Yes, I do,' replied Vince. 'They go around in trucks fixing the streetlights at two in the morning. They spend their evenings sitting on benches waiting to be chosen for clean-up teams. They earn a couple of quid for every thousand envelopes they fill with double-glazing offers.'

'I'm talking about the people with power.'

'We're all born with the same power, Sebastian. Some of us get tricked into never using it.'

'Vincent, Vincent. You've been so bright up until now, it's a pity you've failed to divine the other purpose to all of this.'

'That purpose being?'

'The battle for the leadership of the League of Prometheus, of course. Do sit down, you're making the place untidy. Perhaps I should get you a bandage for that.' He made no attempt to move. Vince warily seated himself near the window while Sebastian poured the last two glasses of brandy and slid one along the table that stood between them.

'Shortly before I met you, my ability to command the League was called into question by the other members. I felt I was qualified to lead them into the next century; they felt otherwise. As a consequence of their lack of faith, I agreed to devise some kind of independent examination. I offered to find a potential candidate for the job and undergo a test of wits. The candidate I chose was you.'

'That's not possible. I chose you.'

Sebastian chuckled. 'I'm afraid not. You contacted me, that's true, but I'd been searching for a suitable player for several months before you called. From the outset you seemed ideal. We had so very little in common. That's what made it so appealing.'

Vince looked in his eyes and saw that beneath the geniality was a hatred born from the fear of anything different, a hatred eternal, dead and pure. 'This country is at a crossroads, Vincent. When the Fabian Society starts suggesting that we disband the Royal Family and replace the national anthem with a song by Andrew Lloyd Webber, you know that something is rotten.' He looked about himself, depressed by what he saw. 'We let our future slip away. Now the nation belongs to people like you.' He gave a disappointed sniff and stuck his hands in his pockets. 'Look at you. Your knowledge is all second-hand, gleaned from TV and the movies. It's left to people like me to provide you with a few real experiences. You know nothing.'

'I know you, Sebastian. You like a bit of strident marching

music. You like Offenbach, Gilbert and Sullivan. And just like Gilbert, you love a good paradox. How could you have resisted this?'

'You're right, I couldn't. I decided to give the leadership contest some bite. It was a chance to further the original purpose of the League. An opportunity to bring the fire of enlightenment to the nation.'

'And a chance to get back at your father.'

'Don't be impertinent. You know nothing about Nicholas.' He pulled a hand from his pocket and drained his brandy glass. 'My father was always aware of my ambitions, right from my fourth-form years at public school. But he didn't believe that I could ever develop leadership qualities. My mother was a "woman's woman". Politics bored her. I was her only issue. Nicholas felt I was too much of a "loose cannon". A favourite expression of his. Felt I lacked discipline. I was allowed a small amount of youthful freedom, but beyond a certain point the parental noose tightened. Do sit down, you're making me nervous.'

Vince remained standing. He doubted his ability to rise again if he sat now.

'I headed off to university. During one autumn break, my father set me a test. Turned out that the old man was a bit of a game-player himself. He threw me a spectacular party, provided me with plenty of temptation, and sat back to watch me throw away my future. He knew my weaknesses, you see. He knew that I would let him down.'

'What kind of father would do that?' asked Vince.

'A pity you never got to meet him. You'd understand a lot more about me.'

'I understand a lot more than you think. I know you want to be me.'

'Oh?' Sebastian raised an eyebrow. 'What is it about you that I covet so much?'

'My freedom. Something you've not had since the night your girlfriend drowned.'

'I wondered if you'd find out about that.' Searching for something else to drink, he located a fifth of scotch beneath the chair. He unscrewed the cap and drank from the bottle. The action was uncharacteristic and sat awkwardly on him, like a badly-cut jacket. 'When I discovered Melanie unconscious on the pier that evening, I panicked. She drank, enjoyed her party drugs, was always pushing the limit, just like the rest of us. Her skin was almost blue. She was so cold to the touch. There seemed to be no pulse. You must understand. I thought she was dead. I thought I'd be blamed. I had already assumed that father wouldn't help me out if there was any kind of trouble. I saw myself losing everything I had worked for.

'I simply nudged her body with my foot and she rolled from the pier into the water. There was hardly even a splash. Then I walked back to the dance-tent and poured myself a drink. Nobody saw what had happened. Her body wasn't discovered for ages. When it was, my father surprised me by offering to help. The old man made sure that the coroner's verdict went in my favour, and that I would be forever in his debt. He understands the power of emotional blackmail. He didn't want to make me hate him. Quite the opposite. He wanted to make me hate myself. He proved how much I needed him. Every time I looked at his smug face I could hear him saying "I told you so".'

'So you searched for a way to get back at him.'

'The League members wanted a test of my abilities. My father wanted the free-migration vote to be passed. And I wanted revenge against you. It was my chance to tie the whole thing up in one neat package, and the beauty of it was, it would only take a single night to sort out the troubling strands of my life – one night, ten hours – and all my problems would be solved. Well, I suppose now they are solved.'

'What do you mean?'

'My agreement with the other League members was that I would admit defeat if you managed to beat me. I do not acknowledge your victory. But I have a feeling that the members will. In which case, I must formally ask if you would be prepared to accept unconditional membership into the League of Prometheus. I am also duty-bound to inform you that if you accept the offer, I must fulfil the final part of my contract with the League.'

'Which is?'

Sebastian looked straight ahead. His pupils had flattened into distant green disks. 'Obviously, I'm required to take my own life.'

'I don't understand,' said Vince. 'You set up this night of challenges yourself. You planned it.'

'That is correct.'

'Then why on earth didn't you make it impossible for me to win? Why did you set me tasks that you knew I would have to solve in order to fulfil your other purpose? If you wanted to get back at your father, why not do it another way? *You could only beat him by allowing me to win.* You deliberately created a situation in which your main purposes cancelled each other out. Why would you do such a thing?'

Sebastian raised his dead green eyes. He looked older in the growing light. 'As you yourself pointed out, I am very fond of paradoxes,' he said, smiling coldly.

'So you've lost and won.'

'That's the best result I could ever have hoped for. The resolution of this night is now in your hands.'

From the street below came the whine of a milk float making its deliveries. The rain was finally easing, but the sky remained grimly dark. Sebastian rose unsteadily and unstuck half a bottle of claret from the sideboard. The atmosphere in the room was fetid and heavy.

'Well, what's it to be, young Vincent?' he asked, tipping the bottle over his glass and slopping wine on the floor. 'Do you accept the offer and take over as part of the League's new "grass roots" order? They'll guarantee you won't be implicated in the night's events. It's simply a matter of a few phone calls. Could you be seduced by the thought of such power and spend the rest of your days with my death on your conscience?'

He set down his wineglass and dug inside his jacket. 'It's a service revolver,' he said, brandishing the dull grey pistol. 'Holds an important ceremonial role in the League's traditions. It's been used many times before, for many different reasons.' Removing the safety catch, he raised it to his throat and tilted his face to the ceiling. 'God, you spend years trying to change the world, only to discover the final hellish paradox.'

'Which is?' asked Vince, watching him and waiting for a chance to snatch the gun away.

'That the good intentions die with you, and the evil ones live on.' His finger tightened on the trigger as he slowly tipped his chair back. 'You'd better get out of here before the sound of the shot brings the others running.'

'No way,' said Vince, shifting forward. 'I want to make sure you pull the fucking trigger.'

Sebastian was so surprised he nearly shot himself.

'Come on, then, do it. You don't get off the hook by chucking me a bit of paraphrased Shakespeare and hoping I'll buy it. Let's see you take the noble way out, do the decent thing. Open the tent flap, look over your shoulder and tell me you might be gone for some time.'

Sebastian held the pose, but his eyes flicked uncertainly back at Vince.

'Go on, join an illustrious gallery of honourable suicides. How old was Brutus when he killed himself?'

Sebastian remained motionless for a few seconds more, then started to waver. 'Jesus.' He lowered the revolver. 'I think it's quits, don't you? You're not about to join our ranks, and somehow I don't think we'll ever be able to join yours. The poor old Prometheans are like this city; we're carrying too much baggage to ever start entirely afresh. We'll still be here next month, next year; a little older and shabbier, but still here. And no doubt it will be the task of someone like you to cancel out each forward move we make.'

Vince gave a rueful smile. 'Then the game would continue for ever.'

'Of course.' Sebastian laughed. 'How could it ever end?'

'But it has ended,' said Vince, seating himself at the other end of the table. 'You see, there's one final paradox you haven't considered.'

Sebastian shifted nervously in his armchair. 'I don't understand.'

Vince's smile broadened. The loaded pistol sat between them.

'I accept the League's offer of membership,' he said, smiling wider as he picked up the gun and aimed it at Sebastian's forehead. 'Get on the floor.'

Sebastian was aghast. He struggled to understand the command. Vince came forward and kicked him from the chair. Drunker than he realised, Sebastian fell to his knees, then rolled over on his back.

'Open your mouth.'

Meekly, he did as he was told, unable to comprehend the turn in events. Vince dropped a mudstained boot to his throat, jammed the steel barrel between his parted teeth and fired once.

The bullet that passed through Sebastian's upper palate also tore through his brain before exiting his skull and embedding itself in the mahogany herring-bone floor tiles. Vince remained holding the gun as the others came running into the room.

'Come on in, boys,' he called, still eyeing the twisted body on the floor. 'The leadership contest is over. I think you can figure out who won. You may as well make yourselves comfortable. We've got a lot to talk about.'

Part Three

'The shouting of democracy, like the singing of the stars,
means Triumph.
But the silence of democracy means Tea.'

– E.V. Knox

CHAPTER FORTY-NINE

The Never-Ending Game

'ALL RIGHT,' said Stanley Purbrick, 'it's my turn. Chameleon. Sculptor. Toucan. Dragon. Furnace. Chisel. Microscope.' He sat back smugly and drained his beer. 'Sort that one out.'

'Pathetic,' mocked Maggie Armitage. 'Hopelessly easy.' She shook the last crumbs of salt and vinegar crisp from her packet and munched them. 'They're all –'

'Don't be a spoilsport,' warned Stanley. 'You always know the answer. Let someone else have a chance at getting it. Jane? Harold? Any ideas?'

'They're all constellations, aren't they?' asked Masters, hardly bothering to look up from his newspaper.

'That does it.' Purbrick folded his arms across his cardigan. 'I'm not going to play this any more.'

'Oh, don't be such a bad loser, Stanley. You hate anyone knowing more than you, and lots of people do.' She examined the inside of her crisp bag and ran an exploratory digit around it. 'Almost everyone, in fact.'

'That *absolutely* does it. I'm going home.' He rose to leave, but was waiting for someone to push him back in his seat.

'Do sit down, there's a chap, I've got you a top-up.' Arthur Bryant had arrived with a tin tray full of drinks. The

Insomnia Squad were seated in what had once been the snug bar of the Nun and Broken Compass. Maggie had been due to conduct a meeting of the Camden Town coven in one of the upstairs rooms tonight, but her secretary had muddled the dates and they had found themselves double booked with the Norman Wisdom Fan Club, so Arthur Bryant offered to buy them all drinks. As no one could ever recall the elderly detective offering to buy anyone a drink before, they jumped at the chance.

'We should have invited Vincent tonight,' said Maggie. 'I'd like to meet him one day. It galls me a bit to think that we helped save lives and nobody knows about it. I suppose that now he's a celebrity he won't want to talk to the likes of us.'

'It's odd that he never even rang to say thank you for all the help we gave him,' complained Purbrick.

'Never mind,' said Dr Masters, 'you can read all about him instead.' He held up a section of the *Independent* for everyone to see.

'What is it?' asked Maggie.

'A review of his book. He already has the critics slavering. According to this he's been commissioned to write another volume.'

'That should please the League of Prometheus.'

'They've gone very quiet, haven't they?' Maggie stirred her tequila and blackcurrant with her little finger. 'Not much good without their leader. One never *really* knows what's going on. You don't suppose they're planning something new?'

'Someone's always planning something,' said Bryant vaguely. 'That's what cities are for. The countryside is where you can settle and be at peace with yourself. Cities are there to disturb your thoughts, your dreams, your complacency. I agree with Stanley, though; it's odd that the boy hasn't been in touch.'

'You don't think something's happened to him?'

'Not if the smiling photograph in the paper is to be believed.'

'Funny,' said Masters, examining the picture. 'He looks just like Sebastian Wells here. Must be the angle it was taken.'

'Be careful of my overcoat, would you Maggie?' pleaded Bryant. 'There's a cat in one of the pockets.'

'I wondered where my crisps had been going.' She eyed the garment warily. It was indeed moving. 'You get cats the way other people get colds.'

Jane Masters pulled aside the curtain and checked the wet inhospitable streets.

'Looks like it's in for the night,' she sighed. 'We'll just have to stay here. As a matter of interest, does anyone know why this place is called the Nun and Broken Compass?'

'Bryant can tell you,' said her husband. 'He heard the story from the landlord. It's really disgusting.'

Arthur Bryant leaned forward with a rare, disgraceful grin on his lips. 'Well,' he began, 'it seems that about a hundred and seventy years ago a beautiful young convent-raised woman worked behind the counter here, and customers used to come from miles around to be served by her. Back then, of course, the place was still called the Cromwell Arms, and one night the saloon door was opened by two monks who had lost their way in the foggy backstreets . . .'

The New Brigands

HE STOOD beneath the melancholy greenery of the cemetery, looking at the white marble sarcophagus which bore so many Wells family names, and thought that even here Sebastian had not been able to escape his father. Sir Nicholas had arranged to have his son illegally interred in the family vault instead of being left beyond consecrated grounds, on the sterile little lawn where all the other suicides were buried. If he had known the truth, he would have been saved the trouble.

Vince raised the collar of his Burberry against the misting rain and returned to the gravelled path. He thought back to the events of that eternal night, and how it had crystallised his vague ambitions. Poor Sebastian had wanted to teach his pupil a few lessons in leadership. If only he had known what an ambitious fire he would fan with that first spark. Prometheus was reborn, but not in the way he had intended.

Vince knew he had been given one chance to attain the good life. It was surprisingly easy to make the jump. After all, what was there to give up? He just wanted what the other League members had, to redress the balance a little. And they had offered it to him. No more was he a child of the streets, but an owner of the houses.

And he had to admit that it was a good life, heading up the League. It wasn't called the League of Prometheus any more, of course. Getting rid of all that xenophobic classical crap had been the first big change. Kicking out some of the more useless toffs and replacing them with smart street lads had been the next. He had dumped the racism, the snobbery, the cruder tools of persuasion. He was even thinking about approaching Louie with an offer.

To cover his tracks, he had still written the book. After all, he still enjoyed writing. Only, what with all his copies being destroyed, he had recreated it from a new angle. Xavier Stevens's secret file on Sebastian (kept, touchingly, in a shoe-box on top of his wardrobe) had been useful for that. Useful for publicly burning the old-style League and damning its leader, while allowing the core of the organisation to go underground in a new, more nineties-friendly form. Buying and selling, creaming profits, hiding discrepancies, keeping secrets, burying connections, bending the rules, cementing relationships, fixing deals, fiddling the books, prioritising, publicising, damning, demonising, and doing pretty much what all government ministers did, only more so. Beating them at their own game, as it were.

The League's public profile had been getting too high, anyway. The others had much to thank him for. Strictly speaking, there were no League members now, only business-men. He had returned the League to its roots, made it truly invisible again. Streamlined its organisation. Modernised its procedures. Now it was on the path to true power.

There had been a major change in attitude. Under the old regime, Sebastian would probably have had Xavier Stevens executed for compiling a blackmail dossier on him. Vince had congratulated the assassin on his initiative, and promoted him. Xavier was now loyal for life.

He never saw Pam any more. She went out of her way to avoid him, never even rang his old home number. It was as though she had sensed a sea-change in his character. He missed her. She and Louie, and the life to which they belonged, were part of the trade. He had not seen Betty again, either. Hey, everyone had to make sacrifices. You couldn't have a new life while still hanging onto the old. It was time to put away the past and look to the future. For him, for the city. The political arena beckoned.

The sleek black Mercedes was waiting at the cemetery gates. Caton-James was his driver now. Not terribly happy about it either, as he wasn't allowed to smoke in the car. He saw Vince appear at the entrance and brought the vehicle to a smart stop, hopping out to open the rear door.

Poor Sebastian, thought Vince as he slipped into the Mercedes. I got to be him, but he didn't get to be me. Prometheus could only pass the light one way. A flaw in the paradox.

Tonight he was taking a young lady to an Offenbach concert, then onto dinner at the Waldorf. The new company – he preferred to think of it in this way, rather than a league, which sounded too Conan Doyle-ish – was turning over a fortune. His book, *City of Night and Day*, was a best-seller.

Apart from one niggling annoyance, Vincent Reynolds felt at peace with the world.

Epilogue

TAKEN FROM the *foreword of* City of Night and Day *by Vincent Reynolds.*

London has changed. Now it is a city built on sand, shifting and eliding into a thousand different lifestyles – ghost-images transmitted through interference. Its residents are finally free to plot a course through the maze of glass and steel and flesh, to locate the coordinates of their dream lives and exist within them. And like waters running over sand, strange new tributaries grow and die with the speed of rolling clouds. The social classes once deemed so necessary to maintain the land's financial structure are being replaced by tribal cults.

London's architecture has been freed of religious significance, its pagan influences purged, its Mycenean alignments to moon and stars forgotten, Solomon, Boudicea, Blake and Hawksmoor no longer forces to be reckoned with. Now it is styled on sterile American lines, freed from the weight of the past.

London is no longer a city of formalities. Its institutions are falling, its stock exchange no longer a closed shop, its companies no longer tradition-bound, its employees loyal to none but themselves, its intentions no longer honourable. The agreements that existed within a handshake, like the silk top hats of the city, have vanished.

The tailored suits were too restricting, too earthbound; flight requires freedom.

Once I referred to London as a slumbering giant, but now the giants are gone and there are only people; people with the ability to redefine the power of this mighty city. Change, of course, is not absolute. Some old ways remain. Two thousand years of dreams live on in the shadows around us. It will take a clever man indeed to unite those ancient dreamscapes with our hopes for the future. To return Prometheus and Dionysus, Solomon and Boadicea, to return the pagan glory of the planets to our streets, to reforge our links with day and night, summer and winter, to bring back the sunlight of Helios and the moonglow of Diana into London lives. The dead hand of Christianity ultimately led us into darkness. Perhaps someone will be ruthless enough to lead us back out of it, and into the light.